DOCTOR COTTON

- □ -

STEPHEN BARRETT

BY THE BOOK PRESS BtB

San Francisco

I want to thank my dear sister Teresa. She and I are the only ones left who remember what really happened on Kerr and Burton. We help each other carry the wounds. I thank her for her zealous and unflagging belief in my abilities.

Most importantly I want to thank my partner, Daniel. This book is for him. He is my soul mate. I thank him for giving me fireflies, true support, abiding love and for recognizing my heart. Our love and the magic it has created is the basis of *Doctor Cotton*. We know.

I would also like to thank my four legged companions throughout the years. Thank you, Pom-Pom, Max, and Courtney. At times you truly were my best friends.

Much thanks to D.C., Alberta, Delia and LaDonna, you know who you are.

Thanks, too, to Chris O'Byrne at www.ebook-editor.com and Rakhi Rao.

Many people converge, like threads in a tapestry, to guide the destiny of a solitary human. If a person is fortunate, as I was, those who shape one's time on earth are as varied as the ocean currents.

1 ❧

"Whoa, didja hear that, Duchess?"

"Dude, that girl ain't hearin' nothin' but the sounds in her mind," the redheaded man replied in a low voice, trying to affect a thuggish demeanor.

"Didja hear that, Frosty? That fallin' star made a sound."

The boyish looking man jerked his head and smiled. "Dude, you are tripping. That was just a firecracker left over from the fourth last month. Now just chill and enjoy your high. You and Duchess just hang here a while. I got to hit it and make a roll," the man replied as he stepped into his car and started the engine. Rap music rattled the dashboard of the shiny white Mercedes. The muffler rumbled as he drove the car out of the parking lot leaving his companions, numbed and disoriented by the heroin he had sold them in the darkness of Lands End, a park at the edge of the city.

"Come on, Duchess, we've got to find a place to hang. I ain't that high yet. Frosty is a cold brotha. He knows he ain't comin' back for us. If he didn't sell the best shit in the bay, I wouldn't be havin' nothin' to do with the white muthafucka."

"You're my Tigger because you make me smile. Cornell says you don't really like me, but I know he's just jealous. But my stomach hurts. I don't think I care, Tigger. I just want to lie down. Did I give you my wallet? I forgot to feed Big Kitty, Tigger."

"Fool, I told you not to call me that. It sounds too much like nigger. Call me P-dog like I told ya."

"Love is all that matters, Tigger."

"Come on, Duchess, lets us follow this path into the bushes. That clearin' we like, overlookin' the ocean, is right through there. I'm really startin' to get high. Frosty sold us some real good shit this time," P-dog said, holding Duchess's arm and leading her through the darkness to the clearing. Pausing briefly he added, "Damn, Duchess, watch out. I'm smellin' skunk funk."

Stars sparkled in the moonless velvety sky. Duchess and P-dog lay on a precipice fifty feet above the rocky coastline. The black ocean waters roared below them. The two gazed silently into the heavens above. Meteors fell from the sky and burned up in bright rainbow hues while disintegrating in the stratosphere.

"Look, Tigger, the sky is falling. My stomach hurts, Tigger."

"I toldja not to go eatin' that rotten ol' burrito you dug out the trash. You gots plenty money to buy regular food. Sometimes I think sumthin' ain't right in yo' head. And, we need to be gettin' you to a doctor somehow, Duchess. I think ya might be pregnant. Look how big yo' belly be gettin'. Now jus' chill, Duchess. I wanna enjoy this ride."

Duchess flinched and replied emphatically, "No doctors, Tigger; you take care of me."

Although the experience was like staring into the refraction of a cluster of brilliant diamonds, they were mostly oblivious to the Perseid meteor shower. The fragments of rock that had travelled through the galaxy for millions of years were turning into bright fireballs as they collided with earth's atmosphere and disappeared in an instant.

A moment later, several tiny glittering meteorites streaked from the sky and landed simultaneously on Duchess's stomach with a muted thud, then exploded in a cloud of shimmering dust. A medium-pitched sound vibrated like a sonar blip for many seconds. Duchess cried out dully because her senses were deadened from the massive dose of heroin she had snorted. Hidden from view behind the tall bushes, P-dog, Duchess, and the land surrounding them were lit briefly by a bright white light. For several minutes, their silhouettes glowed like embers against the black horizon. P-dog and Duchess were both too stoned to comprehend the magnitude of what had just happened.

When darkness returned, Duchess cried out as fluid gushed from between her legs. She was becoming more coherent and frightened as the pain in her stomach intensified. In a panicked voice she said, "Tigger, I think something is happening to my insides. Oh, my God, Tigger, it hurts so much." Duchess clutched P-dog's arm and squeezed it so tightly he winced. "Tigger, my insides are falling out. I think I'm bleeding down there. Am I dying, Tigger?"

Duchess howled and then became silent. She let go of P-dog's arm. P-dog hunkered over Duchess, putting his ear to her chest. Her heart thumped wildly. He smelled blood, urine, and something pungent that he could not identify. His hand reached between her legs where it was wet and a lumpy object strained the fabric of her underwear beneath her long tattered skirt.

A half hour later, P-dog was using his pocketknife to cut the umbilical cord of the newborn that Duchess, still unconscious, had birthed. In the gray darkness, P-dog could just barely make out the features of the pale infant. He wrapped the baby in his jacket and held it close. The baby made no noise and barely stirred. P-dog wept, "Oh, Lord, what have you done, Duchess?" He felt sadness so profound it took his breath away.

2 ❧

"Delia, slow down this instant. You're going to get us both killed."

"Grandmother Ingrid, you've been dead for over twelve years."

"Don't quibble with me, young lady, I said slow down. I still don't understand why you didn't have your chauffeur drive us."

"Certainly, Grandmother. I should have rung for him and asked, 'Crawford, please bring the car around and drive me and my dead grandmother to a truck stop in Godforsaken Buttonwillow at three o'clock in the morning because my dead grandmother insists I need to go save my twin sister.' And don't for a second think that next week the story won't be in all of the tabloids with the headline 'Studio Executive in Drug Induced Night Flight to Save Homeless Sister' and they wouldn't have to distort the facts. I *have* had at least a dozen martinis today."

"Nonsense. You know Crawford can be trusted. You drink too much just like your grandfather and like he you become quarrelsome when you've consumed more than two cocktails. Why do you drink so much, Delia? You have not a thing in the world to be unhappy about. It is not as though you have to clean toilets for a living or scrounge for food like a good portion of the world's population. I wonder if I did this family a disservice by creating such a lucrative media empire? I believed it my duty to provide a legacy of affluence for my daughter and son and their children. I had no idea I was creating generations of the idle rich."

"Grandmother Ingrid, please, your grandfather earned the family fortune in oil long before even you were born."

"The families funds were nearly depleted when I founded Royal Arts. Mine was the first studio to net a billion dollars a year. You would never have been able to amass the money I did. At best I would concede that you have exceptional managerial skills, which you inherited from me. You do have the ability of finding the most competent people to run the media empire *I created*. I think perhaps you don't have enough productive activities to occupy your time."

"Please stop analyzing me in the middle of the night while I'm speeding down Interstate 5."

"See, Delia, you're positively surly. Look there, you nearly careened into the median. You're travelling at such a high rate that you couldn't possibly stop before we were on the other side of the highway directly in the path of another vehicle. You might not care a wit about your own safety but I refuse to be the victim of another fatal car crash. I'm certain the passengers in the other vehicle would concur."

"Grandmother, you can't die twice."

"And what makes you an expert on the subject, Delia? Were you always this tiresome? I don't think you were."

"All right, Grandmother, let's both stop talking. I promise to slow down and drive more cautiously."

"I certainly will address you if I have a mind to, Delia. You may be silent if you wish."

Delia drove on; the gray highway monotonously consumed beneath her car, the white divider being as hypnotic as a spiral wheel. The huge car was nearly noiseless. There seemed to be palpable pressure from the darkness outside of the headlights illumination. It all had a dreamlike quality.

Delia and her grandmother didn't speak until her grandmother said, "Delia, the exit for Buttonwillow is coming up. Shouldn't you be slowing down?"

"Yes, Grandmother, I see the exit," Delia paused and then added, "This seems very ludicrous. I must be losing my mind."

"I should think you'd be the best judge of that, Delia. Why do you think that?"

"Are you kidding? I'm talking to my dead grandmother, who by the way does not seem at all like the way I remember her to be, and she is telling me to go to my sister Anngelie who is supposedly injured or sick and stranded at a truck stop in a speck of a town nearly three hours from Beverly Hills, and even further from Anngelie's last known location in San Francisco. Please, I am definitely losing it."

"*Losing it?* What kind of expression is that? Your family didn't pay a small fortune for your education just so you could be lazy with your vocabulary. You have a lovely lilting voice that defies origin. Though, when you speak like that even your tone becomes abrasive. After all these years I'd think you would have become accustomed to communing with the dead. Might I ask why shouldn't you speak to your own grandmother? I'd be incensed if you didn't. I'll own, I might have changed somewhat since my death, but wouldn't one hope that death would bring about a certain level of enlightenment? Lastly, you did not need me to tell you where Anngelie was and that she needed your assistance. I just came along for the ride, which has turned out to be not nearly as pleasant as I had hoped."

"I'm sorry, Grandmother, the next time I lose my mind I'll try to be more companionable."

"That sarcasm might be fine for the indulged coven of hooligans you call your friends, but I won't stand for it. I might be dead but I'm still your grandmother and in my company you'll be respectful. Honestly, Delia, the way you and your hedonistic friends carry on would cause Fatty Arbuckle to blush."

"Grandmother, please, don't start talking about ancient Hollywood," Delia sighed.

"That ancient Hollywood you so disdainfully refer to paid for the house you reside in and it solely saved our entire family from financial ruin. I can also state assuredly that people were much more interesting eighty and ninety years ago, especially the early cinema stars. Of course there are a few exceptions. In fact I was just speaking to Lillian Gish the other day and telling her how much our dear enchanting Anngelie reminds me of poor Barbara LaMarr--both terribly beautiful and both terribly troubled. Now pay attention, Delia, and don't pass the exit."

"I won't miss the exit, Grandmother. Anngelie is the prettiest woman I have ever seen, even after being ravaged by drug addiction and AIDS. She is so much prettier than I am. Her eyes are such a lovely glacial blue," Delia said wistfully as she turned on her signal and exited the highway.

"Take care to veer east, Delia. You will need to turn on this first street here. The truck stop is the first entrance on our right. In response to your statement--don't drive so erratically, Delia--yes, Anngelie was stunning, but it wasn't the drugs or AIDS that ruined her beauty it was the periods of being homeless. All that exposure to the elements wreaks havoc on the skin and hair. You were prettier than Anngelie though, Delia. Your eyes are purple, which is more rare than blue, like the black currants we used to pick back during our summer trips to Norway. You are even lovelier than your mother, but I was more beautiful than any of you, and you were all lucky, including your children, to have inherited my features, except your mother was born with brown hair like her father. It is a *warm* chestnut brown, though, and somewhat attractive. I was so relieved when you and Anngelie and Winston and Gigi were blessed with my platinum blond hair."

Delia barely heard her grandmother. She was concentrating on her driving as she turned into the large parking lot of a restaurant with a big bank of gas pumps in front of it. Dozens of semi-trailer trucks were parked along the perimeter. "I've tried everything in my power to get her to come live with me, Grandmother, or at least to use some of her inheritance to purchase her own home but she refuses."

Delia parked in front of the restaurant. She scanned the brightly lit interior looking for any sign of Anngelie but she couldn't see her among the horde of weary looking mostly male travelers. Suddenly Delia knew where Anngelie was. She and her grandmother said simultaneously, "Anngelie is out in the field behind the parking lot."

Delia drove slowly and parked in a space behind the restaurant. The bright fluorescent pole lamps made everything look gray. Delia got out of the car and started slowly walking to the darkness at the far end of the parking lot behind a long row of softly rumbling semi-trailer trucks. Delia's heart pounded and her eyes scoured in all directions. Her pace quickened and then she started running knowing instinctively exactly where Anngelie was.

Out by two tanks of some kind surrounded by cyclone fencing, Delia found Anngelie. Anngelie was buried beneath a pile of old clothes and dusty blankets. She was curled up in the fetal position and even in the darkness Delia could see she was covered in blood. Delia gasped loudly, but Anngelie did not stir.

Thirty minutes later Delia was riding with Anngelie in the back of an ambulance speeding toward Bakersfield. Delia had contacted her family physician, Dr. Clayton, in Beverly Hills and informed him that the paramedics had told her a car had hit Anngelie. Dr. Clayton was going to meet them in Bakersfield with a specialist in internal injuries. Delia had a feeling it wasn't an automobile accident that had injured Anngelie. Delia held tightly to Anngelie's cold and limp hand. Grandmother Ingrid was gone and it angered Delia. She wanted her now more than ever. She needed comforting and advice about what to do to help her sister stay alive.

"Sammy up there radioed the emergency room at Kern and told them we were bringing in a probable auto/ped, but I think he's wrong. This is your sister, right?" the paramedic asked in a gravely voice. It startled Delia for a moment and then she nodded her head.

"Looks to me like your sister has been beaten with a tire iron. We've found three just like her near the truck stop in the past six months but they were all bagged--I mean dead. I might be wrong though because we heard they were all prostitutes."

Delia didn't respond. She didn't dare tell the stranger that Anngelie was probably prostituting too. Anngelie's sometimes boyfriend for the past century, Cornell, had been having her sell her body to maintain their drug habit. It dumbfounded Delia that Anngelie would rather sell herself to survive. Delia knew that Anngelie was using her inheritance for something, but she knew it wasn't drugs or the squalid hotel rooms she would sometimes rent.

At Kern Medical Center in Bakersfield, Delia soon learned the paramedic had been correct. Anngelie had been severely beaten and left for dead. Even though Delia had always been expecting Anngelie to come to a bad end it was still a shock that felt unreal, like a nightmare you can't force yourself to awaken from.

Delia sat alone in the waiting room watching a pair of children with restless legs fighting over what looked like a television remote. Occasionally they glanced at her quizzically and poked at each other when she pulled a flask from her purse and sipped the martini mixture it contained. The first pink light of dawn was beginning to show but it did nothing to brighten the dinginess of the room. Dr. Clayton and the specialist had arrived about an hour after the ambulance and they had been examining Anngelie for what seemed like an eternity.

Finally Dr. Clayton entered the waiting room and motioned Delia out into the corridor. A worker had just pushed up a cart filled with trays of noxious smelling morning meals. Delia had to force herself not to wretch.

"I'm afraid the news isn't very good, Delia. Anngelie has regained consciousness but her internal injuries are so severe and her body so compromised by the AIDS disease that without her consent to treat there isn't much Dr. Hufstra or I can do. I don't think she'll survive through the day." Dr. Clayton's voice was soothing and paternal.

Delia was beginning to get very angry and she wasn't certain why. "What do you mean 'without her consent'? Is Anngelie refusing treatment, Johnathon?"

"She won't even allow us to administer painkillers. She knows you located her and she is asking to speak to you. Perhaps you can change her mind. I was informed, apparently inaccurately, that Anngelie had been unconscious from the time you located her."

"Anngelie was unconscious until now. We're twins and we have a special connection, Johnathon. If we make the effort we always know where the other is. I'd like to see her now. Can you make the arrangements to get Anngelie to my home in Beverly Hills?"

"I wouldn't advise moving her until we can operate. Don't you think you can convince her to give her consent for treatment? She has several major organs that need immediate repair. You're just distraught, Delia. I'm certain that if you speak to Anngelie you can change her mind."

"I told you I have a special connection with my sister. She can be as stubborn as I am. I already know she will be asking me to take her home."

A few minutes later Delia was alone with Anngelie. She had to finish her flask before she could look at Anngelie. Most of the blood had been cleaned off but Anngelie's face was so swollen and bruised that Delia would not have recognized her. She couldn't move her head because it was bound and cast. Her beautiful blue eyes were swollen into puffy slits. A strange familiar looking lump in Anngelie's stomach also caught Delia's attention.

"Hello, sis, I'm not a very pretty mirror am I?" Anngelie's voice was weak and barely audible.

"You're the most beautiful woman in the world, and you always will be."

Anngelie knew that Delia's attention had focused on her protruding stomach. "Don't worry, Delia, I'm not pregnant. I feel like I'm pregnant though. It's added another thirty pounds to my weight. It's abdominal lipodystrophy. It's a fat that collects underneath the muscles. They don't know if the AIDS medications or the virus causes it. I have it on my face, too." Anngelie laughed and then continued, "I know how you hate fat, Delia. It embarrasses me, too. You wouldn't think that I would have any vanity left, but it seems I do." Anngelie suddenly winced and clinched her fists.

"Stop, Anngelie. Won't you please let the doctors save you, not even for me?"

"I'm sorry, Delia, I truly am. You already know my answer, though. Now would you just please take me home to die?" Anngelie whispered.

"Dr. Clayton doesn't even know if you'll make it back to Beverly Hills. You have a lot of internal injuries that need immediate treatment."

"I'll make it home, Delia, and I'll die in my old room."

Delia knew it was true. Anngelie was finally coming home but she would die before the night passed. Delia also knew there was something else Anngelie would ask of her. She could have figured it out, but she was too exhausted to even think about it yet.

3

"Delia, you really are here and I'm not dreaming. You promised you would get me home in time and you did. Facing death doesn't seem so scary here in my old room." Anngelie gasped weakly. Her voice had always been soft but now it was barely audible. Delia wondered for a moment if Anngelie was really speaking or if she had imagined it. Anngelie had been slipping in and out of consciousness all day and she hadn't spoken one word since Bakersfield.

"Lillian is on her way too. She just phoned, and she and Mitchell and Katherine will be here in about ten minutes," Delia said quietly. She had been holding Anngelie's hand all day and she squeezed it gently. Her cellphone vibrated in her blouse pocket but she ignored it.

"Oh my gosh, Delia. It must be really late. Mother flew in from Paris? She must have taken the family jet. I'm sorry, Delia. I know you don't like seeing Mother, and Mitchell, and especially Katherine. But I'm glad they aren't here yet. I need to ask you something while we are alone before it is too late." Anngelie's voice began to break and weaken, and tears streamed from her eyes, "Oh God, forgive me. I've done something so horrible. Please try not to judge me too harshly, Delia. God, I don't even know if I can say it."

Delia looked intently into Anngelie's eyes and in moments knew what Anngelie wanted to ask of her. "You need me to find your child don't you, Anngelie?"

Anngelie's face puckered and changed from white to scarlet. "You can't let anyone know about this, especially the family." Tears flooded from her large blue eyes as she gasped, "I love him so much, Delia. If you find him, Delia, tell him how much I ached for him. God, forgive me, I lost him. I'm so stupid and selfish. Something in my brain must be rancid. I just never found the strength to stop using. I really tried, Delia. I barely remember the pregnancy. It seems like some faraway dream. I went to the police and I know they just thought I was crazy. There were no records of my giving birth, only of my miscarriages. I almost started believing my son was a part of my insanity. But I know I had a baby boy. I know it in my heart." Gasping, Anngelie squeezed Delia's hand. Delia could see it was hard for her to breathe.

"Don't try to talk, Anngelie. I'll try to find your baby."

"No, Delia, I need to tell you these things before it's too late. I know everyone thinks I've been squandering my trust fund on crack and heroin, but the money I used from my trust fund was to hire people to find my son. Now I realize they were all ripping me off. Why oh why couldn't I think clearly before now? I was so ashamed and I hated myself so much. I dreamed about holding my son, but I have to honestly say I was more concerned about getting high. Please don't tell him what a disgusting person I was, Delia. If he does find out about the drugs and the prostituting try to explain to him that I was sick. Oh, God, time is running out, Delia, and there is so much I need to tell you. God don't let me die yet. I named my son Daniel Christopher. Daniel for that really sweet piano teacher we had when we were little. You remember him don't you, Delia?"

"He was very kind and so patient. We both adored him."

"Yes, Daniel for our piano teacher and Christopher from *Winnie-the-Pooh*. Remember how I used to love to read those books over and over. When you find Daniel tell him in a nice way that if I hadn't been so fucking fucked up I would have read to him every day. Most importantly, Delia, make sure that he feels loved. That's so important. It's the only thing that matters."

"I will, Anngelie, whatever you want."

"I've been so foolish, Delia. I squandered my life and lost the most precious gift I was given. I'm so tired, Delia. I'm tired of drugs and disgusting tricks. I feel like my entire life has been a battle. When I was young I fought to be perfect for Mother and Dad's approval. I struggled to be the brightest and the most talented. I think I was afraid if I wasn't perfect, people would find out how diseased I really was and I couldn't stand the idea of not pleasing everyone. I was afraid of the darkness and shadows and scared of storms and too bright sunny days, but mostly I was afraid of myself. Most of the time I was so depressed I felt as if my soul were encased in cement and when I wasn't overwhelmingly sad my thoughts raced fearfully in all directions. I was so afraid someone would find out how sick my mind was. I'm sure you knew I started using drugs in high school. It was such a relief to zone out and not think or feel about anything. I fought hard and kept up my perfect façade. Then I met Cornell Van Brundt and it all fell apart. The poor man was more miserable than I was. You know the rest of the tired disgusting story, mostly. The truth is the perfect daughter was the farthest from it."

Anngelie forced out a weak chuckle, "Isn't it ironic that my greatest fear was not making everyone happy and I did the opposite. I guess I redirected it to different people. When I wasn't completely strung out I was the best girl Cornell ever had working for him. I did whatever sick thing my tricks would want and I made certain they believed I enjoyed it as much as they did. I never complained when he or a sicko trick beat me and I willingly gave him all the money I earned. The truth is that my whole life has been a catastrophe. The only thing I did perfectly was be fucked up. But I couldn't even get 'crazy' right. I'm borderline bipolar, borderline personality disorder, and borderline in a thousand other mentally impaired ways."

"Please don't talk about yourself like this, Anngelie. I hate Cornell so much. I think sometimes I could kill him."

"Don't blame Cornell for what I am, Delia. He can't help the things he does."

"Cornell is a monster."

Anngelie continued as if she hadn't heard Delia. "The only times I felt at peace were when we played on the beach in Malibu behind Grandmother Ingrid's summer house. Do you remember that, Delia?" Anngelie asked.

Delia nodded and Anngelie talked on, her voice growing weaker. Delia had to lean in closer in order to hear her. "Oh it was such fun. Remember how I would chase seagulls, then climb on rocks and jump off flapping my arms? I wanted so desperately to take flight and soar as they did, high above the earth and without concern, tethered to no one, except maybe you. You were smarter because you embraced life. When we were little, while Miss Wallcrest was distracted, you'd swim fearlessly so far out into the ocean my heart would stop until you safely returned to shore. When we got older, you were more concerned with watching boys or getting a tan. I'd disappear and build those huts made of driftwood and seaweed. That time I ran away, I went to the beach with our cocker spaniel Sherry and we ran in the sand for hours. Afterward, Sherry and I hid in one of those makeshift houses I had labored over for days. I felt secure there, nestled in the sand behind those gray, timber walls. Life frightened me."

Delia felt her cell phone vibrating again and she ignored it.

"If I were a great artist, then maybe people wouldn't hold me in such contempt. My mental anguish would have validity. But I'm just a sorrowful woman with nothing to show for my pain and nothing beautiful or enlightening to give back to the world. I possess no talent for anything but self-destruction. I've often wished I could barter with God and trade my life for some poor child suffering with a fatal disease. I continually marveled at your courage and fortitude, yet I never resented you. I loved you more than anyone. I know it isn't worth much, but you are one of the few people I care for dearly."

"I love you too, Anngelie. You were just too good and too sensitive. You cared too much and I cared too little. Many times just thinking about how sweet you are to everyone has kept me from being as big of a bitch as I truly wanted to be. I'm the bad twin. You and Grandmother Ingrid are the only people I've ever cared for deeply. I can't even say I love Gigi and Winston the way I should," Delia replied as she stared beyond Anngelie. The muted television caught her attention. Anngelie closed her eyes and labored to breathe. Delia stared blankly at the television that had been scooted up close to Anngelie's bedside. It was tuned to the evening news where a picture of the pixyish actress Sandra Dee and the caption, 1942–2005, caught Delia's attention. Sandra Dee had briefly been her mother Lillian's confidant in the early 1970s, a decade after Sandra's fame had waned. Anngelie reminded Delia of Sandra. They both had an ethereal, sweet quality, and once flawless complexions. Now, it appeared they would be dying on the same day. Delia wished she could smile at the irony. She longed to feel mirth or disdain or anything but agonizing grief.

"Delia, you have so much love in your heart it humbles me," Anngelie gasped.

"Please don't die, Anngelie. I'm afraid of what a cold bitch I'll turn into without you in the world."

"You'll thrive--Daniel Christopher will help you. I'm certain he will. Please do your best to find him and make sure he has the best life possible. I'm just so tired now." Delia realized Anngelie was in a great deal of pain just as Anngelie moaned and grasped her hand tighter. Rousing for a moment, she told Delia urgently, "And please don't tell Mother or the rest of the family about Daniel. I know they would mess things up without even meaning to."

Delia didn't notice what an unusually warm February day it was in Beverly Hills. The temperature had climbed into the upper eighties for the third straight day. Outside, the parched Santa Ana winds had been blowing in from the Mojave Desert and whipping through the winter green canyons, but a drastic change in the weather was fast approaching with the setting of the sun that was vanishing molten red on the horizon.

The central air conditioning hummed virtually imperceptibly and the vast house was silent except for the occasional ringing of the phone in a distant room. Anngelie closed her swollen and bruised eyes, the eyes that had been Anngelie's most arresting feature. They were large, luminous eyes as blue and distant as arctic ice.

Soon their brother Mitchell and his controlling wife Katherine arrived clucking and bemoaning Anngelie's plight. Arriving with them in a cloud of perfume and reproach, her newest "project", Delphine, in tow, was Mitchell and Delia's mother, Lillian, who seemed to blame Delia for Anngelie's condition.

"Why isn't Anngelie in the hospital? I consulted with Dr. Clayton and he informed me Anngelie could possibly have survived if you hadn't insisted on bringing her home," Lillian hissed.

"Mother, please don't be angry with Delia. I demanded she bring me home to die."

"I'm not annoyed in the least, darling. I just wish I could understand your sister better. Now don't strain yourself. I'll see to it that you get properly cared for. I'm not selfish enough to allow you to die." Lillian said imperiously looking pointedly at Delia who returned her look with a glare.

4

"D.C., it's going to be freezing tonight, but thanks to you I can read the tiny numbers on the thermostat. Here, give Alberta's scratch ticket a touch. We need us some luck. Your cousin Latonda in Springfield called this morning and she's gone and got herself in trouble with the law again. Oh Lord, that temper of hers. She pitches a fit just like my Momma used to. Rest her sweet soul." Alberta's voice was playful and husky with the slight hint of a southern accent.

Looking down at the small willowy child, Alberta smiled. She put two Stouffer's frozen dinners into the microwave and pressed the timer. One was Swedish meatballs and the other was Salisbury steak and whipped potatoes. The frozen meals were a luxury Alberta usually couldn't afford, but she had purchased eight for ten dollars with her Safeway Club Card.

Alberta's knotted, cocoa-colored hands ached as she delicately set the dishes and flatware onto wobbly TV trays. Filling two tall plastic glasses with water she spooned instant milk into each. "You want some Ovaltine in your milk tonight, D.C.?"

Looking up at her the child nodded his head. Sighing, Alberta brushed his soft white hair out of his pale blue eyes. "I'm going to have to take the scissors to your hair again, D.C. It grows like a weed but it's so soft and pretty. Many a girl would love to have hair like yours. You can't get this hair from a bottle, though."

Staring at her intently D.C. held Alberta's throbbing hand. His round eyes shut tight and his delicate brow furrowed. Alberta could feel a heat envelop her hand and race up her arm. Both of her hands tingled and her heart fluttered. Within moments, her hands no longer hurt. The arthritis was nearly gone, but every so often it would flare up and D.C. would intuit her need and take care of it.

"In Jesus precious name, we thank you, Lord God," Alberta whispered, as she shifted her gaze upward.

Once the frozen dinners were ready, Alberta set them onto the plates, and carried the trays into the tiny living room. D.C. waited until Alberta had set both trays in front of the new green couch before he took a tight hold of the back of Alberta's pant leg and limped behind her into the adjoining room. The old wooden parquet floors creaked as their slender feet scooted across the squares. Exhaling heavily she sat down on the chenille divan her daughter Madison had recently given her as an early present for her eightieth birthday. At first, Alberta had resisted accepting such an extravagant gift, but Madison had insisted. D.C. was struggling to get up on the sofa beside Alberta so she reached down and sat him next to her. Before picking him up, she pulled up his soft, corduroy pants that were a size or two too large. Once brown, the slacks had faded to tan. Just like the stained T-shirt and cardigan D.C. was wearing, the pants had once belonged to Alberta's son, Phillip. Alberta glanced at her worn, black, polyester slacks and her old, threadbare, gray sweatshirt and said with a mirthful sigh, "I guess we look the dickens in these pitiful old clothes, D.C. But we don't care, do we? As long as we're comfy and warm and clean we're not ashamed."

D.C. smiled in his manner and gently stroked her forearm, nestling in close. Alberta smiled too and picked up the remote control lying on the cushion. The local news flickered onto the screen. Alberta grumbled, "No, we're not going to listen to this nonsense, tonight. All they report is death and lies, anyway, D.C. Let's watch somebody win something on *Wheel of Fortune*. That would be something happy to see."

Alberta continued to chatter to D.C. about God and good fortune and the tastiness of the dinners they quickly consumed. With a full belly, he was lulled to sleep by the sound of her soft voice.

A few hours later, D.C. woke up alone on the couch. The TV trays were gone. The room was dark except for a bluish light the television cast across the room. The sound on the TV was muted but D.C. could still hear voices. He recognized one of the voices as Alberta's but he couldn't quite place the other. Clumsily, he climbed down from the couch and went to sit next to Brownie the old wooly, fudge-colored poodle curled up on the rug in front of the sofa.

Suddenly, Alberta's grandson, Hardigree, came bursting out of the bedroom followed closely by Alberta. D.C. and Brownie both sat up startled. Hardigree was punching the air and breathing loudly.

"Why you got to be so stingy, Grams?" Hardigree huffed. He tugged at his baggy jeans and swaggered across the room to the front door. "You sure got enough to feed that fool child and that mangy old dog. Mama says you are gettin' more feebleminded everyday and that the boy is a freak. Me and her, we don't like him."

"I know all about what your mother thinks. And, never you

mind what I've got enough money for, young man. You know you are welcome to come to your Grandma's and eat anytime. I've fed you more times than I care to count. I surely don't have to remind you that you and your mother and your sister lived here rent-free for many years. Don't you dare question my generosity toward you, just because I won't finance you messing with drugs. I love you too much for that nonsense."

"Dang, Grams, I ain't into no drugs. I don't know why you got to be trippin'. Gettin' up in my business actin' like you know somethin'," Hardigree hollered and then calmed down. He turned to Alberta and gave her a hug. "I'm outta here. I love you, Grams."

"I love you too, Hardy. Now go out and be the good man your Grandma Alberta knows you are," she said, but he was out of the apartment and had closed the door before she finished speaking.

Alberta reached the wall by the front door and switched on the overhead light. She set about doing the things required for what had become a nightly ritual for her, D.C., and Brownie. Alberta opened the door of the small, angled closet that was actually just the enclosed space underneath the outside steps leading to the identical unit above hers. Sighing, she drug out an old fuzzy blanket, a plastic folding chair, and a big canvas purse.

She carried the objects to the back door, then outside to the patio. D.C. could see Alberta through the slats of the blinds hanging on the paned door. Her shadowy figure moved about on the concrete for several minutes.

Finally, Alberta stepped back inside. Wordlessly, she walked over to D.C. and scooped his tiny body up in her thin but still sturdy arms. She clicked her fingers once, softly. Brownie stood up and stretched before following them outside to the darkened patio.

Still silent, Alberta sat in the plastic chair and placed D.C. in her lap then pulled the thick blanket around them like a tent with only their heads peeking out. Brownie scratched at a corner of the cover, circled twice, then lay down next to them. Alberta pointed up at the starry sky. Straight above their heads, a wisp of fog floated like grey lace low in the sky.

Alberta and D.C. continued to stare into the darkened sky as the moon slowly revealed itself from behind a bank of puffy, ash-colored clouds. A yellow light, covered in a netting of dusty cobwebs, flickered on the concrete wall opposite where they were sitting. Neither Alberta nor D.C. noticed.

After several minutes passed without a word being spoken, Alberta finally said softly into D.C.'s ear, "It sure is something isn't it? Remember, whenever someone tries to make you feel like you aren't worth spit that you are a part of all of this wonder."

Alberta's arm poked through the blanket and made a sweeping motion across the sky. "Cherish this, D.C., because the sky in this area of San Francisco is usually so thick with fog that all you can see is the night reflecting back on itself. San Francisco is our city, D.C., it has a spiritual quality that is hard to define. It was named for St. Francis of Assisi, a man with a great love for the earth and all life. He knew what a great gift God had given us. Some people even say that the survivors of the lost city of Atlantis settled here eons ago, after sailing the seas aimlessly for countless days. This is your home D.C. and your spirit will always be safe here."

As Alberta identified the planets and constellations, D.C. listened spellbound. She described the moon and the known planets in the Milky Way. Then she took a meat-flavored, wheat-grain dog treat and a chocolate bar from her canvas bag, handing the treat to Brownie, who sniffed it, then snatched it from Alberta's hand. Alberta broke off pieces of the hard chocolate. She and D.C. shared the candy and gazed at the now cloudless sky. The air was moist and chilly but D.C. felt comfortably warm as his weary body rested under the blanket against Alberta. The two of them began to get drowsy.

When the animals came, Alberta was nearly asleep but she looked about guardedly. This had to be kept from prying eyes. Only two came to D.C. on this night. As if from nowhere an injured feral cat and an opossum with a wounded tail crept timidly from the darkness, Alberta was certain they were healed as soon as D.C. touched them.

The moon was low on the horizon by the time D.C.'s frail little body had gone limp and Alberta realized he was asleep. Alberta was tired too though she waited a while longer but no more animals came. Their neighbor, Carla Kookla, spied down on them from her second-story window. Alberta nodded at her cautiously, but Carla didn't see her.

A figure skulked from behind the hedge surrounding the modest patio just as Alberta was about to carry D.C. inside. Alberta sat motionless and held D.C. close. Brownie sniffed at the air and growled. The cloaked person moved within inches of Alberta. Alberta shivered and her skin prickled. In the dim light from the lamp on the facing wall, Alberta saw the face that was nearly hidden beneath a large, white hood. It appeared to be a short, ancient woman with a long, sharp nose, a fleshy, twisted mouth, and tiny, round eyes that eerily caught the light and appeared to glow. It looked like Nadi Ali, the taciturn wife of her longtime, next-door neighbor Ahmed Ali. But Nadi rarely ventured outside, except in the morning to hang her wash or to put shoes on the window sills. Nadi was afraid of dogs and wouldn't dare be this close, even to Brownie, who was docile. The figure stood motionless like an apparition.

Alberta was rarely frightened, but this silent stranger scared her. Alberta was so startled she couldn't speak. Alberta began to wonder if she was the peculiar new neighbor, Fran, whom Karla had mentioned. Alberta had caught only a brief glimpse but why in the world would she come to Alberta's back patio, stand there shrouded, and say nothing? Alberta stood, moving to carry D.C., still wrapped in the blanket, inside.

In a reedy voice, the phantom figure spoke, "What a lovely, queer child. I don't suppose it has a name?"

The woman pulled back her hood and revealed a mane of crinkly, powder-white hair and skin the color of snow. She was dressed from head to toe in white: white shoes, stockings, dress, and gloves. Her eyes didn't look so ominous when they weren't shadowed and the mouth wasn't as crooked as Alberta had thought. In fact, there was a tenderness to her odd smile. But no, Alberta did not recognize her. Then it struck her that it might be the mysterious, older, mute woman she used to see in the city's Mission district. Alberta and her family had dubbed the strange woman "the white lady" because she was inevitably clad entirely in white. Even her face was dusted with white powder. "The white lady" always appeared suddenly and disappeared just as abruptly. She conjured imaginings of a winter angel or the ghost of a long-suffering nurse. Alberta had not seen her in over twenty years and could not imagine how awfully old she must be, these many years later.

"His name is Henry," Alberta lied, and didn't know why. She held D.C. close and tried not to waken him.

"They call me Sarah. I live over there," the woman said with a soft chuckle while pointing west with her long, ashen finger.

"It's nice to meet you, Sarah, but I better be getting inside now," Alberta replied. Still uneasy, she started to walk away.

Alberta was stepping to the door when the woman cackled again, more forcefully than before. "You take great care of the boy. He has an extraordinary life journey. Be wary of foolish people who will try to harm him. They may be imprudent but they are also powerful." Alberta stared at D.C. Alberta looked up and the visitor had vanished. Alberta rushed into the apartment holding a still sleeping D.C. Brownie hurried in with her. With D.C. in her arms, Alberta bolted the patio door, took one of the dining chairs, and shoved it under the doorknob. Tenderly, she placed D.C. on the sofa, then switched on the lamps and set the phone next to the couch. She retrieved her bedclothes from her room and made a pallet on the floor by D.C. He never roused, as though he'd been drugged. Once Alberta lay down, Brownie climbed on the crumbling old cushion that was his bed and was soon snoring and twitching. Alberta gazed at both of them for a long while and finally said quietly, "Thank you, sweet Jesus, for protecting us. I pray that your hands will keep us safe from our enemies, always. I pray that you will give us and our loved ones well being—financially, physically, mentally, and most of all spiritually."

It was early morning before Alberta finally dozed off.

5

Dust hung heavily in the thick curtains. Gray smoke accumulated like clouds at the ceiling. A giant flat-screen television, its sound muted, cast the only light in the large room. Electronic dance music thumped relentlessly from a closed room on the second floor. Two long, mismatched, black leather sofas were shoved against the soiled, textured wall. Cigarette butts, ice pipes, beer cans, and needles littered the cracked, tiled floors.

On one sofa, a slim, blond young man was having convulsions. His onyx brown eyes had rolled back into his head and his tongue was knotted in his open mouth. He could literally feel his soul disengage from his body and soar upward.

"Gigi, this is Josh again. Winston still isn't responding. He's turning blue, Gigi. Oh, Christ, he's fucking dead, Gigi!" The young man shouted into his cell phone. He hurriedly hung up and shoved it in his pocket while bending over his boyfriend and calling his name.

Winston's soul lingered for a moment observing his boyfriend Josh frantically shaking his body and pounding his chest. Then his soul floated through the ceiling and through the bedroom where three of his friends were having sex. Finally, his spirit charged through the terra-cotta roof and zoomed high into the night sky. All of Los Angeles was lit up brightly and the Pacific Ocean lay like a black, shimmering blanket at its feet.

High above the globe he ascended. The blinking lights of a jet disappeared beneath him in a layer of storm clouds. His thoughts drifted back to when he was very young—to warm afternoons at his mother's estate, splashing in the pool and frisking on the plush lawn with his twin sister. Winston continued to travel back in time before he even existed. At a dizzying pace, he saw the first satellites and rockets burn into space. As his essence flew swiftly around the earth going back further and further into the past, he saw enormous, mushroom clouds and world wars, wagon trains and vast, sailing vessels, giant, extinct megafauna, and long, silent, nearly lifeless ice ages. At last, he observed the mighty dinosaurs as they nobly held dominion over all the lands.

Then it was as if time had stopped or turned in on itself somehow. Winston's spirit floated into the silence of space. He passed the moon and Mars and kept traveling to the edge of the universe. He felt humbled and more connected to every fragment of life than ever before. Winston's journey ended with him resting upon the dusty surface of a tiny satellite of some great, orange, gaseous planet. A large spaceship floated star-like above him. Inexplicably, he had a vision of his Aunt Anngelie standing beside him. She was the same but different— definitely younger, healthier, and lovelier than he had ever known her. She chuckled warmly and reached down to tickle his feet. Then, he was abruptly forced back toward the earth.

"What should we do?" Josh cried out to the stranger who had just walked into the room from the kitchen. Josh's shoulder length, ash-blond hair looked almost silver in the room's low light.

"No shit, he's dead?" The young muscular man said while taking a picture with his cell phone of Josh striking the chest of Winston's motionless body. A shock of dark hair covered the stranger's left eye like a pirate's patch and his eyes were as gold and lifeless as the shell of a bullet. "Well, don't call anybody till I'm out of here, dude," he added, as he put a chunk of yellowish, crystallized meth into a pipe he picked off the floor.

"I've already called his sister at least a dozen times. She's called 911 by now, I'm sure. I guess we'd better get him out of here. Help me get him to my car before the paramedics and the police get here," Josh said urgently, his olive-colored eyes flashing.

The other man groaned, then slipped the meth and the pipe into the pocket of his Diesel jeans. Effortlessly, he picked up Winston's body and slung it over his shoulder. He followed Josh out of the large, Spanish-style mansion to the driveway where Josh threw open the passenger door of his Mercedes G55 SUV. The tall, brawny stranger placed Winston in the seat and closed the door. He swatted at the wet roof of the SUV then raced through the rain to his own car, parked just behind the Mercedes.

Josh was still high from pot and a couple of hits of meth. His thoughts were muddled and he didn't know what else to do but go home. His heart was racing as he sped along Beverly Hills's glistening streets in the direction of the house he shared with Winston in the canyons north of West Hollywood.

Josh couldn't bring himself to look at Winston. Waves of panic rushed over him and he started to cry. Turning right onto Sunset Boulevard, he lost control of the SUV skidding across the pavement over the sidewalk and stopping with a thud against a giant palm tree.

A mile or so away, Delia consoled her dying sister. Still overwhelmed by the thought of locating Anngelie's child, Delia watched her sister's chest move slowly up and down. Anngelie's mouth was open and her breathing was loud and labored. Every few minutes her breathing stopped; she'd wheeze loudly and, with a snort, her lungs rattled. Her swollen, glacial eyes were closed but occasionally they fluttered and Delia could see the bloodshot whites.

On the edge of the bed stroking her sister's arm, Delia repeated, "Everything is fine, Anngelie. Go to Grandmother Ingrid; she is waiting for you."

Delia's cell phone vibrated nonstop for twenty minutes. Finally, she turned it off. The room was dark except for light from the adjoining bathroom. The weather had changed. Rain clicked against the windows, and logs crackled in the fireplace. Delia was comforted that the setting was peaceful.

The household staff had been coming in throughout the day to check on Anngelie's condition. Lillian and Delia's brother Mitchell and his wife Katherine had moved from their overwrought mourning in the library when told Anngelie was moments from death. They were now whispering in the bedroom while seated on a sofa by the fireplace. Delia could hear her mother and brother weeping. Even stony Katherine was crying. Concerned family and friends from across the world had been calling all day for news of Anngelie. Delia wondered what it was like to be so adored.

The spirits of Great-Grandmother Birgit and Aunt Agatha had been materializing at different times throughout the afternoon. Great-Grandmother Birgit kept speaking urgently in Norwegian. They seemed to want to convey something to Delia. She assumed they were there because of Anngelie.

Anngelie roused for a moment and her blank eyes opened slightly. She said weakly, "Please, don't forget what I asked, Delia. I know what a huge burden it is and I can't blame you if you don't want to do it." Tears streamed from her eyes and her voice was more intense: "Oh God, what have I done? I pray that my wretched soul can be forgiven."

What Anngelie uttered next wouldn't make sense to Delia for many months, "Look for Tigger. I think he had a sister." Her eyes closed again and she whispered softly in a tone free of care that Delia hadn't heard since they were little girls, "Look at all the lovely seagulls, Delia."

As Delia was about to get up and hug Anngelie, someone

tapping on the bedroom door and entering the room from the hallway distracted her. Delia was unaware that she had just heard her sister's final words. It was Delia's personal assistant, Greta whispering, "Mrs. Wentworth, may I see you in the hall for a moment?"

Delia started to walk out of the room. Mitchell walked to Anngelie's bedside. As usual he was wearing a dark, featureless suit. His brown hair had recently been cut and Delia noticed his graying temples. Still, he was attractive in a willfully innocuous anchorman kind of way. He glanced at Delia briefly with his cobalt-blue eyes and she felt disapproval. Delia purposely shoved him hard and he nearly fell. Neither said a word.

In the hall Delia asked, "What could possibly be so important, Greta?"

"Well, I don't know how to tell you this, Mrs. Wentworth, but apparently your son Winston has overdosed and died. Your daughter tried to reach you by cell phone. She called on the house line but the staff told her they couldn't interrupt you. Remember, you left explicit instructions that you weren't to be disturbed under any circumstances. Finally, she called on my cell phone," Greta stated in a hushed voice.

All that Delia had heard was that Winston had overdosed. It didn't register that Greta had also said he was dead.

"Well, where is he, now?" Delia asked anxiously.

"The last thing Gigi heard was that he was at a house on Roxbury."

"Don't tell anyone about this, Greta. Call the garage and have Crawford bring the car around front. If they ask, tell my family I'll be back soon," Delia panted, as she ran toward the stairs. She didn't even stop to grab her purse or a jacket.

Delia was all too familiar with the Spanish colonial on Roxbury. It was the old Farrow mansion. It had been a place to buy and do drugs for years. It was called "the shooting gallery." She herself had been there many times in what seemed like another life. Delia didn't know how it managed to thrive under the stringent policing of local law enforcement agencies. There were rumors that someone influential owned the property.

Delia ran down the stairs and out the front door. On the marble steps in the circular driveway, she was pelted by the cold rain while waiting for Crawford. She reached into her blouse pocket and pulled out her cell phone. Hurriedly, she dialed her daughter's number. It rang several times but no one answered. Hesitantly she called Winston's number but it went straight to messages.

A plump, fluffy gull, as white as salt crystals, with a bright yellow beak landed on the step in front of Delia. The bird cocked its head and looked at her quizzically, squawking loudly and waddling closer. Waving her hand, Delia said faintly, "Shoo, bird."

Giving her one final look, the bird flapped its wings and flew majestically into the darkness.

6

Alberta's daughter Madison had driven north from San Francisco on Highway 101. At the northern boundary of Marin County, she exited the highway onto a snaky, two-lane road. After traveling for countless miles into isolation, Madison finally pulled her car along the side of the road and parked beside a sloping field surrounded by rolling hills.

Alberta opened the car door and looked at her daughter. It comforted her to see Madison's lovely face. It reminded Alberta so much of her late husband, except Madison's features were softer. Their hair was the same black color and crinkly texture, but Madison's was long, almost to her waist when straightened as it usually was. Madison's skin wasn't as strikingly dark as his, but it was still an attractive, warm-pecan color. Like her father, Madison was tall and regal. Also, like her father, who she barely knew, Madison was an impeccable dresser. Even that early morning after being dragged out of bed to drive her mother into the country, Madison took time to put on makeup. She wore a lovely pair of tan wool slacks and a neatly pressed, white blouse.

Alberta started to get out of the car when Madison grasped her mother's arm.

"Where are you going, Mother?"

Alberta zipped her old gray sweatshirt and pulled the hood over her head. She looked at her daughter. Alberta's tobacco-brown eyes sparkled with enthusiasm as she proclaimed emphatically, "I've been anticipating this momentous event for weeks, Madison. I'm going to get out and experience all the glory of the Lord's spectacle. Aren't you coming too?"

She had read about the meteor shower weeks ago. It coincided with the return of her vision and Alberta had taken this as a sign from God.

"I'm too tired. Mother, you know you haven't been well for some time. Please, don't stay out there long," Madison said. She wondered sometimes if her mother's mind was failing.

Alberta was disappointed that Madison was not going to join her but she understood and did not fuss. Madison had driven her to the middle of nowhere in the hours before dawn without complaint. Alberta slipped into her worn tennis shoes and climbed out of the car.

This time she remembered to close the door carefully as Madison had asked. The silver Honda was Madison's new car. Alberta had never even learned how to drive but she could imagine how Madison wanted to keep her car in good condition. Alberta opened the back door on the passenger side and reached in to take Desmond Charles from his car seat. Brownie observed her keenly, then raced outside to stand attentively at her heels.

"Mother, you're not going to take that sickly baby out there too, are you? You'll both be ailing tomorrow, and I really can't afford to take any more time off from work to care for you," Madison pleaded. She was annoyed that her mother had decided to raise the burdensome infant. It just wasn't right to take an abandoned baby, especially a white one who was no relation. He was bound to have family somewhere. The peculiar and unhealthy baby bothered her a great deal, but she didn't want to see it suffer.

"I'm grateful for your concern, sweetheart, but never you mind about me and Desmond Charles. We'll be fine as long as we're together," Alberta confided. Alberta had been sick for so many years, she knew it was difficult for Madison to accept that she was no longer ill. A few months ago, she herself assumed the Lord would soon be calling her home, but now that she had baby Desmond Charles everything had changed.

It was difficult to see in the darkness so Alberta held the baby tight and walked carefully down a dusty trail that separated a large pasture bordered by a tall, barbed wire fence. The Milky Way cut a twinkling, chalky swath across the blackened sky. Alberta stared into the night and felt the chill go to her bones. Desmond Charles didn't make a sound. It felt as if he too was staring transfixed into the sky.

The baby had only been with her a few months but Alberta was certain he was endowed with special powers. Her foot—that the doctor said might have to be amputated—had healed. Before the baby came, her eyesight was nearly gone. Now her vision was so improved she no longer needed spectacles unless she was reading very tiny print.

Something moved in the darkness ahead of them, and Alberta heard the sound of dry grass being trampled. She held the baby tighter to her squishy bosom. Alberta listened more intently and stared harder into the darkness. She was barely able to make out the silhouette of a large cow standing about twenty feet in front of her.

When a lone car zoomed 'round a bend in the road about half

a mile north, Alberta turned to look. Its headlamps illuminated the landscape. Two other cars were parked on the roadside near Madison's. Someone was sitting on the hood of one and two people leaned against the other. A dewy fog hung in mocking patches over the parched, hard earth. The car went whirring past and Alberta looked away, again fixing her gaze on the heavens. She waited.

Alberta was beginning to wonder if maybe her eyes weren't as healed as she'd thought when she suddenly saw a flash of color rocket across the sky as it was swallowed by the earth's atmosphere. Then another followed, more vivid than the first. In the corners of her eyes, at the edge of her vision field, she saw others. Everywhere she looked, brightly colored stars were falling from space like a shower of sparkling, multicolored gems. She heard someone gasp and then the sound of hands clapping. Then it was silent again. Alberta tried to tally how many stars she saw streak across the coal-colored sky but quickly lost count past twenty. There were so many falling stars it seemed almost dreamlike. But Alberta knew it was real. It was a once-in-a-lifetime gift from God, just like the frail baby she was rocking gently in her arms.

"Thank you, Lord," she uttered softly.

The baby that Alberta had named Desmond Charles after her great-grandfather was squirming in her arms. Then one of his slight, colorless arms poked through the fuzzy blanket and his tiny hand reached toward the sky. To Alberta's amazement, an infinitesimal fragment of a falling star rocketed from the heavens and its flickering light appeared to land directly in the infant boy's hand. The glow of it lit up the boy's face and it appeared golden. He cooed softly and made a noise that sounded like laughter. Desmond Charles was usually so still, she often checked to make certain he was breathing. Alberta sensed how difficult it was for the baby to make noise so she laughed too. Brownie barked spiritedly along with them. Alberta could feel the poodle's fuzzy, brown tail wagging furiously against her leg.

"That's right, baby boy, you should be laughing. Watching a shower of stars like this is a joy. You are bearing witness to God's infinite majesty. You and I are a part of God's munificence. So you laugh with joy, my little man. The sound of laughter is music to our Lord's ears," Alberta said. She took Desmond Charles's grasping hand and kissed it softly.

Nearly four and a half years had passed since that night, and the child's small delicate body had grown very little. Alberta no longer referred to him as Desmond Charles. He was now simply D.C. He could walk but he limped and Alberta could tell it was a strain for him. He still couldn't talk, but he made sounds that only Alberta could decipher. D.C. never truly smiled. Though no one else witnessed it, Alberta knew that D.C. laughed often. Not what most people recognize as laughter, but a sound Alberta was certain was his way of expressing great mirth. The doctors insisted she was mistaken and the boy simply wasn't capable of real laughter, but Alberta would not be swayed. Those doctors had all kinds of ten-dollar words to describe what was wrong with D.C., but none of them understood how extraordinary he was. Asking the doctors about D.C.'s laughter was one thing but Alberta never mentioned his special healing power to them because she feared the boy might be taken from her and neither one of them could risk that.

It amazed Alberta that God had given her the gift of D.C. at the end of her time on earth. Alberta had loved her family and her late husband with unwavering devotion. Her son and daughter, and her daughter's children had swelled her heart to what she felt was its limits, but she was mistaken. D.C. turned out to be her true soul mate. The two of them shared a rare connection that Alberta was wise enough to recognize. The love Alberta felt for D.C. made her truly aware of the eternal.

Alberta was thankful she lived in San Francisco and not in the town in southern Missouri where she had spent her early grade school years. Back in Springfield, the sight of a gnarled, old, black woman the color of pitch, and Desmond Charles, a sickly, white baby, together, would have set many a meddlesome and sanctimonious tongue to wagging. But in San Francisco no one ever questioned how, or why, she and D.C. had come into each other's lives except for her nosy neighbor, Carla Kookla, and Alberta knew she posed no real threat.

Standing firm against the railing at the back of the ferry, Alberta gazed at her beloved San Francisco. Alberta, D.C., and Brownie were on their way to the home of Alberta's sister Roberta who lived in Vallejo at the top of the bay thirty miles northeast of San Francisco. Roberta was giving herself a party for her eighty-fifth birthday.

The sun was beginning to set, and low on the horizon long narrow clouds were turning bright scarlet. They reflected purple in the blue water of the bay that was unusually tranquil. Fat, insistent seagulls flew just above the white, foaming water of the boat's wake. D.C.

clung to her leg and leaned all his weight into her, but she barely felt him. Alberta scooped him up and walked over to one of the empty, hard-plastic seats where Brownie was snoozing in his carrier. Alberta had made a nest of Brownie's favorite blanket in the bottom of the cage. She sat down next to Brownie with the tiny boy in her lap. The big tapestry bag she had been holding slid from her shoulder and she set it at her feet. As the boat churned slowly through the water, the crumbling, beige-colored ruins of Alcatraz came into view. Beyond it, off in the distance to the north, Alberta could see the purple silhouette of the eastern peak of Mount Tamalpais in Marin County. There was something feminine, stately, and ethereal about the image of the mountain. Alberta resolved to take D.C. there for a picnic.

As the ferry passed Alcatraz, the Golden Gate Bridge turned flaming orange in the sunset. Alberta patted D.C.'s hand and pointed to the sun, framed by the bridge, as it glowed amber through a bank of heavy fog far offshore. D.C. made the noise for "pretty" and Alberta nodded. A snow-white gull with black-tipped wings flew just inches from where they sat. It hovered near D.C.'s face and he laughed in his peculiar way, almost indiscernibly, and made the sound for "nice." The bird squawked twice and flew away.

Alberta had long since become accustomed to the way creatures took to D.C.—all creatures except humans. Most people were uneasy and agitated in D.C.'s company. They would look at him curiously and then express too much pity or, more often, an inexplicable indifference or utter contempt. In turn, he would react poorly toward them, which only reaffirmed their suspicions that D.C. was damaged. Younger children, though, seemed innately aware that D.C. was miraculous and they usually treated him with a degree of reverence. As long as D.C. was in Alberta's presence, he didn't pay attention to the peculiar reactions of other people. On the rare occasions when Alberta was not with him, he would become either agitated or withdrawn.

Because she was afraid of losing track of D.C., Alberta rarely took him around crowds. She was hesitant to take him to Roberta's party. Alberta assumed that the gathering would include only Roberta and her two daughters, her son, their spouses, and children, and D.C. had met all of them. Moreover, Alberta knew that Roberta would pitch a fit if she didn't show up. Their only other siblings had passed many years before.

Suddenly, Alberta heard a sound in the water on the side of the ferry. With a low moan, she lifted D.C. in her arms and stood up. Carefully, she walked to the railing at the edge of the slow moving ferry and peered over the side. A large, spotted seal leaped from the water, then dove beneath the surface with a mighty roar. D.C. made a loud noise that Alberta didn't recognize. It was almost as if he was calling out to the frolicking seal. Within moments, the seal's glossy, pointed head bobbed up and his round eyes stared in their direction. D.C. made another noise that sounded distinctly like the word "bear" and then made another loud noise. The seal barked back several times before disappearing again beneath the water.

The ferry rounded a bend and the green hills of Vallejo came into view. Alberta knew the town well. Her father and uncle had moved to Vallejo many years before to work in the shipyards. They were two of the first African-American men hired by the west coast shipbuilding industry. Back then, they were referred to as "those colored boys," or worse. To keep their jobs they quietly had to endure expressions of racism that still made Alberta's blood boil.

Alberta had spent her junior and high school years in Vallejo but as soon as she graduated, she moved to San Francisco. After finishing some business courses, she got a job as a receptionist in a thriving accounting firm. Two years after settling in San Francisco, Alberta met Armand Sommers, who would become her first and only husband. He was fourteen years older than she was but seemed younger or at least romantically inexperienced. Before Alberta, he'd never had a serious involvement and Alberta could tell that he had avoided women out of a profound, nearly crippling shyness. His manner was austere and for that reason, women hadn't pursued him. Alberta sensed in him a fierce sensuality and a need to express his sexual desire. Even the dapper way he dressed was sensuous. His elegant clothes accentuated the perfect symmetry of his physique. He was lovely to behold with dark, nearly black skin, and thick, nappy hair that he tried to tame with a homemade mix of olive oil, lilac water, and glycerin. He had intense, almond-shaped eyes that were as dark and luminous as polished ebony. To Alberta, he was like an exotic pastry left in the display case because others preferred more familiar treats.

Armand was alluring but troubled. He grew up in a desolate, gray speck on the map in southern Alabama that one day ceased to be, like a long bout of flu. It was there where he had survived a lynching after saying "good morning" to the daughter of a white Baptist preacher.

Armand was only thirteen at the time and his Great-Granny Truitt raised him. When she found him near death, she cut him from the tree branch and nursed him back to health. After he'd healed, she tearfully walked him to the tracks and persuaded him to hop a night train headed west to California.

Armand's half-white father, Pleasant, deserted the family when Armand was five years old. His mother, Molly, cared for him, his thirteen-month-old twin sisters, and the baby left in her belly. Food and money were scarce. Molly took what odd jobs she could find in the tiny town but earned hardly enough to feed her young. The twins weakened, and on a frosty morning in February, they died from pneumonia. Molly went mad from grief and threw herself down a flight of stairs in the boarding house where her sister worked. She lost the baby. Molly struggled for a few more years but her spirit was crushed. At age twenty-three, she died in a field where she and Armand had been picking cotton for nearly twelve hours. Armand discovered his mother slumped in the dirt with her hand clutching her chest. In her fist was a tuft of cotton as frothy and white as spun sugar.

Armand was full of festered rage toward his father whom he blamed for his mother's death and the loss of his twin sisters. Alberta remembered the day Armand got a long-distance call from his father's fifth or sixth wife, Norma Lou in St. Louis, informing him that his father had passed away. His stepmother expected Armand to pay for the funeral. Seething with anger, Armand told her to shove the useless body into a potato sack and toss it into the muddy Mississippi. He slammed the heavy black phone so hard, it shattered.

Armand was angry with more than just his father. He was furious at life itself and viewed injustice as a personal affront. Many of his days were spent lost in a fog of despair. Alberta had known from the moment she met him that he was too fragile for the world he was born into. Armand had survived what most people could only imagine. Instead of making him stronger, his suffering had chipped away at his soul and crippled it.

Alberta tried for years to heal her husband. She bore him two lovely children, kept a spotless home, prepared gourmet meals she taught herself to cook from books she borrowed from the library, and she made certain their home was filled with laughter. But the blues encroached on Armand's spirit like unstable air masses, unexpectedly and often violently. For days that could turn to weeks, he would be sullen, brusque, and withdrawn, which left Alberta feeling lonely and neglected. Then, like musical chords, his mood shifted from minor to major and his dark eyes became full of smiles and happy mischief. Alberta fell in love with him again, even more deeply than before.

Armand found solace in his art and in their lovemaking. He painted ferociously with oils for hours, sometimes late into the night. He painted large, bold portraits of his family and people he met. With purposeful, intricate strokes and nuanced shadowing, he could evoke the essence of a person in a single, unsettling painting. His paintings were marvelous works of art that filled Alberta with admiration. Armand was never satisfied though, and considered none of them complete. During his bouts with depression, he sometimes destroyed a canvas he found particularly frustrating. Alberta never tried to stop him, because the art was his to do with as he saw fit. Yet, she knew he could easily have been a celebrated artist. He never once tried to sell or exhibit his art and allowed only Alberta to see his paintings. The canvases that Armand had not destroyed, Alberta kept locked away in her bedroom closet.

Armand's lovemaking was as skilled, fervent, and thoughtful as his art. Alberta was grateful she had experienced that kind of love with a man. Sex with Armand had nearly always been a satisfying and completely intimate experience. Usually, they were both transported to a state of near euphoria. Alberta still lingered over memories of his electric touch.

At the age of fifty-nine, Armand died after a heart attack. Alberta was inconsolable and left alone at age forty-five to raise Phillip, who was seven, and Madison, who was two. But Alberta was also relieved for Armand's sake. She knew he had gone on to a more peaceful place with his mother and sisters and all the family who had preceded him in death. She even believed he was able, in the rebirth of his soul, to understand and forgive his father. Alberta loved Armand with her entire being, but that love had exhausted her. Even though she was still in her forties, she realized within weeks of his passing she would never again get involved romantically with another man. She was convinced no man could compare to Armand and she no longer had the energy, or will, to maintain a complex relationship.

As the ferry docked at the Vallejo terminal, Alberta couldn't help thinking of the past, of Armand and her family. Many of them were dead and buried, but she could still feel them nearby. With D.C. in one arm and holding Brownie's carrier in the other hand, Alberta got off the ferry and headed up Georgia Street toward her sister's home. She walked slowly through the downtown admiring the historic architecture and shook her head in dismay at the many more empty buildings left to decay. At what used to be Duchess Fiona's Fine Ladies Clothier, the store where she'd worked on weekends while in high school, Alberta lingered for a moment then passed by Taylor's Restaurant. Part of the old, hand-painted sign was still visible on the faded brick. Her oldest sister, Dola, had worked there as a waitress. Whenever Alberta had dropped by, Dola would slip her large bowlfuls of pistachio ice cream and huge, fluffy dinner rolls with sweet melted butter. The memory made her smile.

Teenagers—and adults dressed like teens, mostly in oversized, sports-themed attire, and with cell phones glued to their ears—loitered on the corners. People were also standing in shadowy clusters outside the liquor stores and mini-markets. Alberta was thankful that no one gave her, or D.C., or Brownie, a second glance. They were all too busy making deals and getting fixes. Cautious and watchful, Alberta was startled to hear rustling feathers. She turned to look, then smiled when she caught sight of a plump, speckled gull brashly following them.

7

"Where are we going, Delia?" Adrianna's voice was always low and somewhat hoarse.

"Oh, I don't know, Adrianna. I'm supposed to be going to my sister's funeral. But it looks like I'm too late. My so-called family is getting together after the service at my brother's house in Malibu. I doubt if I'll bother, though. No one will notice if I'm there or not."

"Yeah, I think Constance mentioned something about your sister. I'd forgotten you had a sister. Constance said she was some big drug dealer and she got shot during a raid by the feds."

"Please, Constance must be snorting heroin again. She's got it all wrong as usual. I suppose she'll be contacting *The Enquirer*. I hate the idea of Anngelie being slandered."

"I wouldn't worry about it. No one pays any attention to Constance."

"Adrianna, do you think we have too much money? Doesn't the elite group of people we associate with bore you the least bit? Is it supposed to give me a sense of wellbeing that my closest friends control all politics and that the masses follow along like lemmings? We already have more wealth than we could use in ten lifetimes. What's the value of having it all at any cost? Shouldn't life be about more than money and indulgence?"

"Oh, Delia, I've had too many valiums and too many martinis. I don't know how you do it. I feel like my brain has turned to cotton. Anyway, did I tell you I was going to Manila the end of next month? I'm brokering a deal on a new high-rise. The building has a fantastic penthouse you might want to buy. I still want to go to Paris for fashion week. Melody rented a flat for us. Her divorce was final last week and she plans to stay on in Paris for a few months. Do you think I should have some lipo done on my fingers? They look fat to me."

Delia picked up the receiver in the armrest and said, "Crawford, I've changed my mind. Take me to my brother's house in Malibu. Afterward, you can drop off Mrs. Thurston wherever she'd like to go and then come back to get me."

Delia tried to place the phone in its cradle but it wouldn't fit. Huffing she shouted, "God dammit, what the fuck is wrong with this thing?" She slammed the receiver down hard and it cracked loudly.

"Delia, what in the world? Why are you so worked up? I'm going to tell you again that you need a new boyfriend. I still want you to meet Victor's brother, Anthony. He's a really great guy and you know The Thurston family has almost as much money as your family."

"Are you joking, Adrianna? You're constantly complaining about your husband and his family."

"It's Victor and his mother who drive me crazy. They are both so controlling, but I still love Victor despite his mother. Anthony isn't so bad and he's much better looking than Victor. I wish I had met him first. Anyway, forget about Anthony. I thought we were going to Melody's dinner party. You've got to see her. She's had another round of collagen injections in her lips and they look like Goodyears. She wants us to meet her new boyfriend. Talk about a grandfather complex--I hear he's in his eighties but he's connected to the Du Ponts. I think his name is Victor Beall the third or fourth, but I've never heard of him so he can't be of much consequence. Melody hasn't been the same since our involvement in Guang Chi. She insists she is cured of her sex addiction but I've been hearing stories."

"Oh who cares, Adrianna, please?! Go to Melody's and tell them anything you want about me. Tell them I've charted a shuttle to the moon. Tell them I'm a drug tsar and I'm selling arms to rebels in Darfur. I don't give a shit."

"I don't know what has you so upset, Delia, but I'm not going to let you take it out on me. Constance may tolerate your abuse when you get in one of your moods but I refuse to. You know I really could be a good friend to you, Delia, but that's never been what you wanted. You insist on keeping yourself so detached."

"Oh really, Adrianna, wouldn't a good friend know that I'm missing my sister?"

"A good friend would wait until her friend was ready to talk about something so distressing."

"So I'm a cold, moody bitch and a lousy friend. Is there anything else you'd like to criticize me about?"

Adrianna didn't respond. Delia lit a cigarette and said nothing too. Staring out the window as the car sped along she tried to clear her mind. Anngelie kept haunting her thoughts.

Adrianna got out her phone and started texting. She chuckled a few times.

Soon Crawford was pulling the limousine into the drive of

Mitchell's home in Malibu.

"You never did answer me about my fingers, Delia. They're really bothering me, but Dr. Grifton says I shouldn't have it done again. Anyway, I'll call you tomorrow about fashion week," Adrianna said as Delia was stepping out of the car.

"I'm going away soon, Adrianna. I won't be going to Paris. I have no idea when I'll be returning. Oh, and yes, your fingers are much too fat. While you're at you should really see about getting your toes done too. The last time we were at the spa I noticed how grossly fat they were. You simply must get all your digits reduced." Delia slammed the door and walked away.

Adrianna studied her fingers and slipped off her heels and did the same to her toes. She was teary as she texted Melody that Delia was secretly going to Switzerland to have a facelift, but not to tell another soul.

Delia stared after her limousine for a few moments then she walked to the gardens beyond the house out by the sandy bluffs overlooking the Pacific Ocean where tides were sloshing onto the beach.

Lighting another cigarette, Delia stared out at the water. Four gray pelicans soared low above a white cap, then dove into the water. Delia could hear Lillian and Mitchell and the rest of the immediate family behind her where they had gathered on the back patio by the outdoor pool. Winston and Gigi, her children, waved at her shyly but everyone else ignored her.

"Delia, put out that cigarette this instant. You're not going to use Anngelie's death as an excuse to pick up that nasty habit again."

"Grandmother Ingrid, I was beginning to wonder if you were a martini fueled hallucination the other day. I'm quite accustomed to seeing ghosts after all these years but I've never had conversations with them." Delia said as she took one last puff and let the cigarette drop. With the toe of her shiny black heel she smashed the smoldering butt into the damp ground.

"I am indeed quite real and always have been, before and after death. I wouldn't wonder if you imagined seeing pink elephants with the amount of liquor you consume. Don't you know how unseemly it is for a lady to imbibe more than one or two cocktails an evening?"

"Grandmother, please don't start up with me."

"I can see you're in another surly mood."

"Why does everyone talk about my moods?"

"You're like your grandfather. He was unbearably morose when he drank too much alcohol, which I didn't allow him to do too often I assure you."

"Grandmother, sometimes I feel like I'm a bomb that's going to explode. The drinking and the pills numb my anger to a certain extent."

"What could you possibly be angry about, Delia?"

Delia was about to answer when Mitchell hollered out, "Hey, Delia."

"Oh great, I knew I shouldn't have come. These are not the people I want to be grieving Anngelie's death with," Delia spoke more quietly as she neared her family on the patio.

"Well, something compelled you to come here. Perhaps your instincts are better than you'd care to admit."

"Quit talking to yourself, Del, and join the family. Gidget is about to say a prayer for Anngelie's soul," Mitchell proclaimed in his booming baritone radio voice when Delia got to the large square courtyard at the back of the house. She stood just beyond the gathering.

Delia mumbled, "Whatever."

Tittering oddly Mitchell's stepdaughter Gidget recited her prayer prefacing it by saying, "I didn't know Aunt Ann very good, but I know she would have been happier if she had lived with the Lord." Gidget read from the crumpled notebook paper in her hand. "Dear Lord, please be kind to those we leave behind. Let them know the comfort of your vengeful love that you send to us from above," Gidget recited as she tried to force a tear from her eye.

Mitchell walked over and put his arm around Gidget. He brushed her long, highlighted hair away from her tanned, round face and said, "Kid, you are da bomb. I'm so proud of you. God blesses me with so much. He rewards the righteous."

Gidget smiled smugly and whispered, "Thanks, Daddy Mitch," into his ear so quietly, no one else could hear. She kissed his cheek leaving a mark of frosty pink lip gloss, and then she giggled before taking a handkerchief from his breast pocket and slowly wiping it clean.

"Don't you think Mitchell's relationship with Gidget is a little creepy? Hurry, look at Katherine, Grandmother, she must agree with me. She looks peeved. That mall haircut of hers is a disaster. She is so cheap. All it does is draw attention to her droopy nickel-colored eyes. Why in hell are Mittie and Dirk here? Mitchell can't blow his nose without Katherine and her mother around. I don't think that

Katherine's parents ever even met Anngelie. Mittie is looking mighty frisky with that tight new perm, I must say. Her rear must be at least a half a foot wider than the last time I saw her. And please, polyester slacks at a funeral, even if they are black? I hope Mitchell is taking a good gander because that is Katherine in another fifteen years. Oh look, did you see the scowl Katherine just gave me? I think I'm the only person Katherine hates more than her sister, Wendy, the liberal. She calls Wendy a communist because she's a vegetarian, wears garden clogs to the office and fights for labor unions, including for Eggertson's Grocery store chain, the company their family has controlling interest in. Mostly she thinks that because Wendy married a Jewish civil rights attorney who does a lot of pro bono work. I've spoken with Wendy many times. She is not a Communist, she is an egalitarian and a humanist."

"Delia, what are you muttering to yourself about? You must be inebriated. Why weren't you at your sister's funeral? Wasn't it bad enough that you refused to give her proper medical care? Don't you have respect for anyone? That Psychic in Amsterdam warned me about having twin Scorpions. She said one of them would cause me no end of grief, because I'm a Virgo with Leo rising." Lillian was lacquered to perfection as usual. Even her black, linen dress was unwrinkled. Looking around through her dark glasses at the gathering she added, "You'll have to excuse my outburst everyone. I'm certain under the circumstances you all understand. Why don't you play us one of your new pieces, Delphine?"

Delphine was Lillian's new "find." She was purported to be a wunderkind on the sitar.

Mitchell's Malibu home had once belonged to their Grandmother Ingrid, as did Delia's estate in Beverly Hills. Delia had spent many joyous days camped out at her grandmother's home, usually accompanied by Anngelie. Back when Delia and Anngelie were children, Grandmother Ingrid's property extended a ten thousand yards further in both directions than it did now. When they were little girls who loved to explore, it seemed to Anngelie and Delia that Grandmother Ingrid owned the entire southern coast of California. Many memories of nearly forgotten moments flashed in Delia's head. She felt a wave of anguish engulf her and she stood back for a few minutes as the rest of the family filed into the house. She steeled herself.

"Did you see Lillian, Grandmother? She's trying so hard not to cry because she's obviously recently had cosmetic work done on her eyes. She did look stunning though. I think it must be sheer will that makes every strand stay in place; even her hair wouldn't dare defy her. Why did she bring along that Delphine creature? She looks like an unwashed Lilith Fair groupie. I thought protégés went out with prohibition?"

"Have you never considered, Delia, that perhaps your mother tries to assist these unfortunates because she was unable to save her own child?"

Delia ignored her grandmother. "Father on the other hand looks dreadful. Why did that moose Ethel drag him here? He isn't even coherent. My God the man just had a series of strokes six months ago. All he can do is sit there with a confused look in his eyes and drool into that napkin on his shoulder."

"Your father is certainly to be pitied, Delia. You need to rid yourself of your anger."

"And that pitiful daughter of Ethel's, Cindi; I guess she's technically my stepsister. She's obviously anorexic. I'm still not certain whether it is shyness or hunger that causes her to chew on her brittle hair. Well with a mother like Ethel, what can you expect? Ethel is at least 110 and Cindi is younger than Winston and Gigi. I've heard of menopausal babies but Ethel must have freeze-dried her eggs. They're so ancient now you'd have to carbon date them. I better be quieter. I've seen slimmer shoulders on a linebacker. I guess she needs them to hold up those gravity-defying breasts. Her bra must be wired with cast iron."

"Are you quite finished, Delia? You should be joining the others now."

"I promise I'll stop for now, Grandmother. I just have to mention Ethel's eyebrows. It looks like she uses a piece of charcoal to pencil them in." Delia took the slim silver flask of martinis from her purse and drank it all.

"Hey, Del, if you don't stop talking to yourself we're going to phone Dr. Futterman next door. He's got a lovely sanitarium up in Montecito," Mitchell said loudly as Delia was walking into the family room from the patio. Delia noted the room hadn't been redone since obviously 1981—even then it looked self-consciously trendy and outdated. It was done in muted and murky tones of pink, blue and taupe.

Delia purposely stood near the French doors and gazed outside. Heavy clouds loomed offshore and it had begun to sprinkle. The large windows that faced the ocean did nothing to enliven the room because heavy mauve colored curtains and low draping valances shrouded them.

"Hey, Mitch, why don't you grow a pair. Or do you need Katherine's permission to do that too?" Delia replied quietly.

"What did you say, Delia?" Lillian sighed while tossing her black fur onto the back of a chair where she sat down. Lillian patted her meticulously coifed, chestnut hair. Her skin had recently been acid-peeled. It was as ruddy and shiny as newly sanded and varnished mahogany.

"It doesn't matter, Lillian."

"If I dared to address my mother by her first name she would disown me."

Delia ignored Katherine's remark as Katherine walked from the room. Looking at the gathering Delia noticed Mittie smirking at her. Lillian was daubing carefully at her eyes beneath her sunglasses. Gigi was on a bulky sofa, texting. Delphine stood next to the dusty piano strumming a monophonic drone on the sitar. Ethel was seated at the piano attacking the keys in an odd Dixieland Jazz accompaniment. Dirk stood in a corner looking benign and nothing like the monster Katherine had described him to be. Delia purposely glanced past Winston and Josh. She wanted to see her father, Franklin Stanhope's, or as he was referred to, F.S.'s reaction. In many ways Delia blamed F.S. for Anngelie's troubled adult life.

F.S. had been highly educated and innately intelligent, but he had never had a vocation. F.S. was one of those people who were always going to achieve "greatness" in the unspecified future by writing the next classic American novel, or the definitive treatise on Western culture, or by running for political office and resolving the ills of the world. F.S. was a dreamer and a planner, not a doer. He had actually only accomplished four things in his sixty some years of living and they were alcoholism, being appointed to some figurehead government position by a former college chum, having a stroke and desolating Anngelie's life.

When Delia and Anngelie were young, most of the time F.S. was too self-absorbed to notice Anngelie but when he did he doted on her to unhealthy excess. When he wasn't ignoring her and everyone else, he encouraged and enabled her dreamlike and detached existence. To please him, she grew to believe as he did that they were misunderstood comrades who stood alone as a couple against the ignorance of the perverted masses. Then, Franklin proclaimed loudly, and often, that Anngelie was so much like he that their souls must have been connected in a former life.

In those days, Anngelie lived for the times when F.S. would deign to spend time with her. Together they would moon over sunsets, listen intently to classical music, dissect volumes of poetry and literature, amiably debate mythology and religion and question the value and meaning of everything and everyone. By the time Anngelie was twelve she was even F.S.'s secret drinking companion. At first, they only shared an occasional glass of wine. As time passed they were consuming Glenlivet in equal and awesome quantities. Eventually, the scotch couldn't and wouldn't ease the consuming pain of her wounded spirit so she turned to heroin and dropped out of life altogether. F.S. had given Anngelie the blueprints for addiction and self-destruction.

The "Honorable" Franklin Stanhope severed all ties to Anngelie when she turned to drugs and became homeless. He blamed Lillian's compulsion for her business and the acquisition of wealth as the reason for his daughter's unfortunate life. He usually failed to mention though, that his former wife's assets had paid for all of his custom-tailored, three piece, designer suits, his imported tobacco, his own personal chef, his mounds of rare and valuable collectible books and his vintage Rolls Royce, not to mention the infinite number of bottles of scotch he had imbibed. Lillian was still supporting him and paying for all of his medical bills.

Delia knew when Franklin turned his back on Anngelie, he broke her heart and Anngelie lost any real desire for living. She rarely mentioned him but Delia was certain that up to the moment she died Anngelie longed to reconcile with their father.

Delia studied F.S. sitting in his wheelchair next to his refrigerator-sized wife Ethel. Like an unwanted extra limb, his flesh-colored plastic leg brace sat in his bony lap. His withered left arm was pulled up tight against his chest reminding Delia of the dead branch of a sapling. His once intelligent, sod brown eyes were blank and resembled watery mud. He was so pathetic Delia nearly felt sorry for him, but she couldn't forget the damage he had done to Anngelie.

Looking away Delia saw Katherine enter the room passing through the somber group, holding a platter of skimpy sandwiches and greasy strudels that Mittie had made the night before. Delia shook her head no as Katherine shoved the tray in her direction. Katherine paused for a moment and gave Delia a pointed glance before loudly stating, "At least Anngelie knew the *rest* of us loved her."

Delia nearly laughed out loud. If she had been less sober she would have challenged her brother's wife and nearly everyone in the room about their supposed love for Anngelie. Mitchell had often threatened, at Katherine's urging she was sure, to have Anngelie institutionalized because he believed her homelessness and drug addiction jeopardized his political aspirations. Their mother Lillian had expatriated to France years ago, effectively abandoning her troubled daughter. F.S. was the worst though because he had broken Anngelie's already fragile heart by shunning her.

At that moment Delia took a good look at her son, Winston. He had barely survived an overdose of methamphetamine on the night Anngelie had died. His hair was disheveled and he kept clinching his fingers. There was pained detachment in his expression that reminded Delia of Anngelie. She quickly looked away.

"Come on, Grandmother, I have to get out of here."

Delia could hear Lillian asking, "What did Delia say?" as she hurried out of the house.

8 ❧

"Where are we off to now, Delia, or need I ask?"

"Why am I the only one who can see you, Grandmother? You look so real I feel like I could touch you. Great-Grandmother Bergit started visiting me when I was a teenager. She was much less tangible and she always whispered to me in Norwegian. I never understood her. One time though, when I was really upset she came and stroked my face. And Aunt Agatha came to see me when Robert died, and right after the twins were born. She still comes occasionally."

"That sounds like my mother and sister. I'm surprised you remember your Great-Aunt Agatha. You were so young when she died. Agatha was so very loving and timid. She desperately wanted children of her own, but unfortunately that never happened. Did it never frighten you to see ghosts?"

"Not really. It just seemed natural."

"I shouldn't be surprised. You were never the skittish type. You must realize you have been granted a great gift. I too had the ability to communicate with the other side."

"May I touch you, Grandmother?"

"Go right ahead and touch me. I'm certain you'll get quite a sensation." Reaching over to the ghost of her grandmother, who was sitting next to her in the back seat of the limousine, Delia smiled oddly. "You see, dear, it is an indescribable elation. Most people have the ability to see the spiritual realm but their logic precludes it. I presume you are the only one who sees me because you are the only one who is open to seeing me. In addition you need me here for guidance. In any case you have been bestowed with an ability to use a part of your brain that remains dormant in the vast majority of people. Perhaps your skill is developing rapidly and soon you will start seeing other souls that have left their physical form."

Delia glanced at Crawford in the rearview mirror but his eyes were fixed on the road. He couldn't hear her conversation with the glass partition raised. Still she wouldn't want him watching her having a conversation with what he could only assume was herself. She looked down.

"That little post memorial get together at Mitchell's house was just a farce. I hope the funeral was more comforting. Everyone there acted like they cared so much for Anngelie. With the exception of my own children, I could tell they all resented me. They gave me such hateful looks. And Katherine's snarky remark about how at least Anngelie knew that they all loved her, I could have slapped that smirk off her fat face. They didn't care for Anngelie. They didn't even really know her. What is it with my father and brother? I'll exclude Mother because she at least has beauty and finesse, but F.S. and Mitchell both married ball-busting bitches."

Grandmother Ingrid interrupted, "Delia, don't be so crass. I want you to expunge your anguish, but don't be unduly vulgar."

"I'm sorry, Grandmother, but I'm not sad, I'm mad. Katherine is so controlling. Obviously, she holds the purse strings in that house. Mitchell would never let your house look so dated and neglected. And serving that cheap tray of inedible food, please. Katherine is just like Mittie, she has her eyes on every penny she'll inherit from Mitchell after she's driven him to the grave. And what is up with that nose scrunching facial tic of hers? I heard Katherine and Mittie whispering about some Cheese Festival Mittie was panting to go to in Solvang. That was the real reason Mittie and Dirk came down from Sacramento. They couldn't come just to show respect to Anngelie's memory they also had to include a side trip. Could they be any cornier? Katherine was calling for the maid to come sweep as I was leaving. She is such a slave to her trivial schedule. And father's linebacker wife Ethel, she could frighten Freddy Kruger."

"I don't know this Freddy person you refer to but Ethel *is* a bit caustic. I hope you are quite finished disparaging your family. You are very intolerant, Delia. What makes you think you are a joy to be around?"

"Please, I know I'm a rude bitch, but at least I function on a more elevated level. And I know I'm more evolved than those bunch of buffoons."

"That is only your opinion, Delia. Personally, I think you are avoiding thinking about the things that are really bothering you. Your anger seems very misdirected."

"No, Grandmother, I know exactly what I am angry about. I am angry with nearly everyone in my family. But I'm furious about so much more." Delia gritted her teeth and stared out of the car window, as Crawford turned onto highway 101 and zoomed into the eastbound lane of traffic. "I used to be satisfied with redecorating my homes, or jetting the globe, or shopping for whatever I had a whim to buy. I might sound ungrateful but couture gowns and priceless jewels and luxurious homes and cars and yachts bore me now. Lately I've come to realize this world is painful to live in, Grandmother. People make the stupidest decisions. Children starve and millions die of disease because assholes are too greedy to give up any profits. They destroy the planet, start wars and glorify the mediocre. We've become a thug culture. Might is always right. Everyone is so self-absorbed. People text and twitter and blog to give their lives meaning, but they're so disengaged they've lost their civility. There is no common courtesy anymore. And art is dead. I haven't seen a good film in at least fifteen, probably twenty years. Music sounds so digitized and nursery rhyme like it only appeals to the basest instincts. And books are just formulaic and regurgitated blandness. I don't relate to anyone or anything. I feel like I'm from another planet." Delia paused for a moment staring out at the scrubby and dusty hills surrounding the freeway. "I'm so angry at Winston. I may have been a failure at being a nurturing type of mother, but he had a good upbringing. I made certain he attended the best schools and I hired a nanny with the finest credentials. Nanny Wright was cuddly and cooing and full of demonstrative affection. I wish my own nanny had been so kind. All the things I am lacking. Winston is rich, exceedingly handsome and one of the brightest people I've ever known. Why does he throw his life away using drugs?"

"Delia, you should have learned a long time ago from your sister's illness that addiction is it's own beast. I sense that there is something else that is unnerving you but I'll wait until you're ready to discuss it."

Delia and her grandmother were silent for the next half hour as the limousine drove through the sprawling urbanity of San Fernando Valley. Crawford exited the Ventura Freeway and sped toward Santa Monica Boulevard and the Hollywood Memorial Cemetery just blocks from her families' studio, Royal Arts. As they were pulling into the mostly empty cemetery Delia noticed a disheveled man with a stick of some kind in his hand wandering through the drizzle among the gray tombstones. He looked vaguely familiar but Delia didn't ponder on it but briefly.

A few minutes later Delia was unlocking the gate of the family mausoleum. Soft hued light was streaming in from the stained glass dome. Stepping quietly to the west-facing wall Delia gently began stroking the marble letters that had been etched into the granite midway up the wall beneath an arched stained glass image of a bouquet of flowers. The name read, Robert Frederick, Beloved Son.

"Grandmother, I'm so mad at God or whoever created me. I feel like Anngelie was the good twin and I'm the bad one. She had too much sensitivity and I have none. She could see goodness in even the vilest people and I feel like anymore I only see people's faults. I'm such a failure. You and Anngelie were the only people I think I ever really cared for. Something is lacking in me and it makes me so fucking mad I could scream. I was a terrible wife, and I'm certain Lillian and F.S. would vouch that I was a bad daughter. Apparently, as I was informed today, I'm even a lousy friend. And the whole world knows I have the nurturing instincts of Joan Crawford. But I am very ethical. I made certain my children's lives were safe and confortable. I arranged for them both to have the best opportunities and all the advantages my wealth could offer but I never felt maternal toward either one of them. Gigi nearly destroyed herself trying to force me to show her love. Thank God she rallied herself. She's only a bit vacuous but she's utterly charming and so beautiful. Poor Winston is dying right before my eyes. I can't even look at him without feeling ill. I can't save him anymore than I could save Anngelie. I guess my family is right, I am the reason Anngelie is dead. I should have insisted that she get help. Soon I guess they'll be blaming me for Winston's death too."

"I think you've seen too many movies, Delia. Growing up in Hollywood has made you overly dramatic. There is no such a thing as a good twin and an evil twin. People are what they are. You are so far from being evil, Delia. You are very depressed and very hard on yourself, but you underestimate your own capacity for love."

"Why can't I feel motherly toward Gigi and poor Winston? They are both so lovely and bright. And why can't I cry for Anngelie? I didn't even cry when little Robert died. I must be some kind of monster. How couldn't I cry for my baby boy? There is something deficient in my psyche. No wonder God took him from me. You know what frustrates me the most? I'm aware of all this but I'm unable to change the things I know are wrong or change my attitude about any of it."

"Facing up to pain can often require a herculean strength, my dear. Many of us are not up to the task. Your love for your children is quite evident to me even if as you say you don't feel it. Perhaps you should get some counseling."

"Grandmother, I've talked to so many counselors and psychiatrists over the years I couldn't even name a quarter of them. I've gone through

Gestalt, primal therapy and biofeedback and countless other forms of treatment. I talk until I feel like my head is going around in circles. Even though you couldn't tell it from the way I've been acting today I don't really like to focus on myself too much. I actually like getting out of my own head and thinking about other people. I've even tried religion. I was a Christian, a Buddhist, a Taoist, and a Guang Chiite. For one whole week I seriously considered becoming Muslim. That may have been more about impressing that Saudi prince I was dating at the time, though. Did you remember I wanted to become a Peace Corps volunteer when I graduated from college? Isn't that a laugh? Mother said I was just looking for attention again. She said it would be an embarrassment to the family and I had already disgraced the family enough. I let her talk me out of it. I guess I was foolish enough to believe in all the values that the 1960's seemed to stand for. Maybe it was because I was just a child, but peace and love and brotherhood and helping your fellow man spoke to my heart. All of that just seems dead now. See, Grandmother, I'm all over the map. I hate the world but deep in my heart I want to save it. Wow, I really am an odd person."

"Most of us are a unique mixture of contradictions, Delia. No one is stopping you now from getting involved and trying to make the world a better place. I was always heavily involved in charities of all sorts. But what you really need now is a good cry. It would do you a world of good."

"I haven't cried since I was fifteen and Biff Reynolds broke my heart. You never cried, Grandmother."

"Silly dear, I cried often for myself and others. I suppose people don't usually think of their grandmothers crying."

Suddenly Delia noticed a shadow fall across her feet and she heard her Grandmother say, "Oh dear."

"Who the hell are you talking to, Wentworth? Or have you just gone crazy like your sister?"

Looking around quickly Delia saw a man standing in the shadowy corner opposite her. Longish golden blond hair hung about his sunburned face in matted and greasy clumps. His bloodshot green eyes darted about the stone room. In moments she realized it was Cornell Van Brundt, the man who had helped destroy Anngelie.

"What are you doing here, Cornell? Shouldn't you be in San Francisco pimping out little girls?"

"I see you're still a bitch, Wentworth. I'm here because you and your insane sister sent the police after me. They came to my apartment last night asking all kinds of questions about how Anngelie, and some other worthless bitches, had died."

"Get out of here, Cornell. I don't have anything to say to you."

"Yeah, but I bet you had plenty to tell the cops. Just because your sister was fucked up it isn't my fault. She was the most twisted cunt I ever knew. She liked whoring and she liked getting tortured. I think she would have done it for free, but I was too smart to let her do that."

"Please, Cornell, it doesn't take any brains to pimp out innocent girls."

"Angie was far from innocent, dude. I'm telling you she loved getting screwed by strangers and the rougher they were the more she liked it. I was smart enough to know that a twisted girl like her could make me lots of money. Guys pay good money for the freaky stuff. I was disinherited a long time ago because of the shit you and your mother told my family, and Angie wouldn't let me touch her trust fund. She claimed that money was for her imaginary baby. But I think she just wanted an excuse to have to sell her body."

Delia clinched her fists screaming, "Get out of here, Cornell!" Her voice was so loud it reverberated in the mausoleum.

"Oh, she told you about the baby I see. I bet you believed that bullshit story. She convinced herself she wanted a baby so bad that she talked herself into believing that messed up shit. There was never any baby. It was just another fiction of her delusional mind. Don't you think I would have known if she had been pregnant? Maybe you really are as crazy as your sister. I hear your whole family is screwy. People always wondered why your dad used to be so close to Angie. But who could blame him for wanting a piece of that. She used to be a really hot chick."

Even more loudly than before Delia screeched, "Shut up, Cornell! Just shut your filthy mouth! You're the one who is insane! I'm not going to listen to any more of this garbage!"

Delia turned to run out the door, but Cornell, in a flash that seemed too quick, blocked the door purring obscenely, "You're not going anywhere, Wentworth, until you promise to get the cops off my ass. Or I'll shut your bitch mouth forever like I did your crazy whore sister."

Raising his arm, Delia saw that Cornell had a tire iron in his hand. In that instant she realized that he had murdered Anngelie. A rage overtook Delia that she had never felt and she wrenched the tire iron from Cornell's hand and raised it above his head shouting, "Fuck you, you sick bastard!" With all her strength Delia slammed the tire iron toward Cornell's head and in that instant he disappeared. The iron bar slipped from her hand landing on the floor with a loud clang.

"That was very close, Delia. I was about to intervene but fortunately Mr. Van Brundt's spirit figured out that he had crossed himself over early this morning."

"You mean he is dead, Grandmother?"

"Oh yes, indeed. He hung himself early this morning in the closet of his shabby little room in San Francisco."

"Cornell was evil. I know I am not as evil as he was. Maybe there is a bit of hope for me."

"Dear child, Cornell was not evil. He was mentally unstable. People are not evil like you suppose. At worst people can be petty and selfish and unthinking. Their actions can be evil but most often unintentionally. People aren't as black and white as you presume them to be. Now I must be off. I'll be back when I can. Take care, my dear Delia." Grandmother Ingrid's voice lingered longer to Delia than her image before both were gone.

"But, Grandmother, what about Anngelie's baby? Surely Cornell would know if there was a baby, wouldn't he? Grandmother? Oh great, you leave now when I need some answers about finding Anngelie's baby boy. If he even exists."

9

Alberta climbed the hill and when she reached the corner of Georgia and Napa, she freed Brownie from the cage. Turning right, she stepped cautiously toward the alley. For half a century, her sister Roberta had lived in the yellow Victorian cottage at the corner of Garford Alley and Napa. From York Street, Alberta could see the elegant fence her nephew Jay had built.

Alberta noticed the delicate shadow of a person in a second floor window across from her sister's. It was where Charlotte, the white witch, lived. Alberta paused for a better glimpse of the elusive Charlotte. The light from the old home flickered.

The front gate to Roberta's house was propped open with a cast iron pot while Roberta snapped plump, yellow lemons from the old tree by her front door. She wore a pink nightgown and shiny slippers. A porch light and a streetlamp lit up the small front yard.

"Hello, Ro," Alberta called out to Roberta who was hard of hearing but refused to acknowledge it.

A powder blue Thunderbird pulled up in front of the house and the driver tooted the horn. Roberta raised her hand at the passing car and went back to plucking lemons and stuffing them into a brown paper sack.

"Hello, Baby Sister," Roberta called out in a soft, raspy voice.

"Who was that?" Alberta asked while plopping D.C. on the soft grass.

"Oh, I think that was my neighbor from up the hill but I can't see past my own feet when I don't have my glasses on. " Roberta chuckled and then continued, "She usually comes for lemons. There are dozens of lemon trees in yards all around here, but people still stop by asking for my lemons. I swear it's a sight. I can't be out in this yard more than ten minutes without someone wanting a lemon. You'd think this tree bore the fruit of life. Just last week, I caught two different boys hopping the fence to pick some. I don't mind sharing, but this beats all I ever saw."

Roberta continued, "I'm picking you this bag to take home. If I keep the ripe ones in the front picked, maybe nobody will ask for any."

Roberta wiped the perspiration from her brow with the back of her hand and smoothed her hair. "That woman who drove by, her name is Norma Whitman. You won't believe it, but I know for a fact she's a madam in Washington, D.C."

Roberta chuckled. "You better know it. She runs a cathouse for politicians but she should take care. When you're bedfellows with those two-faced devils, you wake up with more than fleas. She knows too many secrets for her own good."

Roberta took one last lemon and dropped it into the sack, which she placed inside the front door.

"All things considered, Miss Norma is doing pretty well. She's got that expensive new car and she owns the pink house up on the hill you've always admired. Imagine, she runs a profitable brothel right here from Vallejo, all on the Internet. I'm going to have to get me a computer some of these days. They say you can meet a nice fellow on one of those things. It's a far cry from the days when you worked for Fancy Fay right out of her home up on Georgia Street. She made quite the living herself, off the backs of you girls. Why she even had those marble steps right up to the front door. A couple of homosexual fellows own the place now. I hear tell they keep it real nice. In fact they… "

Alberta interrupted, "Why, Roberta, I never once worked for Fay Bissett in that old whorehouse. That was Cousin Cassie and your friend Lavette Finley. I liked sex too much to put a price tag on it. It was always the girls that didn't like sex who ended up selling it."

"That's right. It was Cassie and Lavette who worked for Fancy Fay. I don't know where I got it into my head that it was you too," Roberta replied, finally stepping into the house.

Alberta picked up D.C. and followed her sister inside.

Roberta motioned toward the couch. "Take off your shoes and rest on the sofa."

She picked a piece of lint from the cushion before adding, "You're right about those rent girls not liking sex. Cassie hated sex so much that when she finally got married she used to make her husband, skinny Carver Thompson, bring her home a trinket or a fresh pastry before she'd bed him.

"Lord of mercy, all this talk about sex is getting me hot and bothered. Would you like a glass of tea? I'll put out a bowl of cool water for Brownie, too. I swear that sweet creature may just decide to outlive us all." Roberta called and Brownie followed her into the kitchen.

"I'd love a glass of tea, thank you," Alberta loudly replied while getting comfortable on the red velvet sofa. The wooden floors were honey-colored and gleaming. Two antique chairs with intricately carved arms and legs flanked an elegant armoire. Pale, linen curtains hung from the tall windows. Alberta admired the beaded chandelier hanging over the sofa and envied her sister's flair for decorating. Roberta knew how to create a room that looked lovely without seeming stuffy.

Roberta enjoyed having a pretty home. For more than fifty years, she'd taught high school science and had taken in ironing and sewing too. On weekends and every day in the summer, she scrubbed toilets and floors for some of the wealthier women in Vallejo.

When Roberta was twenty-two, she married a shy seventeen year old. As he grew into a man, Velasco Hill stayed home, and cooked and cleaned, and tended their son and two daughters. Occasionally, Velasco would get a job but never kept it for long. Roberta was satisfied with her marriage and did not complain.

Velasco and Roberta's marriage lasted for sixty-one years until his death. It had been nearly two years since a speeding car jumped the sidewalk and struck him down as he was walking downtown. Roberta mourned so mightily for Velasco that Alberta was afraid her sister would die from a broken heart. She got better with time and the help she received from people in her grief support group.

"Is this a new rug, Ro?" Alberta asked as she reached down to feel the plush fibers.

Roberta returned with two frosty glasses of iced tea. She didn't hear Alberta's question and instead directed: "Grab a couple of coasters out of that little table."

She handed Alberta a glass continuing, "Maybe it's because I'm getting older, but the winters seem to get shorter every year. I never remember it being this hot on my birthday. It is just barely spring and I've already had to turn on the air-conditioning twice this year. I guess it's that global warming. Remember, I used to tell you someday before we died there would be too many people on the planet and it would cause no end of trouble. If the meek do inherit the world it won't be worth a red cent after the greedy are done with it."

With a low moan, Roberta sat on the sofa next to D.C. She gave the silent child a look as if she'd just noticed him. She patted her lap and Brownie jumped into it excitedly. Roberta stroked Brownie's ears and stated indifferently, "I see you still have the boy."

"Of course I still have D.C. Where else would he be?" Alberta replied curtly.

"I'm surprised you're not weary of raising kids. I would think that one as developmentally disabled as he is would be too much of a challenge for you," Roberta said.

"Oh, Roberta, don't you do this to me too. Madison insists D.C. is too much of a burden for me, but he's my joy. She thinks he's too strange and that I'm going senile. If I didn't keep him, he'd probably end up in an institution somewhere, and that's not what he needs. Besides which, I wouldn't be alive today if it weren't for D.C.," Alberta stated.

"Very well, Baby Sister, I know better than to battle with you when your mind is set. Are you ready for our party tomorrow? I've ordered a cake and hired the Chinese restaurant to cater the food."

"What do you mean our party?" Alberta asked.

"Well, you turned eighty last month and I turn eighty-five the day after tomorrow. You're the end and I'm the beginning. It's about time we celebrated together."

Alberta had been born a Pisces on February 27 and Roberta an Aries on March 27. Aries being the first sign in the Zodiac and Pisces the last. Roberta, who had always been interested in astrology, often referred to Alberta as the end of the life cycle and to herself as the beginning.

Indeed, the sisters' temperaments were opposites. Roberta was spontaneous and sociable while Alberta was reserved and shy. They were both tall with smallish breasts and tiny waists. Like their mother, both had wide, sensuous hips and shapely legs. Even their faces were similar, but their hairstyles made them look different. Alberta's sparse, curly-black hair was dusted with strands of white and gray; it was always cut short and worn natural. Roberta's hair was still thick and black and usually pulled back flat against her head into a perfectly round bun. Roberta occasionally wore tasteful wigs. The older sister still wore makeup and had her nails done twice a month. Alberta never wore cosmetics and had never painted her nails.

"I've already observed my birthday, Roberta. Madison took me to a nice restaurant on Nob Hill and she baked my favorite angel cake with seven-minute frosting. Plus, she gave me a new microwave and a sofa too."

"Who says you can't have two birthday celebrations, Baby Sister? Considering how long the two of us have survived, we deserve all the celebrating we can conjure." They both laughed.

"There aren't going to be many people, I hope?"

"No, not many, just enough for good merrymaking."

D.C. sat contentedly on the sofa while Alberta and Roberta visited. Then they all went to the kitchen while Roberta fixed a salad with juicy shrimp and buttery croutons. Alberta had brought a bag of Brownie's dry food and Roberta put it into a bowl and ladled a bit of brown gravy over it. Brownie wagged his tail appreciatively, then gobbled the food. D.C. was delighted by his meal and surprised Alberta by consuming two big servings. The two sisters and the child ate organic chocolate ice cream made from real cream, sugar and egg yolks. Alberta never kept sweet treats in the house. Her blood sugar levels had normalized years before, when D.C. had come into her life but she didn't want to tempt fate by not watching her diet. She only made desserts on birthdays and holidays. It was soon obvious that the chocolate ice cream was the best thing D.C. had ever tasted. Alberta and Roberta laughed warmly when D.C. did a little dance in his chair after each bite.

When they finished eating, they all went to sit in the living room again. Alberta and Roberta talked well into the evening. D.C. was soon sleeping where he sat propped up in a corner of the soft couch. Brownie lay stretched out next to D.C.

Around midnight the sisters went to bed. Roberta had the larger bedroom with the hand-carved, four-poster bed. Roberta offered the big bed to Alberta but she chose instead to sleep with D.C. on the foldout sofa in the second bedroom that doubled as Roberta's home office.

Once the sisters had opened the bed, Alberta carried D.C. into the room and placed him on the mattress. He never roused. Roberta got a soft coverlet and a pillow and made Brownie a bed on the floor. He crawled into it eagerly turning twice before curling up to sleep. After Alberta and D.C. were beneath the sheets, Roberta tossed a cotton blanket over them, then leaned over and kissed Alberta.

"Goodnight, Baby Sister," Roberta said softly. Then she surprised Alberta and kissed D.C. and stroked his pale, tiny arm with the back of her wrinkled, brown hand. "He is something special, Baby Sister. Now get some rest tomorrow is a big day." she added.

Alberta smiled back at Roberta nervously.

10 ❧

It was raining when Delia arrived back at her estate in Beverly Hills. She was growing more frustrated because she couldn't get what Cornell had told her at the mausoleum out of her mind. Was there really a baby? Delia knew that Anngelie was convinced, but perhaps the baby had been a delusion.

The voices of Gigi and Lillian echoed from the library at the front of the house. Delia headed upstairs. Inside her room, she slipped out of her heels and unzipped her dress.

After putting on a robe, Delia walked to her dresser. She called out quietly to her Grandmother Ingrid, but she sensed her spirit was no longer near. Opening the bottom drawer she retrieved a bottle of Chanel No. 5 that was wrapped in an old silk scarf beneath a neatly folded stack of summer nightgowns.

Slowly, she opened the nearly empty bottle and took a deep whiff of the perfume, then pressed the scarf over her nose and inhaled deeply. The scarf and perfume had belonged to Grandmother Ingrid.

Delia stepped away from the dresser to stand by the window. She looked down from the second floor over the swimming pool and pool house. It was still raining and the winter wind was rustling the trees bordering the estate. Steam swirled from the heated water and reflected in the flickering lights. The pool looked almost unreal as it blazed bright blue in the darkness.

On a cold, rainy February night, over twenty-five years earlier, the pool had looked the same. Delia and Anngelie were teenagers then, both summoned home from boarding school for their step-grandfather's funeral. Delia and Anngelie had been left alone at the estate for the evening.

Anngelie was out in the pool house with creepy Cornell Van Brundt. He had brought a group of his friends including, William "Biff" Reynolds IV, who was acting like he didn't care at all that Delia had been forced by Lillian to put an end to their intimate relationship.

Delia stayed in the house secretly trying on her mother's couture gowns, which was forbidden. The clothes Lillian had ordered from the designer's spring and summer collections had arrived a few days before from Paris. Delia was so enamored of the rich fabrics, the craftsmanship, and artistry of the elegant dresses that she couldn't resist the temptation of trying them on. She had been modeling each new collection before her mother had even worn them since she was thirteen, and no one had ever suspected.

Now, a few months shy of sixteen, she was finally the same size as her mother though Delia's waist was an inch and a half smaller and, at five feet eight inches, she stood a full inch taller than Lillian.

Delia took great care in handling the garments, never harming a stitch or pleat on any of them. She had even been so bold in the past year to "borrow" gowns on three occasions for formal dances. She always returned them in pristine condition and Lillian was never the wiser.

Outside Lillian's walk-in closet, Delia admired herself wearing her mother's brown silk Givenchy gown with a hand-beaded bodice. The baby in her belly was barely showing, no more than bloat during her cycle.

Delia stared out the window at the Pacific Ocean. She wept about losing her boyfriend Biff, and for their unborn child. Growing up was more painful than Delia had ever imagined it to be.

Delia also cried for her twin. She was certain that Anngelie cared a great deal for Cornell Van Brundt. Delia also sensed that Cornell was going to be a devastating influence on her twin.

Delia didn't want to risk diminishing Anngelie's adoration so she hadn't told her about the pregnancy. Why hadn't her twin sensed it? They had always known instinctively when something was wrong with the other. Anngelie was slipping away. Delia could feel it so profoundly.

Delia turned from the window knowing someone was in the room with her. Very faintly she saw the image of her great-grandmother, Bergit. Bergit moved close reaching to stroke Delia's cheek. Delia felt a tingling soft caress.

"Slik en søt jente," Great-Grandmother Bergit whispered, as she disappeared. Delia didn't understand the Norwegian words.

Delia wiped stinging tears from her eyes. She lit one of the cigarettes she had stolen from the carton her mother kept hidden in her private bath. Then she swallowed two of the Valiums she'd found while snooping in the pocket of one of Lillian's fur coats. Her stomach felt raw and it ached. Warm tears streamed down her cheeks as she puffed on the cigarette and unlatched the window.

Frigid air burst into the room and Delia began to tremble but she stood firm against the cold, moist wind. It was still drizzling outside. Mixed with the droplets of water were perfect, white flakes of snow. They fluttered perilously and dreamlike in the blackened sky. Just beneath Delia's window the fragile snowflakes were melting in the atmosphere about twenty feet above the earth. She felt compelled to tell someone so that they too could bear witness to the fact that it was indeed snowing in Beverly Hills. Instead, she merely sighed and whispered it to herself.

And now, just like that February night over a quarter of a century ago, delicate, fluttery snowflakes mingled with the raindrops. These flakes, too, melted long before they could reach the ground. It snowed for only a few minutes. Delia observed it as a grown woman wanting desperately to weep.

Eventually, Delia stepped away from the window. When she turned around the faint apparitions of an unfamiliar man and woman appeared before her. They both looked to be around sixty. Their mouths opened but no words were spoken. They lingered for just moments and then they slowly faded away.

Delia asked quietly, "Grandmother, would you please tell me what is going on?" There was no response and Delia shook her head and sighed. Delia called Felinda, her poodle Isobella's new nanny, and told her to bring the dog to her.

Someone tapped on her bedroom door a few minutes later and Delia assumed it was Felinda with Isobella.

"Yes, come in," Delia called out.

"Hi, Mother. I hate to bother you but we need to ask a big favor," Gigi said as she walked into the room followed by her new best friend, Lexy Reichmeyer. Lexy was the slender, blonde, inane daughter of one of Delia's acquaintances, the inexplicably successful, romance novelist, Janelle Stone. Janelle had married Baron Frederick Reichmeyer two or three times and given him a litter of willowy, rather homely heirs.

"If you need more money, just tell Greta how much and she can give you a check. Now I'm really exhausted, Gigi, and I'd like to be left alone."

"No, Mother, I don't need money. We need your permission to use the house for our new reality show. Lexy has decided to help me produce the show and she wants to move in and star in it too," Gigi said expectantly.

Delia took a big swallow of the martini. "You mean this house, my house?"

"Yes," Gigi and Lexy replied simultaneously.

The girls seemed completely distracted as they fingered their cell phones. They kept tittering and nudging each other. Finally, Delia asked, "What are you girls doing?"

"We're texting each other and Lexy's new boyfriend, Ferris Durant," Gigi giggled.

"Ferris is not my new boyfriend. I don't even like his new video. His last CD didn't even break the top ten. I just used to give Ferris and his friends hand-jobs at my brother's recording studio in West Hollywood when I was thirteen and really strung out on pain killers. That was all before I went through rehab. It was no big deal," Lexy said casually.

Abruptly, both girls squealed, "Gross," and started to laugh convulsively, staring at their phones.

"I'm sorry, Mrs. Wentworth, but Ferris is getting his balls pierced and sent us a video," Lexy smirked.

"He must be really high," Lexy said to Gigi.

"Girls, I really don't have time for this now."

"I'm sorry, Mother. We really are serious about our new show. Do you mind if we tape it here?" Gigi said, snapping her phone shut.

Gigi had recently moved back home and legally reclaimed her birth name. After graduating from high school, she had vanished with the Indian-born cosmetic surgeon, Dr. Vani Kamar, who had performed her breast augmentation. They both changed their names and joined a survivalist group in the hinterlands of Idaho that Kamar had discovered on the Internet. Afterward, Delia severed all ties to her daughter but it wasn't until Delia cut off her funds that Gigi begged to come home.

Gigi returned doughy, unkempt, and hopeless as a battered housewife. Delia never mentioned to anyone her daughter was exhibiting some of the same morose behavior as Anngelie.

Yet, in two months, and after hours of therapy, Gigi lost most of the excess weight, overcame depression, and looked forward to taking media and business courses at UCLA. She wanted to become a television producer for the Royal Arts network of which Delia and Mitchell had a controlling interest. She was trying to help her twin brother Winston in his battle with methamphetamine addiction. Delia was mildly shocked that she was developing a genuine fondness for her daughter.

Delia had always felt an affinity toward her son Winston. He had been easy to deal with, before the addiction, relishing the privileged life he had been born into and not taking anything or anyone too seriously. Gigi had always been an enigma to Delia. As a daughter, she had insisted on Delia's approval. If Delia had had her way there would have been no other children after Robert. She knew children deserved more than she had to offer. Delia had only become pregnant because her first husband Kyle had been so unrelenting.

Delia was so relieved Gigi was now interested in something other than gaining weight, organizing bake sales to raise money for neo-Nazis, or becoming the "perfect Christian bride" for her demented fiancé, that she was hesitant to discourage Gigi's plans. A few days before Anngelie died, Gigi had informed Delia the first show she wanted to produce was a reality show about her life as a Beverly Hills heiress, and the experiences she would have trying to create successful programs. Though, Gigi had never mentioned she wanted to film the show from her mother's home. It must have been Lexy's idea.

Just the thought of two pampered and unruly young women living in her house was unthinkable. And she could tell Lexy was as bad an influence as she had been at that age. Moreover, she was not going to have a television crew invading her home and life, once again.

Delia was about to refuse and then she remembered her mother. She could blame it on Lillian.

"I'd hate to put your grandmother through that kind of ordeal, Gigi, especially while she's still grieving over Anngelie. I am almost certain Lillian will want to stay here a while and collect her bearing before she goes back to France," Delia lied.

Delia was positive Lillian would be hopping on her broom and zooming back to her beloved France before the next sunrise. Her mother detested lingering too long in the United States. She considered Americans self-serving, uninformed, and too provincial, even though she had been one herself for the first fifty years of her life. Lillian had only been in the United States two times in the past twenty years and both times it was because of Anngelie. The last time she visited, she had a reaction to Botox and some other bacteria that had been injected into her face and she was forced to remain in California, at Delia's house, for many months. Lillian vowed then she would never return, but she had returned, and Delia was making certain her mother enjoyed excellent health during this trip.

"Yeah, I know what you mean, Mrs. Wentworth. When my older

sister overdosed my mother got really depressed and locked herself in a large cupboard with a bag of marijuana, a case of Perrier, a crate of Wheat Thins, a basket of limes, and an incinerating toilet. By the time she came out she had lost nearly twenty pounds. She looked great. She was almost as thin as you, Mrs. Wentworth," Lexy paused for a moment. Then she fingered her long, lusterless, highlighted hair as she continued, "After that she got on antidepressants and Vicodin. The drugs didn't help much so she went on a sojourn to South Carolina to get a healing from a Yorùbá priestess and became addicted to RC Cola and banana MoonPies. Then she gained back all the weight and more. She looks like she must weigh about one hundred and thirty pounds now. My whole family has an addiction disorder. Mother calls it our *black place*. She's contacted a Romani psychic in Morocco to see if she can get us healed. Mother is convinced the family is under some kind of curse, or something," Lexy said.

Delia decided quickly it was best to ignore Lexy. So she turned to Gigi and told her, "I could buy you girls a house in West Hollywood near your brother Winston. Then you'd be even closer to RAC Studios. At any rate, I just can't risk upsetting your grandmother. She might never forgive me," Delia said, suppressing a smirk.

"Forgive you for what, Delia?" Lillian asked, as she stepped into Delia's room. She stood behind Gigi with her arms folded firmly across her slim, puffed out chest. She glared at Delia with her perfectly sculpted brown eyes.

"Oh, it's nothing, Mother," Delia replied quickly, as she averted her gaze. Then she continued, "You look drained, Mother. You've had an exhausting day. I think you should go to bed. I'll call down to the kitchen and have some tea sent up to your room."

"Don't bother, Delia. I'm not the least bit tired. And all things considered, I look stunning. You're the one who looks a bit puffy and pallid."

Gigi and Lexy were too preoccupied with their cell phones again to notice the tension between Delia and Lillian, and Gigi said distractedly, "Mother, you don't have to worry. Grandmother said she would be delighted to stay here indefinitely and be a part of our reality show. Lexy and I are going to make stars of all of us."

"I am delighted to stay. It exactly the distraction this family needs right now. I couldn't let you down, Delia. I've even invited Mitchell and Katherine to move in and be a part of this too. It will be the perfect opportunity for him to solidify his political ambitions. And your Aunt Maxine and Uncle Vance are coming for a lengthy visit, as well. In fact I've extended an invitation to the entire family. And this is the ideal place to film the program, the family estate. I know what this means to you, Delia. I just had to do something to recompense the selfless care you gave to your sister in her final hours."

Delia ignored her mother's sarcasm and looked over at Gigi and said emphatically, "I'm sorry, Gigi, but you aren't going to use my home for your little TV show. I'm glad we're getting along better and you're welcome to stay here as long as you like, but I won't allow you and Lexy to use my house. As I said, I'll be happy to buy you a house to use. Or we could even find one to lease. I just really am not prepared for this right now." Delia thought of the home next to her own which had been empty since Penelope had been murdered but she didn't dare mention it.

"I understand, Mother. I'll figure something out," Gigi replied wearily.

"No, Gigi, I've made my decision and this is where you will be filming your program. Need I remind you that this is the family estate, Delia?"

"Mother, this is not the family estate. I bought this house from Grandmother Ingrid's estate before she died. Anyway, we've been through this a hundred times and I will not have a reality show filmed here."

"The decision has already been made. Gigi, you and your friend Lexus go right on with your plans. You have always been completely self-involved, Delia. Your attempts at parenting throughout the years have been a fiasco. This is the least you owe your daughter. I won't allow you to destroy Gigi's life the way you did Anngelie's. I'm utterly disappointed in you as a person. I'll stay in this house as long as it takes to make certain my grandchildren are taken care of. What are you going to do, Delia, have us all thrown out?"

"Mother, I know I haven't been an adequate parent but I don't think you want to compare mothering skills. You might discover a few unpleasant things about your own character. I'm in no mood to squabble. Gigi, you and Lexy may use my home. Just take care of everything for me. I'm going to instruct Greta to have my irreplaceable objects put into storage or shipped to me. My wing of the house will be locked up. Stay as long as you please, Lillian. I'm leaving town tomorrow," Delia said making up her mind.

"So you're going to abandon Gigi? You truly are egocentric, Delia. I'm ashamed to claim you as my daughter."

"Gigi, would you and Lexy please excuse your grandmother and me. We have a few things to discuss." Delia waited until her daughter and Lexy had left the room and closed the door. Then she glared at her mother and sneered. "So you're ashamed to claim me as your daughter? Well, likewise, I'm sure. What is this nonsense about how I ruined Anngelie's life? I loved her beyond words and I'm completely devastated that she is gone."

"You certainly don't express any genuine grief. You are the one who introduced her to the drug culture."

"Are you kidding me, Lillian? I'm not even going to broach this subject with you. I would just like to know why you don't like me?"

"What a ludicrous question. I love all my children. I hardly think this is the day to discuss *your* feelings."

"You're absolutely right, Lillian. And since you seem to be such an expert on motherhood you can take my place for as long as you desire. I'm relinquishing my rights to you. You're so skilled maybe you can even cure Winston of his addiction to drugs. You were so adept at helping Anngelie."

Delia paused simply adding, "I'd like to thank you, Mother."

"Thank me for what?" Lillian asked snidely.

"You helped me make a decision about something. I was looking for a sign, and the fact that you're staying is all the portent I need. Just so you're current on my plans; your selfish bitch of a daughter is moving away indefinitely, to fulfill your other beloved daughter's final request. Mull that over in your poisonous little mind. Now get out of here before I show you what a real bitch you reared. Get out! Get out before I throw you out," Delia roared.

Lillian gave Delia one final puzzled glance, then scurried from the room. Delia poured herself another martini and swallowed it. She chuckled and then let out a low groan. Lillian had incited Delia to take flight to San Francisco. But the thought of staying in Beverly Hills and braving her mother's presence and the onslaught of family and a television crew, and the terrifying prospect of witnessing Gigi transformed into the next Paris Hilton, suddenly sounded more endurable than attempting the onerous task of trying to find Anngelie's child that might or might not exist.

11 ❧

Alberta and Roberta didn't awaken that following morning until around ten. D.C. had already been up for nearly two hours. With much effort he had quietly crawled out of bed and gone outside. For much of that time he had sat in the yard underneath a Japanese maple tree stroking a scruffy, black cat that had curled up purring next to him. Apple blossoms from the tree next door dusted the ground around him like fat snowflakes. The cat eventually left in search of food and D.C. went to sit next to an immense, old gardenia bush. He then turned his attention to a squirrel that had scampered up beside him.

Alberta was getting dressed when Roberta rushed into the spare bedroom and frantically asked, "Where is D.C.? I've searched the whole house."

Alberta looked at her sister and replied calmly, "Oh, D.C. is fine. He's probably outside enjoying your yard. Your gate is locked."

"Oh, Baby Sister, he shouldn't be out there by himself. We've got a vicious stray cat that hangs around here. It's as black as night and ferocious. The animal attacked my neighbor's little granddaughter last month," Roberta said breathlessly, as she hurried to the front door.

"Why, Roberta, animals never harm D.C. They know how special he is," Alberta called out after her sister, as she slipped on her tennis shoes and followed her to the front of the house.

When Roberta opened the front door, she and Alberta glimpsed an emerald green hummingbird D.C. was cupping gently in his hand. D.C. was making noises to the tiny bird and stroking it gently. As soon as the bird noticed Alberta and Roberta it clicked a few times and went whizzing away, D.C. reaching up after it. Alberta marveled at how sweet and normal D.C. looked with his fleecy blond hair and his entrancing ice blue eyes. Looking at him here, no one would ever imagine that he was severely physically and mentally disabled.

"Well, I swear. That beats anything I've ever seen," Roberta said, as she looked over at Alberta with a mystified expression.

"Let's go have coffee, Ro. D.C. will be just fine," Alberta said stepping away from the door. As she walked toward the kitchen she suggested, "Maybe we could go down to the farmer's market after we eat. I saw the signs downtown when I walked here from the ferry last night."

"Just get that idea right out of your mind, Sister. That's the most worthless excuse for a farmer's market that you'll ever see. Apparently, Vallejo gets the vendors that Berkeley, Oakland, and the rest of the Bay Area won't accept. As usual, this town gets the chaff," Roberta replied, with disgust. "Besides, the party is supposed to start around noon. I'll only be eighty-five once, and I'm ready to party," she added, as she raised her arms and swung her hips back and forth.

Alberta smiled nervously. She was certain now that the birthday party her sister had planned was going to be a bigger deal than she had said. Alberta prayed that D.C. wasn't going to get too distressed.

A few hours later Alberta was sitting with D.C. and Brownie in the kitchen with the door closed. At least thirty family members had gathered inside Roberta's modest home. The crowd was so boisterous that Alberta had taken D.C. into the kitchen where it was quieter. She was at the window watching for Madison and her children to arrive. The many people coming and going from the dilapidated, mustard-colored apartment building that was across the alley from Roberta's house had caught her attention. Like most of the newer multi-resident dwellings that were sandwiched into narrow lots amongst the picturesque Victorians in the Heritage District of Vallejo, the building didn't even look up to code. The newer buildings blighted the whole midtown area like the insidious yellow oxalis that encroached on the better-maintained yards.

"Hi, Grandma. What are you and D.C. doing here in the kitchen? Oh, and there is Brownie. " Julia, Alberta's granddaughter, walked over and sat at the table in the chair next to Alberta. She kissed Alberta and D.C. and he gurgled his version of hello. Brownie licked her ankles and wagged his tail.

"Hello, sweetheart. When did you get here? I've been watching out the window but I never saw your mother's car."

"We just got here. Momma parked out back in Aunt Roberta's driveway. She was afraid to park her car on the street. There's a lot of people hanging around outside at the apartments next door. Vallejo is kind of scary. Momma says she hates to come here because it depresses her. She isn't in a good mood. We've been fighting all the way here."

"You know how D.C. doesn't usually like crowds so I thought we'd wait in here for you and your mom and brother to arrive."

"That's okay, D.C., I don't always like crowds either. You are so cute, D.C., I'm going to eat you up," Julia said, tickling D.C.'s belly. He couldn't really smile in a way that Julia could perceive but she did notice that his eyes lit up.

"There you are, Julia. Why did you walk away from me? I wanted you to say hello to your cousin Sondra." Madison said as she entered the kitchen. Alberta felt D.C. tense up and he leaned in closer to her. She wrapped her arms about him and patted his arm.

"I wanted to come find Grandma and D.C. Brownie is here, too, Momma." Brownie leapt into Julia's lap.

"Did you come in her to whine to your grandmother? Mother, I bet you took her side. Why do you always side with everyone against me?"

"I don't know what in the world you're talking about, Madison, honey. We were just saying hello to each other. Julia mentioned you weren't feeling real good."

"It's well, Mother, not good. I hate coming to Vallejo. I can't believe so many of our family still lives here. Derelicts roam the streets and everything is so rundown. That downtown area is a disgrace. I don't even want to discuss what I saw going on next door at the apartment building across the alley."

"They look like prostitutes, Grandma," Julia interjected.

"See, Mother. I don't want Julia exposed to trash like that."

Alberta had noticed an older rather shabby looking BMW with no license plates going past the house several times as she was watching for Madison's car. An attractive, middle aged, white man with black hair and a thick mustache was driving the car. Two young black women and a skinny young white girl were riding around with him. Every so often the car would stop in front of the apartment building and one of the three young women would sashay into the entrance followed by various men. It hadn't taken long for Alberta to figure out that the girls were prostituting.

"I don't know what you want me to do about it, honey. I'm not crazy about Vallejo, either. It has always been a rough town." Alberta replied.

"I just don't know why someone in your family is always having a party or family gathering of some sort. Someone is always angry with someone else. Melva Lou, whoever she is, is in there now arguing with someone named Rosalie about some garage sale money. I don't know how you can stand being around that. I guess I'm more like Daddy's side of the family. They never get together as a big group. They visit individually. There is none of this whole messy family in one place stuff."

"Maybe you take after your mother, too, Madison. I'm getting so as I don't much like crowds either. More and more I'm like I was when I was young. When I was living back in Missoura I always got so nervous at family gatherings that I almost always made myself sick. It doesn't look like these family gatherings will last much longer, anyway. The younger ones show up less and less."

"It is pronounced Missouri, Mother, not Missoura. Why do you always sound more country when you are around your family?"

Alberta knew that when Madison was in a fussy mood there was no arguing with her. She decided to change the subject, "Where is my handsome boy, Hardigree?"

"Mother, don't start in with me about Hardi. He just didn't feel like coming. He's a good boy. He's just going through normal teenage phases."

"I know Hardigree is a wonderful young man. I just worry that he is mixing with the right people."

"Hardi is not Phillip. I have my children well in hand."

Alberta wanted to reply that she too had been a very attentive and involved mother but she kept silent.

"I'm going in the other room to visit. Julia, I want you to come out soon so I can introduce you, although I don't know half the people here myself. I don't plan on being here all day. Mother, don't let Julia sway you into agreeing that she needs a cell phone. Twelve is too young. She needs to be saving her babysitting money and her allowance."

"Aren't you going to say hello to D.C., Mother? You always like babies." Julia asked.

"D.C. isn't a baby," Madison replied and then she left the kitchen.

"Why doesn't Mother like D.C., Grandma? He is so sweet and so special. One time when my belly was aching a whole bunch and I was scared because I thought something was really wrong with me he touched my stomach and I felt all hot and the pain went away. I think he is a gift from God."

Alberta was about to speak when her cousin, Cassie, burst into the kitchen followed by her daughter, Judith, and her daughter-in-law, Joan.

Cassie was barely five feet tall but she had a voluptuous body, large facial features and a larger voice. She bellowed, "There's my gal and her sweet baby D.C. I'll swear till my dying day that he cured my emphysema. I'm as serious as a heart attack. What in hell are you doing hiding in here, Alberta? It's just like when we was kids back in Missoura. My kid cousin gets all shy and timid in a crowd. Well, not me. The more people around me the better. And if there is a sexy man or two in the mix I'm as happy as a suckling pig. There ain't no men here except family. I don't know why I bothered putting on a bra. The other day I was working at the Mission House and 'long 'bout five o'clock I told Wilma that I was feeling pretty comfortable and then I realized I had forgotten to put on my bra that morning. You'd think I'd have noticed these big udders dangling loose."

"Cassie, you are a sight," Joan said sheepishly. Her voice sounded like a little girls even though she was in her sixties.

"She's one to talk. Look at her trying to look so innocent. Last week she was up to the mall in Fairfield buying tennis shoes for my great grandbabies and as she was walking up to the counter, Gwen told me she walked plum out of her slip. It fell right down to her ankles. Must have been a sexy man that was a waiting on them. Don't you love those heels Joan has on, Alberta? She always dresses so cute. I'd love to wear high heels again but I get too dizzy when I try to wear even a low heel. Hell, I'm just plain dizzy." Cassie laughed loudly and everyone laughed along with her.

"Oh, Cassie, you're not supposed to tell that story. I didn't even know my slip had fallen until I looked down at my feet. I was so embarrassed." Joan tittered, her face turning red. Joan had been a dancer on *The Carol Burnett Show* in the '60's and '70's and she still had her lithe dancer's body and very shapely legs.

"Yeah, but I bet the clerk was good looking," Cassie challenged.

"He was too young and too short for me. I don't even remember what he looked like."

"Sounds like you got a pretty good look to me. A young one, huh? Short, tall it don't make no mind to me but I like 'em young. The old ones can't keep up with me. I'm going to have to go shopping for me some tennis shoes this weekend. I better go to Charlotte's for a sex potion first. She can conjure up anything."

Everyone was really tickled at this point. Alberta was laughing so hard she began to cough. She was surprised that D.C. had relaxed in her lap and was making happy noises.

"Who is Charlotte, Grandma?" Julia asked.

"She is a white witch that lives across the street," Cassie answered.

"Is she really a witch?" Julia's eyes got big.

"That's what people say, sweetheart," Alberta said.

"I've got many potions from her. My momma and my grandma swore by her powers. Oh Lordy, is that Metamucil on the counter there? Hand that to me, Judith. And find me a spoon," Cassie said.

Judith was as quiet as her mother was loud, although she looked like her mother's twin. Cassie began rummaging through her large purse and finally pulled out a Mason jar filled with a clear liquid. Judith handed her the Metamucil and a spoon and Cassie ladled a heaping spoonful of Metamucil into her jar and stirred it briskly.

"Here top that off with a dash of water," Cassie directed Judith.

"Mother, you're not going to drink more of that homemade liquor and Metamucil, are you? You know better than that. Remember what happened at the beauty college last week when you were getting your hair set?" Judith said paternally as she added water from the tap to the jar her mother had handed her.

"You can take the doctor out of the hills but you can't take the hillbilly out of the doctor. I had that accident because I had taken too many Zydones and Tylenol PM's. If I hadn't had to wait so long under the dryer everything would have been fine. Julia, don't ever get old, child. Everything just dries up including your insides. Ask your grandma. She's younger than me but only by 8 years. The older we get the shorter that distance seems." Cassie said, and then she drank the contents of the Mason jar in one long swallow.

"Guess what this one did in the other room not more than ten minutes ago? Are you sure you haven't been sneaking into my stash of corn liquor, Jody?" Cassie continued, pointing at Joan. "She bumped into the window air conditioner and said 'excuse me.' You have to love a gal who is even polite to appliances."

"Cassie, you are terrible. I thought I had bumped into someone. There are so many people in the other room. I didn't know it was an air conditioner until I turned around."

"Can I take D.C. into the back bedroom, Grandma? I brought two of my old stuffed animals to give him," Julia whispered in Alberta's ear. She reached for D.C. and he didn't resist when she took him in her arms.

"I guess so, honey. Be careful. Stay in the spare room. I know I don't have to tell you not to get into Aunt Roberta's things. D.C. has another half of a peanut butter sandwich in the refrigerator that he hasn't finished. See if he'll eat it now. Are you hungry, honey?" Alberta asked quietly.

"Not yet," Julia replied

"His sippy cup is in the fridge, too. I've got washcloths in his diaper bag. If he gets fussy just bring him back to me. I'll come check on you two in a little bit. And don't go outside, honey, it's getting too hot for the both of you. Do you need me to help you carry him?"

"No he's really light, Grandma," Julia said carrying D.C. to the refrigerator grabbing his sandwich and cup and leaving the kitchen. Brownie followed closely after them.

"Now that the little pitchers are gone I don't have to watch my filthy mouth. Lordy, forgive me but I'm horny. My neighbor was out washing his car this morning with his shirt off. I forget how pretty a man's chest can be."

"I remember when you hated sex, Cassie. Roberta and I were talking about how you used to make Carver bring you home a gift before you'd bed him," Alberta said.

"Even then he always got the better end of the deal. All I ever had were those filthy pawing men at Fancy's and old 'Slim' Carver. I got to where I hated the sight of men. I even wondered for a while if I was one of those lesbian girls. There was quite a few of them at Fancy's. But women are too soft and panicky. Then I met Albert Duncan, Judith's daddy, bless his soul. He was all man and such sexy hands. He gave me a good learning about sex. I haven't had another man since Albert died fifteen years ago. I've waited long enough. What was the name of that shoe store you went to, Jody?"

Everyone laughed again.

"Sounds like all the fun is in here. What are you all laughing at?" Roberta asked as she walked into the kitchen.

"We're talking about sex and how I ain't getting any," Cassie shouted.

"Oh don't get me started on that subject. Hot weather always makes me provoked. All the men our age either want the young ones or they're six feet under," Roberta said.

"That's why I'm on the prowl for a young buck. If I get my hands on one I'll wear him out good."

"Oh stop, Cassie, I'm getting flustered. I don't want to think about it. The food just arrived, maybe that will calm us down. My baby sister is frowning anyway. Alberta is getting offended," Roberta said.

"I'm not offended at all, Ro. I can listen to other people talk about sex."

"I can tell Alberta is a doer and not a talker. I like to talk about it, think about it, picture it, taste it, touch it, do it and see it. I watch them soaps just to see those pretty young boys loving up on a girl," Cassie added.

"Let's go eat. Ursula and Edie set up my buffet table and decorated it real nice in the other room. Edie and Jay brought a huge birthday cake for Alberta and me. Vivian scheduled a psychic to come over. She is going to tell fortunes. Vivian knows how I like things like that. Alberta, Madison says she's going to leave when the psychic comes, she and Sondra seem kind of offended for some reason," Roberta said as everyone followed her out of the kitchen.

"Remember Beulah's mother-in-law, Mrs. Akins, up on Virginia Street who used to read our tea leaves, girls?" Cassie asked Alberta and Roberta.

"She was good. She told me all about Velasco before I had met him."

Alberta walked away from her sister and cousin. She searched for Madison in the living room but she wasn't there. Fixing two plates of food she carried them to the spare bedroom. On her way down the hallway she saw Madison and Sondra whispering in Roberta's bedroom.

With her elbow Alberta tapped on the spare bedroom door. Julia opened it. D.C. was on the rug playing contentedly with a stuffed elephant. Brownie was curled up beside him.

"I brought you kids some food, sweetheart. Did D.C. eat the rest of his sandwich?"

"He ate most of it. He drank all of his juice. Grandma, why doesn't Momma let me talk about Daddy?"

"Probably because she misses him so much. She loved your daddy a great deal and it was very shocking when he fell off his Uncle Fred's roof and died. He was always helping somebody fix something."

"Sometimes I can't remember him. People say that the spirit lives on but how do I know?"

"Let me think." Roberta pondered for a moment or two and then continued, "Picture your daddy as best you can and tell me something you do remember about him that requires one of your senses besides sight, like scent or sound or touch?"

"I remember how he smelled all soapy and nice after he took a shower in the morning. He used to let me comb his hair sometimes and it was all crinkly and soft like yours."

Alberta set the plates of food on the desk and took a rose from the vase. "Smell this flower and touch it. I'm going to smell it too."

"Um, it smells good," Julia said, touching the petals.

"Now come over here to the closet." Alberta held the rose in the dark. It was no longer visible. "Now was that flower real?"

"Yes."

"I think it was real too, but how do you know?"

"Because I touched it and smelled it."

"Yes, but you can't see it anymore. Are you certain it was real? And is it still there?"

"Yes, because I remember how it smelled and what it felt like to touch it. I know it is there because you're holding it there."

"The same is true of your daddy, sweetheart. As long as someone holds a memory of him in their heart he will always be around. When no one remembers him anymore that means all the people who loved him have joined him in heaven."

Julia thought for a minute. "I think I understand, Grandma. Did you love Daddy, too?"

"I loved him very much. He was one of the kindest men I ever knew. He reminded me of my Great-Grandfather Desmond. Your daddy was like another son to me. He was a wonderful husband to my daughter and an excellent father to my precious grandchildren." Alberta held back her tears but her eyes got misty.

"I love you, Grandma. I remember Daddy told me he loved me all the time," Julia reached out and hugged Alberta tightly.

"I love you too, you precious thing."

"There you two are. I've been looking all over the house for you. Your cousin Hannah wants to see you, Julia. I think she is in the kitchen. She wants to know if you're going to be at Sunday school tomorrow. Now go find her and tell her you will be there," Madison said as she entered the room. D.C. looked up at her and dropped the stuffed elephant he had been gnawing on. He scooted to a corner of the room and hid himself behind a chair. Brownie hid with him.

"Don't forget your plate, sweetheart. There is cake in the other room too," Alberta told her granddaughter.

Julia let go of Alberta, picked up her food and left the room.

"Why haven't you ever told me about Cousin Cassie?" Madison asked in an insistent whisper after the door was closed.

"There wasn't any need for you to know. What Cassie did was a long time ago and she was a very different person then. What should it matter to you, Madison?"

"I've always considered Cassie vulgar, but when Sondra told me she used to be a prostitute I nearly flipped. I thought Cassie used to be a doctor? Everyone used to call her Dr. Cates. I don't want my daughter being around people like her. Forgive me for saying it, but Sondra is right about D.C., too."

"These people are your family, Madison. Cassie was most definitely a doctor and was and still is one of the smartest and finest people I know. She put herself through school and became an internist when she was in her forties. Then she went and did missionary work and tended to the sick and destitute in places all over the world. Why Cassie would give you her last dime if you needed help. I think she is a wonder and a riot. She is 88 and still as vital as any woman a quarter her age. And what in the world could Sondra possibly have to say against D.C.?"

"Besides the fact that she agrees with me that you are too old to have the responsibility of caring for him? She says what he does is not right before God. God's children are not supposed to heal unless they can claim the healing in the name of Jesus Christ. Then Sondra tells me a fortuneteller is coming to the party. We might as well slaughter a lamb and start worshipping the devil."

"Children are the innocents, Madison. God created D.C. and gave him his special abilities. I have too much faith in my God to question his actions or require some kind of sanctification from any religion. If this is the kind of thinking you've adopted from that church Sondra has you going to I don't want to hear anything about it. Throughout the years my cousin Sondra has espoused the wonders of Buddhism, Feng Shui, Free love, Taoism, Paganism, Atheism, Scientology and for several years she was one of those Moonies. I don't like talking about people, but you and Sondra have made me really angry, Madison. She's always been as flaky as a biscuit and as spoiled as curdled milk. Carl and Jewell always gave her anything she asked for. She never had to work a day in her life and they left her several million dollars. Try to get a dime out of her if you're ever hungry."

"Why don't you ever listen to the things I say, Mother? Just because Sondra introduced me to my new church does not mean I don't have a mind of my own. Give me a little credit."

"I give you a great deal of credit, Madison. But I'm just tired of you fighting me about D.C."

"I'm sorry for arguing, Mother. I'm just in a horrible mood today. Coming to Vallejo really does make me depressed. I better go find Julia. Do you want me to give you a ride home?"

"I'd like for you to. When I mentioned that I was thinking of having you give me a ride back to San Francisco, Roberta pitched a fit. She wants me to stay for another night."

"I'll call tomorrow after church and see if you want me to come get you. I hope you realize I love you, Mother. I just worry about you."

"I know you do, honey. I love you too. But you shouldn't worry about me. D.C. and I are just fine."

After Madison had left the room Alberta found D.C. behind the chair.

"Everything is okay, D.C. Madison doesn't mean to scare you. She just doesn't understand." Alberta picked up D.C. and held him tight. She kissed his soft neck and chuckled into his ear. She checked his diaper and changed it. Taking a jug of tap water from the diaper bag, Alberta refilled D.C.'s sippy cup. Together they sat on the sofa bed and ate the honey sweet, walnut chicken and rice.

A half hour later Alberta carried D.C. into the living room. The house was still full of people but D.C. didn't seem to mind. Alberta sat with D.C. on the sofa next to Roberta. Brownie sat at their feet. Everyone was silently listening to the psychic who was telling Cassie's fortune.

"Please tell me you see a dark, I mean awfully dark young stranger in my future," Cassie crowed, only half joking.

In an instant the psychic's expression changed. Even her features appeared to transform. In a low male voice she turned to Madison and said, "Maddy, I remember the peaches. I'm sorry I didn't listen to you." Alberta quickly recognized her son-in-law, Rick's voice.

Alberta looked over at Madison who was standing near the front door with Julia. Madison visibly gasped and stood frozen for a moment. Then she grabbed Julia's arm and hurried her out the door.

After Madison and Julia were gone the psychic's expression changed again. Nearly inaudibly she whispered, "Kommer til mig, min gutten." D.C. wriggled out of Alberta's lap and hobbled over to the psychic. The woman lifted him gently in her arms and levitated a few feet in the air. For a few seconds they disappeared. Brownie went to sniff where they had been and he yipped twice.

Cassie rubbed her eyes and said loudly, expressing what everyone felt, "Lordy, have mercy. They just vanished. I wouldn't have believed it if I hadn't a seen it myself. It's like one of those Las Vegas magic shows." Most of the people in the room found it easier to believe the vanishing was a parlor trick.

When the psychic became coherent again she carried D.C. back to Alberta saying, "That was certainly exhilarating. I've never experienced anything so profound before. This child has an extraordinary spirit with a strong connection to the other side. Your child astounds me," She told Alberta meaningfully.

The psychic spent the next hour telling everyone's fortune that requested it. Each one she spoke to listened intently and believed.

After the psychic left everyone but Edie and Ursula and Jay filed outside to leave. They stayed inside to clean up. Alberta and Roberta walked out with Cassie and the rest of the family. They quickly stepped to their cars ignoring the loud throng of miscreants who had gathered outside in the yard of the apartment building on the other side of the alley. There were so many people that they spilled out into the street.

"I might have to go next door, Cousin Roberta. It looks like they're having quite a winging over there. It puts me in mind of those rent parties folks used to have years ago. Lordy, it is hot as a firecracker out here. Well, I'm out like a light. I feel that Metamucil kicking in. Bye, baby cousins. I love you like sisters," Cassie said as she walked to the gate. A few moments later her car was driving away.

Alberta was certain the mercury must have climbed to one hundred degrees. If there had only been a breeze the heat would have been more tolerable. Alberta sat with D.C. in one of the rocking patio chairs on the front porch shaded by the roof. Brownie reclined under the chair.

As the family left, Alberta noticed a carload of teenage girls drive past the house several times. They shouted out for another young girl, Remy Martin, who was at the party next door with her toddler, Britney, and her drunken mother, Mona. Mona lived in the wretched apartment building next door. She had a flabby shapeless body that was bowed and aged beyond its years, hair the color of mortar, tiny severe eyes, and a thick long nose. On a face with stronger features the nose might have looked noble but on Mona it dwarfed her face obscenely. Remy was more petite than Mona and only slightly overweight. She and Britney had brilliant red hair and creamy pink complexions. Mona seemed more agitated by the girls in the car than her daughter was. Soon Mona was shouting out threats and insults at the teens in the passing car.

Earlier that morning Roberta had told Alberta all about Mona. Alberta recalled her words, "Oh, she's just a hopeless alcoholic, Baby Sister. It's just pitiful. She reminds me of our Dola. Most every night she's wandering around outside wailing about, or to someone. I've nicknamed her *Moanin'* Mona. She'll be moving soon though. Sugar, my neighbor up the street, says she hasn't paid her rent for months. The court gave her two months to get caught up and that time has come and gone."

Roberta came back from the edge of the fence where she waved at the last carload to leave. She sat in the rocker next to Alberta. "I'm about done in, Baby Sister."

"Yeah, I can't let D.C. stay out in this heat too long. I don't care for it much either.

The two sisters shook their heads and watched Mona hollering as the car full of young girls passed the house again.

Finally, one of the girls shouted back, "Shut the fuck up, you crazy tweaker bitch. Just tell your slut daughter to stay away from the father of my son."

Alberta quietly asked Roberta, "What in the world could get them so worked up?"

Mona's face instantly blanched and then she let out a ghastly howl and hurled a bottle of beer at the passing car. It smashed deafeningly. The people out by the street quickly backed away and filed into the yard of the apartment building. They expected the carload of girls to stop their car and start a fight. Instead, the car disappeared down the street. When it didn't cruise back by the house, people relaxed and started talking again.

Slender white clouds drifted across the sky like bands of smoke formed by the broiling heat. Green hills to the south had a blue cast to them and they looked deceptively cool. Even the long shadows that the sun was casting offered little relief. Alberta had forgotten how hot Vallejo could get when there were no ocean winds.

Just as Alberta was about to take D.C. inside out of the heat, a tiny unmistakable clump of gray fog floated across the sky from the west, the wind chimes on the porch of the white, Victorian house across the street on the corner of Maine began to ring. Within moments, strong, cool breezes were bristling through the trees. A blue plastic recycling bin clamored as it bounced up the alley, caught by a powerful gust.

Then there was a low rumble that Alberta first mistook for the blustery wind. The sound grew to a roar and soon it was all you could hear. With screeching tires, the car full of young girls came rocketing up the street. Alberta looked over just as the vehicle struck Remy who was standing out by the curb holding little Britney in her arms. The toddler and mother soared into the air like lifeless rag dolls. They flew for about thirty feet and then landed in bloodied heaps within inches of each other on the hard asphalt. Everything seemed to stop for a few moments. Even the wind settled down. Then Alberta and several others rushed into the street behind Mona who let out a scream that made Alberta catch her breath. Over the shoulders of the people in front of her, Alberta saw the motionless bodies of Remy and her little girl. She wished Cassie hadn't already left.

"Oh, God, my babies are dead!" Mona shrieked as she dropped to her knees on the pavement between her daughter and granddaughter. Sugar rushed from her yard and ran over to Mona and tried to put her arms around her but Mona pushed her away gruffly. Mona's face turned scarlet and her head dropped back. Her mouth gaped open without a sound coming from inside. Then she began to weep violently.

Alberta realized that D.C. had been clinging to her leg, just as he limped away from her and headed toward Mona and the broken bodies. He stopped briefly, and then went over to Remy. Her head was twisted in a queer direction and blood oozed from her mouth and nostrils and ears. Alberta was certain that the teenager's neck had been broken. It looked as if she was dead but then her eyes fluttered open and she looked directly up at D.C. who was about to put his hands on her.

"No, go to my baby," Remy cried out distinctly.

"Get that retard away from my babies! He stinks like shit!" Mona howled. She rose quickly to her feet and started to shove D.C. away. D.C. must have had an accident because of all the excitement. He didn't have accidents too often, only when he was stressed or tired.

"Stop, Mother. He has to save Britney," Remy muttered distinctly. Her eyes closed again.

Mona stopped and glared at D.C. as he hobbled over to Britney's unmoving body, a misshapen heap lying on the hard street in a pool of blood. Alberta began to sob quietly looking at the little girl. Britney's whole body was bent and mangled and her head was turned backward. Her left leg had been almost completely severed at the hip. A raw piece of flesh was all that kept it connected to her body. D.C. leaned over the child who was only slightly larger than he. Then his hands traveled over the girl's body. With a grunt he turned Britney's head around slowly. Next he pushed Britney's leg back into place and held it for several seconds. No one said a word. They just looked on transfixed, even Mona.

Suddenly, Britney stood up. She looked over at her lifeless mother and then she waddled over to Mona and started to bawl. Mona checked Britney's body thoroughly and then she shoved her aside and went to kneel over Remy.

D.C. started to amble away. He was covered in blood and Alberta could see that he was physically weakened. She was walking to him, when Mona grabbed his slim arm and jerked him back.

"I don't know what kind of devil child you are, but you save my Remy, you retard. Somebody make this freak save my Remy!" Mona screamed furiously.

D.C. tried to pull away but he was helpless. Alberta didn't understand why he wasn't healing the teenager either, but she wasn't about to allow him to be mistreated in any fashion. And neither was Brownie, he had followed them out into the street and was standing next to Alberta. He started to growl and Alberta reached down to restrain him by holding his collar.

"Why won't you help Remy, you retard? Now you get down there and fix my baby!" Mona wailed, as she shook D.C. and then shoved him violently on top of Remy's body.

Brownie tried to break free of Alberta's grip and lunge at Mona and she commanded him back into the yard and he obeyed reluctantly. Alberta turned to go pick up D.C. and tell Mona to leave D.C. alone, when a tiny woman with waist-length, golden hair came running out into the street and snatched D.C. up in her arms. Alberta knew at once that it was Charlotte, the white witch. Her faded house with a roof as pointed as a sorcerer's hat on the other side of the street was nearly hidden behind a soaring wall and an immense and spindly pine tree. Alberta knew the legend of Charlotte from when she was a little girl in Vallejo, but she had never laid eyes on her till that moment. The night before, she was certain she had seen Charlotte's shadow behind tattered lace curtains in a window on the second floor when she was walking with D.C. and Brownie from the ferry.

Charlotte had been living in her house even before Roberta moved into hers. People in Vallejo referred to her as the white witch because she sold homemade love potions and rare herbs for healing. She also read Tarot cards and tea leaves and told fortunes. Most people who had availed themselves of her services swore by her mystical powers. There were even rumors that she had been around since the Gold Rush and that she had outlived three husbands, a dozen or so children, and scores of grandchildren and great-grandchildren.

To Alberta, Charlotte appeared perfectly beautiful and barely old enough to even have grandchildren. Her silky skin was the color of alabaster. She had large, kind, teal colored eyes, and refined, delicate features. She was like something out of an old-fashioned illustration or a hand tinted, antique photograph.

"You leave this child alone. He's worth a thousand of you," Charlotte said with composed forcefulness. The wind whipped around her and her golden hair billowed around her beautiful face. She cradled D.C. in her arms and placed her cheek against his forehead. Alberta was stunned that he seemed perfectly content to rest in Charlotte's arms.

"Why won't you make him save my Remy?" Mona pleaded.

"Don't be such a fool, woman. It's not this child's choice. If it is somebody's time to pass on he can't stop that. Now, go sober up and tend to your granddaughter and let Remy move on in peace," Charlotte said, and then she instinctively nodded her head at Alberta. Still holding D.C. close, she started to walk over to the sidewalk in front of her house. Alberta followed after her and Roberta did too. Charlotte handed D.C. to Roberta and then she motioned Alberta closer. Roberta held D.C. tight, kissed him gently and turned to walk away.

Charlotte leaned nearer to Alberta and whispered, "Hold tight to that child. He has a remarkable destiny. He must have been born with a veil. He is a profit. He has awareness of the Knowledge of Five. He is here to help us unlock the powers that lay dormant in our brains. I'm afraid he may have been born too soon. Most people aren't ready for such miraculous change and that can cause them to be very scared. Fear causes people to do desperate and sometimes evil things. Someone very powerful is going to try to take him from you." Alberta instantly recalled the ghostly Sarah and her warning from weeks ago.

Charlotte glided to her tall, old, wooden gate. Fittingly, it groaned when she opened it and then she vanished behind the stone wall that surrounded her house. Just before the gate closed, Alberta glimpsed a lush, colorful garden on the other side of the ivy-covered wall. Alberta lingered briefly by the gate hoping to catch another look at the exquisite Charlotte and her lovely garden. Then she walked back across the street to Roberta's.

Sirens blared in the distance as Mona lay on top of her daughter's body sobbing. Britney was still streaked with blood; she stood alone next to her grandmother whimpering and looking bewildered. Alberta thought she heard a crow caw loudly when she was passing them in the street. She looked up and saw that it was only a guileless, silver mockingbird high up on one of the telephone lines. And above the mockingbird, higher still, floating in the sky was a white seagull.

12 ∾

The six women were hushed and apprehensive as the driver
traveled slowly down the remote and deserted road, a few miles
southeast of Springfield, Missouri. It was oldies night on the FM station
the radio was tuned to, and "Respect" by Aretha Franklin was just then
ending. Parking along the side of the road the driver turned off the
ignition and the headlights. Gravel crunched under the tires and then it
was as if the car and its occupants were swallowed by the night.

LaDonna Cofax's heart was pounding in her throat as she tried to
focus her eyes in the darkness. Cicadas and crickets chirped loudly in
the typically warm and humid May night in southern Missouri. The sky
was clear and raven black except for a few storm clouds rumbling on
the horizon. Ladonna knew the storms would arrive with the sun unless
they stayed north and drifted east.

"We've got about fifteen more minutes," Tammy McLaughlin
said lighting up the dial of her wristwatch and checking the time. Her
long, tawny hair shone in the light from where she sat in the front
passenger seat. Tammy's younger sister April was driving the car they
had "borrowed" from their Uncle Orville's auction lot. LaDonna didn't
know the make or model of the long black car, but she thought it was a
Cadillac. It had the same plush leather interior, crests, and wood grain
accents her former husband Jerry Cofax Sr.'s Cadillac SUV did. It was
certainly much nicer than any of the featureless and derelict vehicles he
had allowed her to drive.

With the air conditioner turned off, the car quickly heated up.
LaDonna began sweating under the black wool cap that she had pulled
down tightly over her short dark hair. She was a little frustrated because
she had just had her hair cut and styled by Judy at Ruby's Gold Crown
Beauty Shop for her trip to California, but it couldn't be helped.
Long beads of perspiration trickled down her spine beneath the heavy
black sweater she was wearing. Even her hands were moist inside the
thick, black leather gloves. She was growing so warm it was difficult
to breathe. Stifling as it was, LaDonna was so frightened she was
trembling.

LaDonna had lost count of how many of these missions she had
been a part of in the past two months. Weeks ago she had accustomed
herself to the slight guilt she felt, but she could not rid herself of the

overwhelming fear she was going to be caught and exposed.

If only she had kept silent about Jerry, Sr.'s abuse then possibly she would never have gotten involved with these women and their furtive and illegal activities. His cruelty had grown so monumental that she had to share it with someone. The women in her Red Hat group were her only friends.

LaDonna confessed every detail of Jerry, Sr.'s wicked deeds to her best friend Laurie Kuntz while they were shopping for a Noah's ark collectible for her Red Hat secret sister. That night at the weekly meeting, Laurie insisted she tell the other women in the Red Hat group what had happened to her. Not long after, everything spun out of control.

LaDonna hated thinking about Jerry, Sr. and their failed marriage, but every time she committed another crime with the gang her mind flooded with memories of him. She would recall all of the bad experiences and the ones she had believed were good. Over time she had grown less angry toward Jerry, Sr., while a simmering fury directed at herself had begun to fester. Why was she always so afraid of everything?

Signs of Jerry, Sr.'s abusive behavior had been evident since the beginning of their relationship but she had ignored them. Now she resented her own dread and ignorance throughout the marriage. Ultimately, fear had been the guiding force of her entire life. Worse, she had passed on many of her worries and insecurities to her fifteen-year-old daughter Jean Anne, or Jeena, as she now preferred to be called.

Although LaDonna had to admit that she had made many mistakes in raising her two children, Jerry, Jr. and Jeena, she would never concede that she had been an unfit mother as Jerry, Sr. had told her, their children, and the courts. The courts might have believed him but she was certain her son and daughter weren't thoroughly convinced.

At the time of their divorce, Jerry, Sr. had her so confused and beaten down that she hadn't put up much of a fight against his demands. Afterward, it was too late. The kids no longer wanted to be with a mother who was always despairing and completely unsure of her own future and her ability to take care of them.

Jerry, Sr. had so cunningly manipulated the divorce that both of her teenage children freely asked the judge to give their father sole custody. But they didn't know the whole story. They weren't present on the last night she was allowed to stay in the house.

For nearly the past twenty years, besides the house she grew up in, it was the only other home she had ever lived in. Rightfully, both homes had belonged to her parents. It was their money that paid half of the seventy-five thousand dollars it cost to buy the home Jerry, Sr. insisted they purchase just weeks after the marriage. And it was LaDonna's mother and father who had given her money sixteen times in the past eighteen years to keep the home out of foreclosure. Astoundingly, at the time of the divorce, after the house was paid off and its value had tripled, he was able to persuade LaDonna to give up her interest in the house for the sake of the children who would be living there with him. She felt as ignorant and helpless as a six-year-old who has been conned out of his milk money by the classroom bully.

Through the many years, LaDonna had devotedly, gladly, and tirelessly maintained the home and kept it looking lovely for her children and her husband. She would often laugh to herself as she was dusting or polishing or putting away another load of clean clothes wondering whether Jerry, Sr. thought magical fairies came during the night to keep his home and his clothes so meticulous. He apparently didn't think that LaDonna was doing the work because, in eighteen years, three months and four days of marriage, he had never once thanked or even acknowledged her for all the countless hours of dusting, mopping, disinfecting, scrubbing, washing, drying, ironing, folding, sweeping, cooking, and sewing she had done.

Jerry, Sr. had even laughed at LaDonna that last night when no one else was around to witness his meanness. He called her a curse word idiot for sacrificing her life to raising children and being merely a housewife. He didn't know she had done it all with a glad heart, because she believed it was her duty as a loving wife and mother.

How easily Jerry, Sr. forgot that it was he who had insisted LaDonna resign from her job at the church. She had made herself nearly indispensable at the job she had grown to love, and she had still managed to maintain their home and care for the children. He had been so adamant though, that after two years of working in the church office she had finally relented and given her notice. Inanely, she had laughed along with him when he merrily reprimanded her because she didn't need all that "mad money." If only she had saved the money she had earned then she wouldn't have been left homeless with so few options. But instead, she had paid off most of the delinquent bills Jerry, Sr. had amassed and given some of the money back to her parents.

In a way, LaDonna was grateful that her parents had passed away a few months before the divorce. If they had been alive they would have been aghast at how their daughter had so willingly relinquished everything that mattered to her; her possessions, her home, and, most importantly, her children. They would have never understood the overpowering sway that her husband had over her and the terror he instilled in her.

Thinking back on it, LaDonna was certain that Jerry, Sr. had been plotting the divorce for years. She realized later that he had callously taken advantage of the anguish and dread she was cast into by the sudden loss of her parents in a fatal car crash. It was as if he had been waiting for just such a circumstance to manipulate the dissolution of their marriage to his ultimate benefit.

That last night, two months ago, Jerry, Sr. basically confessed it. In fact he admitted all of his transgressions and his enmity toward LaDonna. LaDonna wasn't surprised by some of it, she was already well aware of his affair with the church pianist, Darlene Wellman. She was surprised though, by his pride in how miserably he had treated her, and much of it was without her knowledge.

"The divorce was final today and it's too late to do anything about it, LaDonna. I could have told you that grass was purple and you would have just said, 'Uh huh'. Actually, you're so pathetic it's nauseating." Jerry, Sr. taunted, as he stood leaning against the entry into the dining room in his favorite gray Haggar slacks, his white, short sleeve Arrow dress shirt, and his burgundy and gray striped tie. It was the outfit she had bought him for his last birthday with money she had saved by doing her own permanents and hair coloring at home.

LaDonna stood by the front door on the other side of the living room. Jerry, Sr. was sipping on the coffee that LaDonna had made for him to his strict specifications: seven rounded scoopfuls of coffee beans ground for eleven-seconds precisely, brewed in seven and a quarter cups of water. For the eighteen years of marriage and the two years they courted she had done everything he had told her to do, without question or resentment, and now he was mocking her for it. Between sips of coffee he took bites of one of the pork chops that LaDonna had made him for dinner. He was making that smacking sound with his lips that LaDonna now realized she loathed.

"Why are you saying such hateful things? Jerry, you promised in front of God that you would devote your whole life to me. What have I done? What is so wrong with me? Tell me how I can fix it, please,"

LaDonna said in her soft voice. She stood by the front door on the tiny squares of pearl white tiles that she had laid herself in the foyer.

"I'm tired of being married to a little girl who looks like a fat old woman. That naïve act of yours was cute when you were young and slim and pretty, but now it's just disgusting."

LaDonna nearly pointed out that he too had aged a lot. His waist size had gone from a trim thirty inches to a paunchy thirty-six inches. Now he had more hair in his ears and on the back of his neck than he did on the top of his head. Even the skin on his face was lined and weathered. None of that had mattered to LaDonna. She hadn't married Jerry, Sr. for his looks. He was an average looking man with alluring eyes that were as yellow as pine, hidden behind thick eyeglasses. He had a funny, crooked nose, small, delicate, effeminate hands and one of the most infectious smiles she had ever seen.

"I think you're just going through a phase, Jerry. I know the stress of taking care of a family must be overwhelming. So, of course another woman with no children or responsibilities is more appealing. But Darlene Wellman can't make you happy. She's too much like her sister, and you know they call Anita Wellman the 'black widow of Reed Springs'. Darlene and Anita pretend to be such pious Christians, but all they do is go after married men. I just hope you don't die like Anita's husbands have. Maybe Darlene isn't as bad as Anita, but she does only get involved with married men. She and Anita just covet what they aren't supposed to have. What if getting you away from me is all that Darlene is after, Jerry?" LaDonna was so concerned with analyzing Darlene that she wasn't aware Jerry, Sr. was grinning at her. When she first noticed his smile her pain lifted. Then she realized it was merely a menacing smirk.

"Is it the kids, Jerry? All teenagers go through a rebellious stage. My whole junior year of high school I used to skip P.E. with two Vietnamese girls. We'd go smoke cigarettes at the 7-eleven around the corner from Parkview High. One time I rolled out a whole roll of toilet paper from the girl's third floor lavatory, for no good reason at all. I know Jeena and Jerry, Jr. have done more serious things, but I think the pressure is much stronger on kids today. Dr. Phil says that..."

Jerry, Sr. interrupted, "You just don't get it LaDonna. It's not the kids. You've pretty much ruined them anyway. I would have let you get custody of them but then you would have been granted the house and I would have been bled dry by child support. Besides, I'll make certain that they're both gone in a couple of years. I know all about your rebellious streak in high school. Maybe you really are as ignorant as you act. Darlene insists that you're very calculating and one of the most passive aggressive people she has ever met. She's convinced that you're the one who stole all of her sheet music from the piano bench at church. She says that any girl who has a baby to trick a boy into marrying her, and then gives that baby away without a second thought, is plain devious. This is not a phase I'm going through. You are the problem, LaDonna. You're fat and ugly and boring and scared of your own shadow. Maybe you really did go psycho when your folks died. What about all the pills you took last month? I'm beginning to think you need professional help. If you don't get out of here and leave me alone I think I'll contact a doctor and tell him how crazy you've been acting. I could tell him that I think you might be planning to harm yourself or someone else. I think I'll tell him you've been making threats against me and the kids. You already heartlessly gave away one child with no second thought."

"You promised you would never tell about my baby. I was only fifteen. I told you how heartbroken I was when my parents made me give up my son. What a hurtful thing to do. I've kept your secrets. For your information I miss my child every day of my life. Maybe some day I'll go to California and find him."

"You'd never have the courage to even leave Springfield. You'd get all panicky." Jerry, Sr. shivered mockingly.

With one final smack of his lips, he finished the pork chop he had been gnawing on. Then he turned and tossed the bone onto the platter that lay on the dining table. The bone missed and landed on the beige carpet that LaDonna had vacuumed two hours before.

LaDonna started to pick it up just as Jerry, Sr. shouted furiously, "Leave it!" so forcefully that LaDonna stopped and then began to tremble.

Perhaps Jerry, Sr. was right. Maybe she was crazy and she just didn't know she was crazy. How could he know about her strange dreams, the floating sensation or the panic attacks she kept hidden from him.

"Jerry, if you don't want Jerry, Jr. and Jeena, I'd love to keep them. I could stay here and you could move in with Darlene, or your parents in Strafford. Then, when you're ready you can come back home."

Suddenly, Jerry, Sr. took his nearly empty cup of coffee and hurled it against the wall right by LaDonna's head. The cup shattered and left a wet brown spot on the wall. Then he raced across the room and stood right in front of LaDonna. He was so close that LaDonna had to breathe in his hot, stale-smelling breath. His left hand took a tight hold of her face. LaDonna closed her eyes and winced as he balled up his right hand. A second later his fist hit her hard in the stomach. She felt as if she might vomit or pass out, but instead she got that strange tingling sensation again. She had only felt it two other times. The first time was the day that her parents had been buried. The second time was only a few weeks ago when Jerry, Jr. got lost at church camp in The Mark Twain National Forest. Both times she had felt it necessary to take a tight hold of something sturdy.

The beginning of the weird feeling always started deep inside her head. Her temples would throb and a part of her brain ached like a muscle that had never been used. Then the sensation shifted quickly to her loins and it started to feel like the orgasms LaDonna had only when she masturbated. It always ended with the intense and unmistakable awareness that she might ascend straight into the air if she didn't hold onto something heavy and grounded. At her parents' graveside service LaDonna had thrown herself on top of her mother's coffin and clung tightly to the brass handles. Everyone assumed she was merely grief stricken, and she never confessed the truth. When she got the call at home about Jerry, Jr. being lost she had rushed out into the front yard and wrapped her arms around a tall oak tree until the sensation passed.

After Jerry, Sr. hit her, LaDonna was certain she was going to rise off the ground. Instinctively, she reached for the handle on the front door and grasped it firmly. When she felt like her feet were still going to lift off the tile floor she instantly wrapped her arms around him. He mistook her embrace as affectionate and shoved her away roughly. La Donna fell back and her shoulder hit the door with a loud thud. When she landed on the floor the eerie sensation left her body. He was right, she was deranged, but she couldn't let him know.

LaDonna stood unsteadily. Her stomach and shoulder throbbed with pain. Jerry, Sr. looked at her and smirked again. Neither of them spoke as LaDonna opened the door. She picked up her suitcases and quietly left the house for the last time. She didn't even flinch when he slammed the door shut behind her.

Somehow, Jerry, Sr.'s spiteful words and unexpected physical violence had shifted her attitude. Elation began to chip away slightly at the crippling despair and fear. She actually found herself humming as she placed her bags in her twelve-year-old Ford Escort with the rusted hinges, the cracked muffler, and the slipping transmission. She wasn't fretting about signing over to her husband her one hundred thousand dollars inheritance from her parent's in lieu of child support, or her rights to the house and its furnishings, or her rights to the new, grotesque, Cadillac Escalade SUV. She wasn't even concerned with the children at that moment. Something told her it was all going to be just fine. She would have a better house and the Lexus hybrid she had wanted instead of the Cadillac. Not long from now her children would choose to be with her again.

No more would she have to relinquish her control or her choices to Jerry Cofax, Sr. She'd never have to endure his noxious farts and belches, his offensive and unfunny racist and sexist jokes, or his uninformed and unenlightened pontifications on every subject under the sun. Never again would she have to scrub the stains out of his underwear with an old toothbrush and Scrubbing Bubbles because he refused to wipe or wash thoroughly. No more having to get down on her hands and knees to clean up the pee splatters around the toilet. He would in no way even one more time decide what she was going to cook or when she was expected to serve it. If she wanted to bake chocolate chip cookies at midnight or have a light salad as a last minute dinner, he had no control. And if she got as big as a barn he wouldn't be around to taunt or berate her. Even the remote control for the television she didn't yet own was going to be in her control, finally. And if she decided to move to California to be with her brother like she had talked about for years, she wouldn't have to listen to her husband's famous harangue: "Only nuts and fruits live in California; which do you plan on being, LaDonna?"

"God, thank you," LaDonna said aloud as she started the noisy engine of her car. It took her three hard shifts to get the car into reverse. Carefully, she looked behind and positioned her car so that it was right next to Jerry, Sr.'s Cadillac in the double drive. Slowly she backed up, making certain that her car made contact with his. There was a loud screeching sound as LaDonna's tiny car sideswiped the Cadillac. Even in the darkness she could see the long red scratch her car had left on his beloved arctic white SUV. She wished that Jerry, Sr. could behold her bright shining smile that grew wider knowing that he was eating another of the pork chops he had insisted she fry even though she had told him they had been left out all night by accident. Maybe she had been angry with her husband for a long while and just didn't know that she was angry.

That was how it all started. When the ladies in her Red Hat group learned what Jerry, Sr. had done to her, they were furious. Unfortunately LaDonna's own anger toward Jerry, Sr. and sense of empowerment only lasted a day or two. They were quickly replaced by the nearly crippling panic.

LaDonna couldn't remember for certain but she believed it was Teresa Rogers who first suggested the notion of exacting some kind of retribution against abusive men, specifically Jerry, Sr. The other women were quick to get involved with the plotting. Five of the eight Red Hatters had suffered similar abuse, or worse, from their former or current boyfriends or husbands.

It was decided over coffee and pie at The Village Inn restaurant that they would organize and retaliate with violence. Two weeks later, the Red Hatters in LaDonna's group went out in a borrowed car to attack Jerry, Sr. The women waited in the middle of the night wearing coordinating black outfits that they had gotten off the clearance rack at the Fashion Bug at the Plaza Shopping Center. They located him at Darlene Wellman's house out by the Battlefield Mall, where he had spent most of the night. LaDonna fumed because he had left their children at home alone, but the other women managed to calm her down and keep her focused.

The women waited and watched anxiously until finally at about half past three o'clock in the morning, he came out of Darlene's house and walked to his still scratched Cadillac. Just as he was opening the car door, the Red Hatters attacked. LaDonna was so frightened that she closed her eyes and her first punch landed on Rosella Huffland's back. With sticks and gloved fists the six women pummeled Jerry, Sr. to the ground. He didn't put up much of a fight; mostly he cried and begged for mercy.

Five minutes later, when the alarm on Inez Butcher's Timex watch chimed, the women stopped as they had planned. Before they left, Teresa kicked Jerry, Sr. one last time and then she tossed a single red rose on top of him and said, "If anyone asks you who did this, just tell them it was the mad hatters."

LaDonna couldn't help snickering quietly as she and her friends sprinted back to the waiting car. Earlier that night at the Village Inn, when they had concocted the plan to attack Jerry, Sr., all the women had howled when LaDonna had said in a hushed tone, "Well, I guess we're not the Red Hatters anymore. I think we should call ourselves the mad hatters."

Soon word spread and their family and friends were entreating the "mad hatters" to beat up other men who had abused their spouses or girlfriends or children. It wasn't long before the mad hatters' covert acts of vengeance became part of the local folklore in and around Springfield. The core group of eight women quickly expanded, splintering into numerous female-only gangs. Often the women gathered for an assault knew no more than each other's first names and the domestic crimes of the man they were going to attack. Of course LaDonna had no real statistics, but she had personally witnessed men in Springfield behaving more thoughtfully to the women and children in their lives.

That night, parked in the darkness outside the city limits, LaDonna's mind was so worried about the fact that she would be boarding a bus later that afternoon to move to San Francisco that she was finding it difficult to concentrate on the attack she had agreed to participate in. She had forgotten whether it was April's boyfriend or husband they were going to assault. All she remembered was that the man had beaten April so severely that she had lost the baby she was carrying. The man had only spent two nights in jail because his father was a prominent local attorney who had connections to Greene County officials.

LaDonna could hardly compare what Jerry, Sr. had done to her to what had been done to April, but still she had lost everything to his scheming. Now she was forced to go live with her brother Donald and his partner in California because she had no place else to go. She had been imposing on the kindness of her friends for weeks. For the past two weeks she had been secretly living in her car. The little bit of money she earned at her part-time job at the Stop n' Shop convenience store barely paid for her gas and food, and her bus ticket to San Francisco.

Suddenly, the headlights of another vehicle appeared in the distance. Gradually the lights grew closer and then abruptly the truck turned down a tree lined drive and the lights faded away. LaDonna's heart raced even faster.

"Let's go, girls," Tammy said excitedly. The pack of women left the car and stole into the night. LaDonna could not see where they were going in the darkness. She just followed after Tammy who was holding a flashlight to guide the way. All LaDonna could discern in the bouncing beam of light was tall grass and stalks of prickly weeds directly in their path. A fluttering bug landed on her face and she nearly tripped and lost her glasses.

April whispered, "Stay together. We're about there."

After April spoke, LaDonna began to see a gravel covered clearing lit up bright by the lamp on a large, metal shed about fifty yards ahead. Next to the shed was a mint green mobile home. A tall, brawny man was just then climbing out of a shiny, red truck he had parked in front of the trailer.

Moments later, one of the women shoved a metal rod into LaDonna's hand hissing, "Here, you'll need this. Rex is a big ole boy and he's tough as nails. He'd just as soon whip a puppy as to sit still and take a licking." LaDonna was fairly certain it was Lydia, the short, bony woman with a ratted and lacquered mound of rust red hair. She had been introduced to Lydia earlier that night when the six women had met in the parking lot of the twenty-four hour Wal-Mart on the south side of town.

The thought of Rex, a giant brute of a man hurting puppies or someone as nice and tiny and meek as April, and the memory of Jerry, Sr. and all that he had stolen from her, enraged LaDonna. She was so incited that she raced ahead of the other women. Holding the metal pipe high, LaDonna barreled toward the towering man. Just as Rex started to turn around, LaDonna yelped shrilly, jumping on his back. Pounding on his muscular chest with all her force, Rex effortlessly removed LaDonna from his back tossing her to the ground.

Scrambling to her feet LaDonna was about ready to pounce on Rex again when one of the women shouted, "Watch out! He's got a gun!"

All LaDonna could think was to run away as fast as she could. But when she turned around Tammy and her flashlight had disappeared, so LaDonna sprinted out of the clearing into the darkness. A gunshot rang out and she heard Rex shout some obscenity so she ran faster. She raced blindly for several minutes, stumbling twice. Some kind of thorny plant tore her pants and scratched up her legs but LaDonna kept running. Just when she was beginning to feel safe, she heard Rex shout something behind her and she ran even faster.

A light flashed in front of her and LaDonna heard Tammy call out, "Come this way. But be careful, the river is in front of you and the water is really deep." The beam of light moved exposing the thirty-foot wide gully that was several yards ahead of her. LaDonna knew instantly that the James River was raging in that gorge. A low-pressure system had been stuck over southern Missouri and it had been raining heavily every morning for the past three weeks. The James River was nearly at flood levels.

Rex was still shouting and he was gaining on her. Another gunshot crackled and LaDonna heard a bullet go whizzing past her head and then slice through what sounded like the branches of a tree. LaDonna couldn't see it in the darkness but she could hear the James River. It was now steps in front of her. Tammy and the other women had crossed a narrow footbridge a quarter of a mile east. LaDonna had run so far from the group that if it hadn't been for Rex's hollering and the gunfire, Tammy would never have located LaDonna.

Overwhelmed with panic, LaDonna knew that even if she could swim, the currents in the river were so strong they would carry her away. She couldn't stop because Rex would catch her and shoot her or turn her over to the police. LaDonna was so terrified she thought she was going to pass out.

The tingling sensation raced through LaDonna's body. The feeling came much more rapidly than it had the other three times. Without anything to cling to she quickly felt her body becoming weightless and soon she was ascending into the air. Closing her eyes she felt a rush of wind engulf her as she heard the James River surging below. When she opened her eyes she could see Tammy holding the flashlight about thirty feet beneath her. Shutting her eyes again, moments later her feet were touching the ground.

Tammy stumbled against LaDonna. She turned her flashlight on LaDonna briefly asking incredulously in a whisper, "Where did you come from, LaDonna? How did you get across the river?"

"I guess I just swam across," LaDonna lied.

"I don't know how you did it; but never mind that now. Follow me. We need to get back to the car PDQ."

LaDonna heard the car's engine idling not far ahead. Opening the door of the car, LaDonna spied two falling stars flashing orange as they disintegrated in the earth's atmosphere high up in the moonless sky. A longing for California, a terrain that she had only seen in movies, came over her. Tears of exhilaration flooding her eyes, LaDonna couldn't possibly consider that maybe she had flown and she just didn't know that she had flown.

13 ❧

"Oh, excuse me," LaDonna said startled, even though the other person had bumped into her at the bus stop. Staring off at Merced Lake in the distance LaDonna had been somewhat distracted, but she was nearly certain she had been alone at the corner stop. The woman, clad entirely in white, who had shoved past her to get on the bus, said nothing. She did turn around for a moment revealing her powder white face before scurrying to a seat at the front of the bus.

Before she could stop herself LaDonna panted, "My goodness."

"It takes all kinds, doesn't it? That's why I love living here," said the older woman in very short shorts who came running from the other corner boarding the bus behind LaDonna.

Smiling, LaDonna turned to nod at the woman noticing several more people running to the bus. The woman said briskly, "Let's hurry this along, you're holding up the line."

Moving to the middle of the bus LaDonna spotted a pair of empty seats. She sat on the aisle. Removing her backpack, the woman behind her stepped over her and plopped down in the seat by the window.

"How's my Peanut?"

LaDonna saw that the woman was speaking to a large yellow bird. The lining on one side of the backpack had been cut out and replaced with mesh wire and the bird was perched inside. Looking away LaDonna smiled. She observed the white lady at the front of the bus and noticed she had a slim box in her gloved hand.

LaDonna *did* love San Francisco. People weren't particularly friendly but there was a pervasive "live and let live" attitude. How could she leave and go back to Springfield? LaDonna was terrified. She had been in San Francisco for nearly two weeks and she still had no prospects for a job. She couldn't bear the thought of leaving. San Francisco felt like home. The moment she had spied the skyline of San Francisco, peeking from a thick nest of silvery fog as she was crossing the Bay Bridge on the Greyhound bus, her heart had been instantly charmed.

San Francisco was indescribably picturesque. The countless, colorful Victorians that hugged the steep hills were so lovely, like elaborately decorated wedding cakes. Cradled in the valleys were neighborhoods like West Portal and North Beach with their quaint little shops and cafes. There was something about San Francisco that felt very European. But it was the blue Pacific Ocean that surrounded San Francisco and tempered its climate that LaDonna loved the most. It also gifted San Francisco with the romantic and mysterious fog. The fog often cloaked the city for days like a diaphanous, pale gray cloak. Sometimes it gusted through the streets and chilled you to the bone; other times it pillowed in the trees silently and was so heavy with water that the branches showered rain on the sidewalks. It never seemed the same and it continually stimulated the imagination. LaDonna didn't feel so afraid in San Francisco. She hated the thought of leaving and knew that she would carry images of San Francisco in her mind forever.

LaDonna had been living with her younger brother Donald and his husband Arthur. They were very accommodating and insisted that they enjoyed having LaDonna stay with them, but LaDonna knew it was putting a strain on their already stretched budget. And their apartment was a tiny one bedroom with barely enough space for their furniture. LaDonna tried to be inconspicuous and she mostly kept her two suitcases hidden under the sofa that she slept on. She spent as little time in the one bathroom as she could. She ate just enough to keep from starving, but she could still sense the tension her presence was causing.

During her first week in San Francisco, LaDonna had submitted her application or résumé, or both, to dozens of employers and all the employment agencies in town but there were no offers of a job. There hadn't even been one callback for an interview. LaDonna was beginning to wonder if she possessed any marketable skills or sufficient education.

The other major problem LaDonna had was that Arthur worked from home. He taught piano and his students began arriving at ten o'clock every weekday. Donald informed LaDonna politely that Arthur preferred privacy when he taught. The piano was in the dining area that was just a section of the living room next to the tiny galley kitchen. The only rooms with doors were Arthur and Donald's bedroom and the bathroom, and LaDonna couldn't shut herself away in either of those rooms for the entire day, so after looking for work in the morning LaDonna roamed the southwest section of the city out by Merced Lake where Donald and Arthur's apartment complex was located.

After the first few days of staying at her brother's, and having explored nearly every street nearby, LaDonna decided that she was going to venture farther out and enjoy San Francisco for as long as she could. Using a city map that she bought at Walgreens, a transit map she got on the city bus, and cash advances from the one credit card she had, LaDonna began to get to know the city. LaDonna had never travelled more than a few hundred miles from Springfield, and never alone. It was a new and exhilarating experience.

LaDonna lunched in tiny neighborhood cafes and bought trinkets for Donald and Arthur at unique shops. There was only a thousand dollar limit on the card so LaDonna didn't spend much money, still it made her feel empowered. She already had her return bus ticket, and if she was going to have to go back to Springfield anyway she wanted to get some kind of vacation out of her stay.

During those last days in San Francisco, LaDonna had gotten even more adventuresome and had decided, with Donald's guidance, to visit the public parks. There were famous parks like Golden Gate, which stretched across half of the city to the ocean, and the Presidio that was so lush with foliage you could forget you were in a major city. Also there was bustling Washington Square Park in North Beach by Saints Peter and Paul Church. In the heart of the city was Alamo Square Park bordered on the east by the Painted Ladies, the famous row of vibrant Queen Anne Victorian houses on countless postcards.

Though, it was the smaller almost hidden parks that LaDonna enjoyed best. These parks she often found by accident, or by exploring an area pinpointed by a tiny green mark on her map. With its shady palms and a large windowed octagonal gazebo nearly hidden from the street, the Sunnyside Conservatory Park seemed to echo sounds of a gentler era. It was at Ina Coolbrith Park situated on the top of a steep bluff with views across downtown where LaDonna was inspired to take up writing again. Her favorite of all the parks was possibly Fay Park on Russian Hill with its small yard of terraced gardens, its sweet apricot colored roses, and views of the North Bay. It was here where she first spied the famous constellation of peridot green, cherry-headed, and blue-crowned parrots. They flocked in the trees and raced overhead, their squawks as loud and mirthfully mocking as their plumage.

LaDonna loved the city but she was also intrigued by views north of Marin County. With only a few days left, Donald encouraged her to explore the Marin Headlands. It was already Thursday afternoon and LaDonna had given herself till Friday to find a job. There weren't any prospects, so she had resigned herself to the fact that she would be going back to Springfield after the weekend. What she was going

back to she had no idea. Still it was much less expensive to survive
in Springfield. She could only pray that she would find some kind of
employment there even if it was washing cars or gutting turkeys at the
Belfarms poultry factory. It was all just too depressing and frightening
to contemplate.

So here she was on the bus surrounded by distracted strangers, but
still feeling like she belonged. It was her last Thursday in San Francisco
and it was an impossibly beautiful day. LaDonna was determined to
relish it. She had set out from her brother's apartment at Parkmerced.
She planned to have a meatball sandwich at a cafe on Nob Hill and
then transfer to the bus that took her through Sausalito and up a hill
to an entrance into the Marin Headlands, which was a section of the
preserve known as the Golden Gate National Recreation Area. Donald
mapped out her route and recommended the restaurant.

LaDonna took slight notice of Alberta and D.C. when they got
on the bus two stops from where she had boarded. Brownie was in his
carrier and the three of them were going to the Marin Headlands too.
Alberta had packed a picnic lunch for herself, D.C., and Brownie. They
would stop for sodas at Longs Drugs in Marin City. Alberta planned
that they would eat on the hill by the water tank where they would have
views of the bay and the houseboats. Then the three would walk along
the trail at the top of the ridge.

On the bus, LaDonna sat a few rows back from Alberta, D.C.,
and Brownie who were sitting in the seats at the front reserved for the
elderly and the disabled. LaDonna tried to be discreet as she watched
Alberta and D.C. They were extremely attentive to each other. Alberta
was careful with D.C. and made certain he was secure in his place
next to her. She looked at him with much tenderness. Once they were
settled, Alberta took three books out of her large, worn bag; one was the
Bible, the next was *The Sonnets of William Shakespeare*, and the last was
Winnie-the-Pooh. Quietly Alberta began to read to D.C. from the Bible.
He sat there focused on Alberta, but LaDonna could not see his eyes.

At one point the white lady walked over to D.C. and placed a
narrow box in his lap. Alberta opened the box and handed D.C. the
gleaming piccolo that was contained inside. LaDonna had played the
instrument for many years when she was young. LaDonna realized
she was staring so she looked out the window watching a seagull that
appeared to be following the bus. When she glanced back the white
lady had vanished.

Just before Market Street, LaDonna transferred off of the bus. She wanted to catch Alberta and D.C.'s attention and give them a smile but shyness overtook her.

By mid afternoon LaDonna had arrived at the Headlands. D.C., Alberta, and Brownie had been there for a few hours and they had finished their picnic lunch and were walking along the main dirt trail about a quarter mile ahead of LaDonna. The clouds were the color of wilting blue irises and there was a mild grumbling in them that hinted at storms but at the moment it was very still. Because of the approaching inclement weather and the inaccessibility of this part of the Headlands there were no other people about.

At almost the same moment, LaDonna, Alberta, Brownie and D.C. heard the lilting music of bagpipes. The sweet, plaintive sound echoed in the windless air like the call of a Siren. Intently, they all followed the sound, curious of the source.

It was not long before LaDonna was near Alberta, D.C. and Brownie. LaDonna slowed and kept several paces behind them. LaDonna recognized them from the bus ride earlier that morning. As a group they walked south, deeper into the wilderness, for at least a mile.

After a while D.C. charged ahead. LaDonna could not know that he was stepping faster and more nimbly than he ever had before, and Brownie scampered after him right at his heels. The smell of bay and eucalyptus and butter-colored Scotch broom scented the warm, moist air. Soon the trail narrowed beneath the canopy of a grove of oak trees. Just beyond the trees, and past a hedge of bay, the path suddenly forked and the diverging trail took a sharp western turn. It was here where Alberta turned and looked at LaDonna. They both smiled and said, "Hello."

D.C. turned to look too and LaDonna was struck by how lovely his blue eyes were. His expression was so strange and enchanting. LaDonna felt an instant reverence for him.

The music of the bagpipes had intensified and LaDonna could tell they were getting closer to the person playing so hauntingly. D.C. didn't hesitate at the fork and he seemed to instinctively know to follow the new pathway. It was much narrower; more of a deer trail, but it was deeply rutted as if it had been there for untold years.

Suddenly it began to rain. LaDonna first noticed it clicking on the leaves and the brush. It was a soft feathery rain that made the surroundings appear impressionistic. Then a beam of sunlight peered from the edge of a cloud and a brilliant rainbow arched above them, ending yards ahead on the other side of another hedge of bay.

D.C. and Brownie had raced so far forward that LaDonna could not see them. Brownie barked spiritedly but the thick, dark leaves of the laurel bushes hid the two. As the trail led into a clearing LaDonna spotted them. To LaDonna's surprise, D.C. was adroitly playing beautiful music on the piccolo the white lady had given him. The sound brought tears to LaDonna's eyes. Then LaDonna stepped farther out into the clearing and caught her breath when two men and a woman came into view about fifty feet ahead. Through the thickening rain they looked illusory like the images conjured by bedtime fables.

One of the men and the woman were tending a large square garden. The other man was standing beyond the garden blowing into the chanter of a set of bagpipes. He was wearing a red plaid kilt and a tall furry hat. Both men's hair was as light yellow as buttermilk and their eyes, even from a distance, shone as green as spring clover. The woman was dark with black hair pulled into a tight bun. Wisps of hair that had loosened fluttered around her head like dark birds. She was wearing a full-length faded black muslin dress with a frayed hem that grazed the ground. Parts of the fabric had worn away on the full skirt and the crinoline underneath was exposed. The three disregarded everyone but D.C. whom they acknowledged with a slight nod.

Beyond these men and woman was a small stone cottage. LaDonna noticed that the end of the rainbow landed on the gabled roof of the pewter-colored house. The tin roof was aged with rust and a cobbled path led to the wooden door. Next to the house was a jacaranda tree as purple as grape juice. At the foot of the tree were three timber crosses with faded hand painted names on them, marking three graves. The earth over the holes was still mounded but tall grass blanketed them. D.C. walked over to the wooden markers and patted at each one tenderly.

Suddenly there was a loud clap and a streak of light flashed from the sky miles above, and D.C. reached out and appeared to catch the bolt of lightning in his tiny hand. The light streamed for several moments twinkling like the dust in the tail of a comet. The sky in the area from where the beam emitted became iridescent. D.C. made a noise that sounded like chortling and Brownie barked twice. Alberta stood away from them by LaDonna but she joined them with a mirthful laugh.

As if on command, hundreds of golden finches as yellow and radiant as daffodils flew from the purple jacaranda, twittering as they fluttered around D.C. and Brownie. The birds landed fearlessly on them. Brownie stood on his hind legs and D.C. wrapped his arm about the dog. It was a sight to behold there in the mist in The Headlands. LaDonna was overwhelmed.

Then the wind suddenly grew fierce and whistled through the air. LaDonna heard a branch snap behind her and she turned to look. The unnerving floating sensation quickly engulfed her and she took hold of an oak tree behind her. It was the first time the sensation had not been roused by fear. The feeling passed quickly but when she turned back around, the music had stopped and the two men and the woman, the cottage, the purple tree, the exaltation of golden finches, and the three lonesome graves were gone.

D.C. and Brownie were still yards ahead of LaDonna, but they were standing in a now empty meadow on the edge of a bluff. Alberta stood just a few feet away and she turned again and smiled warmly at LaDonna. D.C. and Brownie started walking back to where Alberta was waiting. LaDonna felt compelled to linger. D.C. struggled to hike to where they were waiting and in a few minutes had ambled directly to LaDonna. He made a few noises and then he reached up his hands to her. She noticed that he had objects clutched in both his tiny palms, one thing being the piccolo. LaDonna reached down to him and he emptied the objects into her hands. Then he reached into his pockets and retrieved more items. LaDonna smiled down at him and quickly said, "Oh, Honey, I can't take your things, especially your piccolo, but thank you very much."

D.C. made an urgent noise and Alberta told LaDonna, "He wants you to have those things for some reason. He's never done anything like this. Please take them. It would make him very happy."

LaDonna hesitated briefly and then replied to D.C. "Thank you very much, sweetheart. Nobody has given me a gift in a long time." She touched his cheek softly and Alberta noted that he didn't recoil.

D.C. made another noise as he looked up at LaDonna.

"Is he trying to tell me something?" LaDonna asked Alberta.

"I don't understand it but he's calling you his sound for bird," Alberta replied.

As she walked back to the main trail, getting far ahead of D.C., Brownie and Alberta, LaDonna studied the objects the child had given her. Along with the piccolo there was a feather, an acorn, a smooth pebble, and a tiny cutout from a photo in which LaDonna recognized the child, the dog, and the kindly lady he was with that day. LaDonna was instantly certain that these objects held great significance. She would study them until she knew what they meant. LaDonna wondered if maybe she had witnessed a miracle in the meadow at the Headlands that day.

14 ❧

LaDonna drove by the address in Sea Cliff several times before she finally parked across the street. It wasn't quite time for her interview. She had seen a young girl go into the house carrying a leather satchel. The girl was quite pretty and looked very professional. LaDonna was certain the girl would get the job. LaDonna wasn't even sure if she was qualified to be a personal assistant. She only had a vague idea of what her duties might be. The two suitcases with all her belongings were locked in the trunk. She was afraid of returning to Springfield, but she accepted it as inevitable.

"I have a Masters in Communications. I think I could be an indispensable employee." The young woman LaDonna had watched enter the house was saying eagerly.

Delia had to scan the résumé to remind herself of the interviewee's name. "Yes, I'm certain you would be, Crishel. I hope you understand I'm looking to hire a personal assistant and your duties will have nothing to do with my media company."

"I don't mind starting at the bottom. I have to admit I Googled you this morning, Ms. Wentworth. There were over half a million results."

"How fascinating. Well, thank you for coming by. I won't be making a final decision for several days. I have a lot of applicants to consider."

Watching the girl exiting the house Delia shook her head. The difficulties of settling in San Francisco had been so stressful that she hadn't given much thought to Anngelie's final request to find her baby. It took a month to find the right house to buy. The residence she finally chose was a modest 8,000 square foot, French limestone, neoclassical house at 100 Sea Cliff Avenue, a couple of blocks away from Robin Williams. The stone house had a pool and a private beach, both amenities a rarity in San Francisco real estate. But it still took her twin decorators from Montecito, Tobi and Toni Shafter, another two months to have the house refurbished to her specifications.

Even after it was redone to Delia's tastes the house still felt desolate. The moderately sized rooms had been redone in vibrant, jewel toned colors with opulent furnishings and the finest appointments. The designers had used much of Delia's current favorite colors, amethyst and carnelian, but Delia didn't feel comfortable in her new home. Perhaps it was because of the location. It was situated at the edge of a stony windswept bluff, high above the churning metallic blue waters of the ocean. Although the house had an abundance of immense windows it always seemed gray and shadowy throughout. Of course the fog that season was relentless. Day and night the mists made everything appear muted. Even the views of the lofty green Headlands on the other side of the bay were usually obscured, except during early morning. Delia usually slept till noon.

If only Delia hadn't sold her ranch in Marin County she wouldn't have had to do anything but hop on her jet and relocate to the Bay Area. It was generally sunny in Kentfield and the acreage she had owned there had been bucolic and secluded. But after the Guang Chi cult scandal, and her involvement in it became tabloid fodder, she wanted to erase the whole revolting episode from her life so she had impulsively sold the sizable ranch two years ago.

Consequently, she had been forced to endure the Penthouse Suite at The Fairmont Hotel for three, interminable months. Twice she had been coaxed to relocate to another suite of rooms to accommodate the demands of a visiting dignitary. She refused to move for Cher and Donald Trump when they stopped over in San Francisco.

Delia wanted to make certain moving to San Francisco to find Anngelie's son remained a secret. So she decided to hire a whole new staff that had no possible connection to her life in Beverly Hills. She had been conducting interviews for a new personal assistant for more than a week. She still needed a chauffeur, a butler or maid to oversee the domestic staff and the workforce for that person to oversee, a stylist, a manicurist, an acupuncturist, and a private investigator. She also needed a nanny and a nutritionist for her poodle Isobella. But her personal assistant could handle all of those tasks, if she could only find one who fit her qualifications. She had never had to shoulder so many burdens by herself.

For one week Delia had basically been living out of her luggage in her master suite on the third floor. She was subsisting on the dinners she had arranged to have delivered from Aqua restaurant and the martinis she mixed in the wet bar in her room. She had only visited the kitchen twice. The first time was to evaluate the refurbishment and the second, that very morning, to put some liquor in the pantry. Mostly she roamed the house like a solitary wraith, the sound of her movements echoing through the dim rooms and corridors.

More frequently there were moments when Delia was not alone, but only in the spiritual sense. The unknown older couple she had seen in Beverly Hills the night before she left appeared often, but they never said anything. Great-Grandmother Bergit and Aunt Agatha were also common visitors, Bergit always speaking in Norwegian and Aunt Agatha seeming to want to comfort. Often Delia called for her Grandmother Ingrid and Anngelie. She had even tried a couple of times to summon the spirit of Cornell Van Brundt. Delia had serious doubts about the existence of Anngelie's child. There were moments when she felt quite ludicrous having left Beverly Hills because of a request to find a boy who quite possibly could be a delusion of her sister's troubled mind.

At that moment though, Delia had no time to ponder ghosts or think about finding her sister's child. She needed competent help. She had been meeting with applicants for the position of personal assistant for nearly a week. Greta, her current personal assistant, was back in Beverly Hills handling Delia's affairs. Delia was primarily depending on Greta to take care of her estate while it was being invaded by her relatives and a television crew.

Again Delia had spent that entire afternoon interviewing more overqualified prospects. It was the usual parade of former Ivy League students who had gotten frustrated, for various, tiresome reasons, of pursuing professional degrees. Furthermore, each one of them knew who Delia was and she could sense they were hoping to acquire entrée into the vast media empire she had inherited. They obviously assumed that by first proving their competence as her personal assistant she would be so impressed she would move them into more lucrative and prestigious positions at her movie studio, her television network or her publishing company. It was always so difficult to find a proficient person who had no greater ambitions than being a highly paid and overworked personal assistant.

It was now nearly five o'clock. Glancing at her date book Delia saw there was only one more applicant expected that afternoon. She wasn't very hopeful when the doorbell rang and she went to answer it.

"Oh, your home is so lovely, just lovely. It looks like a palace. My goodness, are these marble floors?" LaDonna said impulsively, knowing it sounded silly.

Delia studied LaDonna's appearance. Delia noted that she had short brown hair and pink-framed glasses that were too large for her face. Maybe, in 1984, the mauve polyester dress she was wearing would have been the height of shopping mall couture. The dress hung loosely on her squishy looking body that had probably never had more exercise than low impact aerobics. At five feet three inches tall and weighing at least one hundred and forty pounds she was about fifty pounds overweight by Delia's estimation. She wasn't wearing any make-up except for some glossy pink gunk on her lips. Delia didn't even have to think about it; this woman was just too plain looking to hire.

"The floors, oh, yes, I guess they are marble," Delia replied, as she led LaDonna down the hall to the library. She knew this was sure to be the shortest interview of the day.

Once they were seated in the library on opposite sides of Delia's desk, LaDonna handed Delia her résumé and stated timidly, "My name is LaDonna Cofax." LaDonna shifted in her seat and then rattled on nervously, "I just divorced my husband, Jerry Cofax, Sr. Oh, but I guess you see that on my résumé. Not that I just got a divorce, but that my name is LaDonna Cofax. I'm sorry, but I've forgotten your name. I had your name and address written down on a piece of paper, but I left the notepad in the car."

"I'm Delia Wentworth," Delia told her indifferently, as she took a perfunctory glance over this LaDonna creature's résumé. She thought she better say something or the visibly anxious woman was liable to chatter ceaselessly. Delia was impressed, in a strange way, that the woman didn't know who she was. Doubtless, it meant that she was either totally incompetent or totally ignorant, probably both. But Delia had been very specific about her requirements to the employment service she had contacted, and so far, the thirty or so people she had interviewed had been highly qualified. Apparently, this LaDonna woman had some worthy qualifications that weren't readily apparent. Delia couldn't deny that she was intrigued because LaDonna was the first applicant who hadn't Googled her name prior to the interview.

"It says here that you attended the University of Missouri," Delia said as she gave the résumé another glance.

"Yes, and before that I studied at Baptist Bible College in Springfield, Missoura," LaDonna said, as she gazed at the antiqued paneled walls and the countless shelves filled with important looking books. She didn't want to look at Delia because she was afraid she might stare. Delia was the loveliest woman she had ever seen. Her face was so perfect, like that of a beautiful porcelain doll. There was something extremely familiar about her dark blue almost purple eyes too. After a moment, she quickly added, "But I'm not a fanatic. I no longer believe in organized religion. I don't think I do, anyway."

LaDonna was trying her best to stay focused. It was Friday and she had decided earlier that morning before she got the call for the interview, that she would not wait until Monday after all and that she would take the evening bus back to Springfield. It was a terrifying and depressing prospect. More than worrying about getting a job and being able to stay in San Francisco, LaDonna couldn't stop thinking about her experience the day before at the Marin Headlands with D.C and Alberta and Brownie. The enchanting little boy had left a huge impression.

"So, you've never been a personal assistant before? What exactly were your duties at this Atlantic Avenue Baptist Church?" Delia asked, setting the paper down and looking at LaDonna. Studying her, Delia realized LaDonna had some very fine features that she didn't know how to, or didn't want to accentuate.

LaDonna cleared her throat nervously and then answered, "Well, I did everything at Atlantic Avenue except wipe the pastor's you know what. I managed the office, the church library, the ladies' choir, the outreach mission, the daycare, and I kept the church books; and the church brought in over three million dollars a year. On top of all that I was Pastor Street's right hand girl. I did all the research for the Theological Doctorate he was pursuing. I wrote many of his sermons and typed and corrected the ones he wrote. I even managed to keep his wife, my best friend Nyla, from knowing about his countless affairs. I raised two active children, kept my family's home pristine, and made certain that I cooked well balanced and nutritious meals for my children and my former husband."

Delia was slowly beginning to change her mind. She had always been an excellent judge of people and this LaDonna was intriguing. Delia leaned back in her tall, suede chair and said, "Persuade me to hire you, LaDonna."

"Oh, I hate it when employers ask this. I really don't know why you should hire me," LaDonna replied. She paused for a moment and then she continued more resolutely, "You should hire me because I'm a very hard worker. I enjoy taking orders and fulfilling people's needs. I have excellent typing and phone skills. I'm proficient on the computer.

I'm also organized and I learn things quickly." LaDonna paused again, before she added, "Oh, And I'm always finding out that I know things that I didn't know that I knew. Most of all, I really need a job."

"I have to be honest, LaDonna. I can be a real bitch sometimes."

"Well, maybe you have reason to be, or maybe it's just poor digestion. I need this job, Ms. Wentworth."

"I demand expertise and you'll be expected to perform any task I ask of you, promptly and efficiently. My needs and wishes come first, before your own, in other words."

LaDonna didn't even flinch. She responded without even a hint of sarcasm, "Well, that sounds just like a man or a baby, and I've had plenty of experience with both."

Delia smiled slightly and asked, "Why do you say you need this job?"

"To be honest, I haven't had much luck finding the right job in San Francisco. I don't have a professional degree, or connections. And I don't live and breathe computers. When I think about it, I think I'm perfectly suited to be a personal assistant."

"The job pays one hundred and of course you get all benefits. If I decide to hire you, it will be on a trial basis for at least the first few weeks. Then I'll have my attorneys draw up the necessary contracts. I do require that you sign a confidentiality agreement. I don't know how long I'll be in San Francisco, but if your job performance is exemplary I'll find you a position with my current staff in Beverly Hills or Manhattan or with one of the companies I have an interest in."

"Do you mean one hundred dollars a day, plus benefits?" LaDonna inquired keenly.

Delia shook her head and replied, "Certainly not. I mean one hundred thousand dollars a year." Barely noticing the look of astonishment on LaDonna's face, she continued; "Now I want you to contact the most competent private investigators in the area and set up a meeting with the owner here at the house. Then arrange to have my poodle Isobella flown here on my personal jet. She's going to need a nanny and nutritionist while she's here. I need to find an experienced chauffeur and a domestic who will be responsible for hiring the staff to maintain this place. I don't suppose we'll need more than nine or ten full time servants. But first, get me a pitcher of very dry martinis. Just before you arrived I put a couple of bottles of gin and vermouth in the kitchen pantry. You'll find the phone numbers to make the arrangements for bringing Isobella to San Francisco in this folder that my personal assistant Greta in Beverly Hills prepared," Delia instructed, handing the folder to LaDonna.

"So I'm really hired?" LaDonna asked astonished.

"Yes, LaDonna, you're hired, but only on a trial basis. I'm going to call the employment agency and make certain that your references check out and that you aren't evading the police," Delia said with a chuckle. Her instincts told her that the biggest crime that LaDonna had ever committed was allowing her hair to be butchered by a completely unskilled hairdresser.

"Oh, I've never been arrested in my life," LaDonna exclaimed, feeling her face flushing. She was almost compelled to confess the crimes she had committed with the mad hatters but she stopped herself. She needed the job too desperately to jeopardize it. Anyway, she wasn't a real criminal like a bank robber or a drug dealer. And she hadn't lied to Delia. Truthfully, she had never been arrested.

About thirty minutes later, LaDonna tapped softly on the heavy wooden door of the library. She knocked so softly that it took Delia a few moments to notice. She already appreciated how unobtrusive LaDonna was, but she wondered if she was aggressive enough to handle the demands of the job.

"Come in," Delia called out.

"Sorry it took me so long," LaDonna said, as she entered the library carrying a tray with a pitcher of martinis, an empty glass, a jar of olives, and a plateful of some kind of food.

LaDonna carefully placed the tray on the desk. Then she poured Delia a martini and said, "I couldn't find much food in the kitchen but there were a few vegetables and some plain Greek yogurt in the refrigerator so I fixed you crudités. There were some herbs growing in planters on the back patio so I made a thyme and rosemary dip with the yogurt."

"LaDonna, I'm not much of an eater. A couple of martini olives usually fill me up. Occasionally, I'll have a light dinner or a salad. So you can take this food away. Just come back when you've finished the other tasks. If I'm not in here I'll be in my master suite on the third floor," Delia said as she took a sip of the martini. She was surprised and delighted that it tasted as good or better than the ones she herself fixed. And it was perfectly chilled.

"Oh, I've done everything you asked, Ms. Wentworth. A Mr.

Devlin Barlow from Barlow and Associates Investigations is coming here tomorrow at one o'clock. He offered to meet earlier, but I thought you might want to sleep in. Your Isobella arrives tomorrow afternoon and I've arranged for a limousine to pick her up at the airport and bring her here. I've got two very qualified applicants coming tomorrow to interview for the chauffeur position and three applicants for head domestic. I'll interview them in the morning for your final approval. I've also lined up interviews for a household chef, and a nanny and a nutritionist for Isobella. I also took the liberty of contacting a dog masseuse. I noticed that the roses and the gardenias looked a bit stressed so I contacted a landscaping service to maintain the grounds. Perhaps I should cancel the interviews for a chef unless you are planning to entertain?"

"I always like to have a chef or two on the staff," Delia replied. She was a bit astonished by LaDonna's proficiency, though her instincts had told her LaDonna was the right choice. She had barely had enough time to fully check out LaDonna's references but had discovered, as she had surmised, LaDonna had no police record. But something had to be done about her frumpy appearance. If she decided to employ LaDonna permanently it would be necessary to contact a professional stylist.

"I'd like you to move in immediately. This afternoon if possible."

"You mean I get to live here?" LaDonna asked incredulously.

"I need my personal assistant to be available at all times. You can occupy any of the guest suites on this floor or the lower level."

"This is just too wonderful. Thank you, Ms. Wentworth. I'll do my best to satisfy you," LaDonna said as she picked up the plate of uneaten crudités and started to walk out of the room. She stopped in the doorway and turned to say, "Oh, and I programmed the house phone so that you can ring for me from any room in the house."

"By the way, LaDonna, where did you ever learn to make such an exquisite martini?" Delia asked.

"To be honest, I had to call my brother. The gays always seem to know those kinds of things," LaDonna answered. Then she asked, "Is it all right if I leave now to get my things?" LaDonna didn't want to tell her that everything she owned was already out in the trunk of her brother Donald's car. She'd have to drive around for a while so Delia wouldn't become suspicious.

"Now would be a perfect time for you to go get your belongings."

As LaDonna left the room, Delia whispered, "I suspect you might be a treasure, LaDonna Cofax."

When LaDonna was gone the ghosts of the older unidentified couple appeared to Delia in the library. They were more distinct than ever before. Their faces appeared brighter and they were smiling. They lingered for mere moments. Delia was left with a warm feeling.

Delia was going to her room, a half hour later, when her Aunt Agatha appeared on the staircase. She was holding a baby in her arms. Delia could not see the infant's face because Agatha held it close to her bosom. Delia thought of Anngelie. If there was a baby perhaps it had died at birth.

"Anngelie, I miss you so very much. Why won't you come and tell me what to do? And where are you, Grandmother Ingrid?" Delia asked loudly, her voice reverberating through the house.

15 ❧

At a weathered picnic table Alberta sat staring south out over the redwood-covered valleys that surrounded Mt. Tamalpais. She was eating a buttery chocolate chip cookie and sipping on the coffee that Madison had bought for her at Peet's in Mill Valley. D.C. was sitting in her lap. They had just finished eating lunch, and Madison was cleaning up. Between slobbery bites of the cookie, D.C. stared at the tasty treat as if he was mesmerized. Chocolate chip cookies were D.C.'s favorite and Alberta had baked a double batch of them for his birthday.

It was D.C.'s fifth birthday so Alberta had made a picnic lunch of roast beef sandwiches on croissants with red pepper jelly and horseradish. She had also packed a bagful of grapes, slices of sweet peaches, a container of green olives, radishes, and carrot sticks. She had even mixed some tiny chunks of the roast beef into a bowl of Brownie's dry food.

On the way to the mountain they had stopped at the store and D.C. had picked out a big bag of salt and pepper potato chips and some cold bottles of black cherry soda. Alberta had surprised D.C. with the cookies when they got to the top of Mt. Tamalpais. She had stayed up the night before and baked them while he was sleeping.

Alberta was glad Madison no longer made a fuss about celebrating D.C.'s birthday. The first couple of years that Alberta had D.C., her daughter had refused to be a part of something she considered "absolute nonsense." Alberta knew Madison had been concerned that she was getting too attached to D.C. Those first months, Madison had been certain that someone was going to come and claim D.C. at any moment. It had been five years now, though, and Madison hadn't wavered much in her negative opinion and dislike of D.C. Alberta had hoped her daughter might develop an affection for the innocent and helpless little boy, but it hadn't happened. Madison often mentioned, almost gleefully, that someone was going to come and get D.C. someday.

Alberta had known from the beginning that no one would ever come to retrieve D.C. The child belonged to her. He was her gift from God, her late husband Armand, and her son Phillip. Phillip had told Alberta on the dark morning he passed on that he had been compelled by God to bring the child to her.

In some ways it seemed like it was just yesterday when Phillip had pounded on her door at three o'clock on that cool and foggy July morning. Alberta was in so much pain she never slept soundly; she instantly heard her son's insistent banging on the door. She knew it was Phillip and that he was in trouble again. Still it had taken her some time to crawl out of bed and turn on the overhead lights as she slowly ambled through the apartment on her ulcerated and infected foot. When she had finally opened the door, Phillip walked in hurriedly carrying a baby that was so emaciated, still, and pale Alberta thought it must be dead. The infant didn't even stir when Phillip tossed it carelessly onto the recliner, before he lay down on the sofa.

Even though Alberta could barely move because of the rheumatoid arthritis that had crippled her limbs, she rushed over to pick up the motionless baby wrapped in a soiled beach towel. At the moment she held the child to her bosom he stirred. Seconds later, Alberta felt heat surge through her entire body and the aching pain in her joints and foot lessened. Even her eyes that were clouded from diabetes focused, and she began to see clearly for the first time in years.

Phillip sat up suddenly and said agitatedly, "I brought that baby to you, Mother. He's got special powers. God told me to bring him to you. His mother doesn't deserve him. She didn't even go to the hospital to give birth to him. I don't even think she named him. She's just an AIDS riddled, worthless junkie like I am and his dad is a murdering rapist. She forgot him in the car like a bundle of trash tonight when we went to shoot up. She forgot all about him yesterday too, and he was in the room all day by himself. He's too weak to even cry. I know he's going to heal you, Mother. Sweet Jesus, he is going to heal you." When Phillip finished he collapsed back on the cushions again.

The baby made a noise and Alberta recognized he was in pain, so she held it closer and rocked it back forth. "I know child, everything is all right; you just rest in Alberta's arms," she whispered soothingly.

Alberta looked over at Phillip and saw that his eyes had rolled back in his head and his breathing had become more labored. He was overdosing again. She had seen him like this so many times in the past dozen years she was almost numb to her own feelings about it. Yet, he was different somehow this time. He wasn't talking in his usual street manner. He was agitated but he sounded like he used to before the addiction.

She had accustomed herself to the routine, though, and Alberta knew what she had to do to save her son one more time. Carefully setting the baby back down on the recliner she called out loudly to her son, "Phillip, stay awake for Momma. You've taken too much drugs again. You know I have to call for an ambulance."

Alberta leaned over her son and reached for the phone on the table next to the couch. Suddenly, Phillip took a tight hold of her wrist and said plainly, "No, Mother, please don't. I'm ready to meet Jesus and live in peace. Even that baby couldn't save me now."

Alberta looked down into her son's eyes. They were clear and fearless. It reminded Alberta of a day over thirty years before when she had walked him to school for his first day of kindergarten. She knew he was petrified because he was unusually silent, and his little hand was clasped so tightly to hers, the whole way. Then, when they arrived at the school he took a deep breath and suddenly let go of her hand. With a determined expression in his dark brown eyes, her son had looked back at her just once before he entered Lowell Elementary.

Tears welled up instantly in her eyes and she replied earnestly, "You are my son, my child. I can't sit here and watch you die."

"It's been a long time coming, Mother. I've been flirting with death for years," Phillip said, as he stared unwavering into her eyes.

Alberta tried to loosen his grip on her wrist but he held fast. He seemed so alive and so coherent that Alberta could not believe he was really passing. Phillip had been ill with AIDS for almost three years and he had been an addict for at least ten years longer. She had seen him near death many times, but this time was different. He was lucid and his eyes were so bright.

"Phillip, let me call the ambulance. The doctors can help you and then you can go into a treatment center our Madison found. I've still got a little money and she promised she would help too. I've been praying and I believe this time it will work," Alberta told him lovingly.

"Mother, you've wasted too much money already. We both know I can't be helped. You keep that baby, though. He's had a hard first few days and I don't know if he's strong enough to live much longer. But you love him as long as he lives, like you did me, Mother. He deserves that. Did I tell you his mother left him in the car while we were shooting up?" Phillip asked, as his eyes clouded over. He looked away from his mother and over at Brownie who was standing against the sofa staring intently at him. Then he added, "Tell her to let me go, Brownie."

"I've not wasted one red cent on you, Phillip. I'd do anything to get you well. I love you with all my heart. I'd give up my life for you. Just let me call for help." Sobbing, tears rolled down Alberta's cheeks. Even though she knew her God did not barter she looked up and closing her eyes she prayed aloud and fervently, "My dear sweet, Lord, please don't take my baby away from me. Take me, your humble and grateful servant instead, Sweet Lord. I beg of you, God, ruler of the earth and all the heavens."

"Mother, before I got here I shot up myself and that poor wretched baby's mother with enough heroin to kill two elephants. She's probably dead where I left her on the park bench by the fountains in Huntington Park. She didn't even know what was happening and neither will I," Phillip said. His words grew softer until they were barely audible as he spoke. His grip loosened on her wrist and she could sense him slipping away quickly.

"Phillip!" Alberta cried out, as he shut his eyes and she thought he had died.

Within moments she saw tears streaming from his still closed eyes. Phillip's chin puckered as he gasped with a mixture of joy and anguish, "Daddy, it's me, goy-boy. Hi, Pom-Pom. Aunt Dola, it's me."

Alberta's body began to shake as she sobbed harder. She could feel her heart breaking for the second time in her life and she whispered, "Oh, God, help me." "Goy-boy" was the pet name Armand had given to Phillip when he was just a toddler because Phillip sucked his thumb while he rubbed the nap of his blanket and chanted goy-goy continuously. From the time he was five years old Pom-Pom was the adoring, scruffy, white poodle that had been Phillip's closest companion. Alberta longed to see the dog, her husband, and her sister. She cried for them too, and then she took a deep breath and mustered more strength than she knew she possessed. Her voice trembling, she told her only son, "You just go to them, Phillip."

"I can't, Momma. You're holding me too tight," he moaned, almost silently.

Alberta lay across her son and wept. "I'll stop holding on, son. You just go on to your daddy and Pom-Pom and your Aunt Dola," she whispered into his ear. Then she kissed him gently as he inhaled deeply and snorted. It was his final breath. Alberta pressed her face into his motionless chest and screamed out a soundless, "No!"

Alberta couldn't help but weep quietly as she remembered that

morning five years before. She calmed herself quickly, though, because
she didn't want Madison to know she was upset. Anyway, it was a day
to celebrate D.C. Over the years she had learned with all she had lost
that she couldn't afford to wallow in grief. So she smiled because it was
the day D.C. had been brought into her life. She had no knowledge
of D.C.'s history or even his actual age but this was the day she had
designated as D.C.'s birthday. That day had been kind of a rebirth for
Alberta, too; D.C. had healed her of all her ailments and the love they
shared had given her the will to live again.

Alberta had named D.C. after her great-grandfather who had
fought in the Civil War, Desmond Charles. The first time Alberta had
looked into D.C.'s haunting, ice blue eyes she had been reminded
of her father's grandfather. Desmond Charles had been born on a
large tobacco plantation in North Carolina. His father was a second
generation Swedish American who had fallen in love with Suffrona a
young slave who was maidservant to his wife. Desmond Charles was
the product of their brief affair. Alberta remembered him as a kindly,
pale skinned, old man with silky, white whiskers and hands as soft as
polished stone. Most of her memories of him were faint but she could
still recall his stories of traveling out West on one of the first trains as
he gazed upon dust tornados and vast herds of buffalo that covered the
prairie like a dark restless sea. He didn't speak often but when he did he
usually quoted the Bible and Shakespeare. She still kept an arrowhead
and a buckeye he had given to her just before he died when she was
seven years old.

Even though his eyes and something about his spirit reminded
Alberta of her great-grandfather she secretly referred to the second
Desmond Charles by another name. Because of his special healing
powers and his complexion that was the color of chalk dust, when they
were alone, she called the child Doctor Cotton. Over time Alberta and
her family had just started referring to him simply as D.C.

Despite everyone's warnings, Alberta had fallen in love with D.C.
To Alberta, their inexplicable bond and unwavering love for each other
was destined to be, as if it had been written in some celestial book of
life. In her heart, she knew that through D.C. she had been shown the
true magic and infinite possibilities of life. For D.C., Alberta was in
his life to help him grow into manhood. She had known long before
Charlotte had told her that D.C. was destined for a greatness she could
scarcely comprehend.

Alberta chuckled softly. D.C. was concentrating so intently on the cookie he was eating. Anyone who observed this infirmed child would call it utter nonsense that he was going to be a very important man one day. Even Alberta's family would be quick to point out that D.C. had never spoken even one word, not to mention he still wasn't completely toilet trained. The notion he would even be able to function on his own one day, let alone achieve great prominence, was the height of improbability. But Alberta knew otherwise.

Why are you crying, Mother," Madison asked, when she sat back down at the table next to Alberta. She had been loading the now nearly empty cooler back into the trunk of her car.

"I'm not really crying. I'm just a bit misty because it's so pretty up here."

"Well, I wanted to give D.C. a gift. You simply must be exaggerating about D.C. playing that piccolo so proficiently a few weeks ago. I still don't believe it. Why you accepted a gift from a total stranger in the first place blows my mind. Even so, I thought this would be easier for him to handle." Madison said pulling a slender box wrapped in silver paper from her purse. She placed the package in front of D.C. and he looked up at Alberta.

"Go ahead and open it, D.C.," Alberta said.

Tentatively, D.C. picked up the box and stared at it for a few moments. He dropped the cookie he had been eating and it landed in his lap. Then he put the edge of the box in his mouth.

"I knew this wasn't a good idea." Madison stared out across the parking lot behind them. She wanted to like D.C. to please her mother, but she had such repugnance toward him. Yet it was difficult not to have pity for him, as well.

It was a late Tuesday afternoon and the lot was practically deserted. Nervously, Madison ran her fingers through her recently straightened hair. She was nearly thirty-seven but she looked years younger. Only the expressions in her eyes hinted at her true age.

"Don't be so impatient, Madison," Alberta said, and then she patted her daughter's long, shapely leg. Detachedly, Madison brushed cookie crumbs off of her neatly ironed linen shorts. She took a tube of peach colored Chanel lip-gloss and a compact out of her purse. Expertly applying the lip color to her heart shaped lips, as she glanced into the mirror of the compact. After studying her image for a few moments she put her sunglasses on.

"You don't give D.C. enough credit, Madison. He has wisdom that you and I could not handle," Alberta said quietly.

Madison inhaled deeply and then replied in clipped tones, "I know all about his healing powers, Mother. I know what you think he did for you. And the family can't quit talking about what happened in Vallejo at Auntie Roberta's party. All of that supernatural nonsense is impossible for me to comprehend and accept. I still strongly oppose it because what he does is against God's law. Beyond that D.C. isn't even able to function normally. Don't you think it's time you thought about getting him some professional help? There are people who are trained to care for children with special needs. You should think about his future. You won't always be around to take care of him, Mother." Madison paused for a moment before she continued in a hushed voice, "I've been thinking a lot about it lately. Maybe it's time we tried to locate his real family. His mother has to have had relatives somewhere. They're probably closer than we think."

"I am D.C.'s family. I give D.C. all the care and understanding he requires. I'm assured God will keep me here as long as D.C. needs me. The God I believe in makes no mistakes. D.C.'s special abilities could not possibly be evil. He has a pure heart. D.C. and I are essential to one another, Madison. I just don't know what I can say to make you understand. It's all just something I know in here," Alberta said, as she pounded hard on her chest twice. Since the moment D.C. came into her life it had been obvious to her that Madison was envious of the attention she gave to him. This latest objection to D.C.'s healing power was just another excuse for wanting to get rid of D.C. Alberta knew Madison's animosity for D.C. was increasing. Her daughter's malice was becoming wearisome.

Gruffly, Alberta snatched the box from D.C.'s hand. Madison and D.C. were startled and they watched Alberta as she clinched her mouth ripping away the paper and ribbon from the box and letting them fall. Madison quickly picked them up. With a huff, Alberta opened the slender box and folded back the tissue paper. Inside was a shiny red and gold harmonica. Alberta's mood instantly shifted. She chuckled and then placed the instrument to her lips and blew hard. It blared noisily.

"I know, Mother, it is ridiculous. I'll take it back and get him some new clothes or something else he needs. I was just in the store the other day getting sheet music for Julia's piano lessons and the harmonica caught my eye. I felt compelled for some reason to buy it for D.C.,"

Madison said, reaching to take the harmonica from her mother. "No, Madison, let's see what D.C. thinks of it. If you had heard him that day in the Headlands playing that piccolo you would realize it is the perfect gift. " Alberta placed the colorful instrument in D.C.'s tiny grasping hand and said, "Here you go, D.C. This is your birthday gift from Madison."

D.C. looked at the harmonica quizzically. He nearly dropped it. Then he grasped it tightly with both hands. Finally, he brought it to his mouth and started to gnaw on the edge of it.

Madison sometimes even hated looking at D.C. She reached to take the harmonica from the boy's hands, saying, "See, Mother, it was a silly idea. He'll just destroy it. I'll return it and get him something more practical."

Alberta pushed back her daughter's hand and told her, "Leave him be, Madison." Then she leaned her head down next to D.C.'s and she blew hard into the harmonica again. D.C. looked up at her bouncing excitedly in her lap.

"I won't fight you, Mother. But it's getting late." They both watched as a cluster of boisterous children piled out of two shiny SUVs that had just pulled into the parking lot. Then Madison continued, "If you still want to walk around the top of the mountain, we should start now."

Alberta set D.C. on the ground. He held fast to the harmonica. Brownie was sitting patiently under the table. When Alberta picked up his leash he stood and wagged his tail and stretched. Alberta looked back at the squealing children who were bouncing merrily and effortlessly toward the picnic table they had just left. Each child was wearing some kind of swimming attire and they all had silky, tanned skin. Two weary women with blonde ponytails and dark sunglasses followed after the horde. The women were toting big boxes and lugging a giant cooler behind them. One of the little boys with glossy, black hair, who was dressed in red swimming trunks, stood out to Alberta. The young boy bore a golden crown on his sturdy head. The boy didn't look much older than D.C. but he walked haughtily with the confidence of a grown man.

Madison had to call out, "Mother," twice, to catch Alberta's attention. Then she, Alberta, D.C., and Brownie set out to walk the lower and more level path that snaked around the top of Mount Tamalpais, about fifty feet beneath the peak.

Madison charged ahead and Alberta followed holding Brownie's leash and D.C.'s hand. They started on the shaded side of the mountain where bluish green hills rolled out to the horizon. To the northwest, the tip of Point Reyes jutted out prominently from the coastline into the Pacific Ocean. The blue of the water merged with the cloudless sky and it appeared to flow into infinity. A warm wind was blustering around them. It was so thunderous that Alberta and Madison didn't even try to speak.

Rounding a bend, Madison turned and pointed as the glistening waters of Phoenix Lake came into view in one of the valleys far below. It nested in a valley like a misshapen hand mirror. Even D.C. seemed enthralled by the majestic scenery. Brownie's eyes were beginning to cloud over from cataracts, but his nose twitched in the air excitedly.

The four of them walked slowly for about a half a mile until they came around to the east side of the mountain. San Francisco Bay and the rest of the continent lay before them. A pale pink, nearly full moon was just then rising over Mount Diablo in the East Bay and they stopped to admire it. The tension between Alberta and Madison had eased and Alberta looked at Madison and they both smiled.

Just as they were about to walk out of the shaded side of the mountain into the sun, the wind slowed down. D.C. pulled his hand free of Alberta's. He ambled over to a dusty gray rock in a niche of the mountain. Alberta let go of Brownie's leash and he went to sit by D.C. A moment later, a strange melodic sound echoed in the air. Madison and Alberta turned to look at D.C. in astonishment. He was sitting on the rock pulling air into the harmonica. Sweet haunting chords filled the air.

D.C. moved the instrument expertly across his mouth and his tiny hands agilely cupped the instrument. He wasn't playing music that was familiar to Alberta or Madison. It had a complexity and a dissonant proficiency that flirted over several bars in unstable chords until it resolved into soothing consonance. There was an ancient quality to the music, but at the same time it sounded entirely new. Alberta thought it sounded as if the seraphim were singing. The sound was overwhelming and beautiful, more beautiful than the piccolo music he had played in the Headlands.

As he played, D.C. seemed to be transported. His spine stiffened and it looked as if it was no longer a struggle for him to sit upright. The tiny body that was so ungainly and stressed was now poised and serene. For the first time, there were no visible signs he was a severely developmentally challenged, little boy. He looked powerful and as old as time. The expression in his eyes was no longer vacant, it held an unfathomable wisdom. Even the creatures were mesmerized by the magical music D.C. was playing. Brownie sat up on his hind legs at D.C.'s feet. Amazingly, a furry chipmunk and a fat black crow sat unmoving on the ground next to Brownie. Two green speckled lizards inched their way up onto a rock by his left shoulder, and a red hawk swooped down to perch on the limb of a bay tree by his right shoulder. A bobcat and her cubs stepped up to listen from behind the glossy orange branches of a Manzanita. The sight was nearly unbelievable but Alberta thought it right, somehow. Above it all, Alberta noticed a fat seagull that had landed in a crevice just over D.C.

When D.C. finally stopped playing, the creatures scurried away. His body became twisted again and his eyes were once again expressionless. Brownie walked over to Alberta and she picked up his leash. D.C. grunted as he climbed off of the rock and hobbled over to Alberta and took hold of her hand. Madison snatched up the harmonica that D.C. had left sitting on the rock and quickly shoved it into her purse. Alberta noticed her do it but she didn't say a thing. Afterwards, they all walked wordlessly into the warm sunlit side of the mountain.

Just then the group of children they had seen earlier came barreling past them. The raven-haired boy in the gold crown was leading the pack. As they scurried past, the boy ran into D.C. causing him to fall. The other children scampered on and the boy turned momentarily and Alberta looked at him warily. He had a cell phone glued to his ear and he was mumbling something. His golden paper crown was embossed with the words BIRTHDAY KING. There was an unmistakable glint of smug imperiousness in his eyes when he stared down at D.C. It seemed as if he was going to say something but he just smiled wretchedly and ran off after his noisy companions leaving a cloud of dirt in his wake.

Alberta shook her head and then reached down to help D.C. to his feet. As she dusted him off she noticed that one of his hands was cut. Alberta dabbed at it gently with a handkerchief she got from her purse. She kissed D.C. softly on the forehead as she lifted him up and carried him the rest of the way. It forever surprised her how weightless he was.

16 ❧

"I'm sorry we don't have anything more substantial to report to you regarding your sister's son, Ms. Wentworth. So far, we have been unable to find any evidence that there ever was a child. Without any new leads we will not likely make any headway. If you would like me to refer you to another agency I will be happy to do that. My expertise tells me they won't uncover any more facts than we have been able to do," Devlin Barlow informed Delia as they spoke in the privacy of the library. He was a trim man with steely eyes. Most women would have thought him quite handsome but he was a bit predatory and his pristine appearance too forced for Delia's taste.

"Your company has exemplary credentials. I would never have engaged your services, otherwise. I'd like you to continue looking for at least a few more weeks. I understand you most likely won't be able to give me any new information."

Devlin moved to the door. Delia could sense his restlessness. She felt it so often herself.

"It is never hopeless. People just don't necessarily get the answers they want to hear. I'll call you next week unless there is a development sooner." Devlin couldn't help but stare at Delia for a moment. She was so beautiful. "I'll show myself out," he said as he left the room.

Fleetingly, Delia wondered why Devlin had looked at her so oddly before he left. She waited to hear the front door close and then she whispered, "Anngelie, if your baby exists I need to have some help finding him and soon."

Delia was about to ring for LaDonna when she remembered it was her day off. In fact the entire household staff was out. Delia made certain no one was around when she had her Friday evening meetings with Devlin Barlow.

As Delia was passing LaDonna's darkened bedroom the computer on LaDonna's nightstand flickered on. Delia stopped and saw the apparitions of the strange man and woman, who were visiting her more often, floating in LaDonna's room. The screen glowed brighter and they both pointed at it. Delia stepped into the room and read the monitor. She clicked through several pages. It was a novel, and a quite interesting one.

There was a popping noise as Delia was leaving LaDonna's room to go upstairs to her suite. In the alcove behind the staircase Delia thought she saw a shadowy face. Her skin prickled instantly. Then there was another pop and the lights went out. Feeling her way along the wall she flicked the light switches by the front door and nothing happened. Delia suddenly recalled her cell phone and she turned it on. It emitted only scant light in the darkened house, just enough to see a few feet. Delia cast the light in the direction of the alcove. There was definitely a face there, one she certainly didn't recognize. The unfamiliar face recoiled into the dark when Delia shone the light on it. It looked like a young African American man. Delia rushed to the alcove and cast the light. No one was there.

A car drove by the house and its headlights illuminated the house for a few moments. In the corner opposite the staircase by a powder room and coat closet Delia saw a cloaked figure rushing toward her. A slight waft of air whooshed past her and she heard a moan. The large chandelier overhead tinkled and Delia felt the gust pass her again.

"Call LaDonna," Delia said into her cell phone.

"Yes, Ms. Wentworth?" LaDonna answered on the first ring.

LaDonna only heard Ms. Wentworth say her name and "please" before the call was dropped. LaDonna noted the unmistakable urgency in her voice. LaDonna tried to return the call but her cell phone was out of range.

LaDonna had hiked a mile or so from Delia's house just before sunset along Land's End Trail to a deserted rocky beach where she had been trying to discern the significance of the five objects D.C. had given her in the Headlands a month ago. She had been staring at the waves not noticing how dark it had gotten until the call from Delia. When she turned around she realized she couldn't see the trail. The coastline would lead to Delia's home but it was too rugged to walk all the way, especially in the dark.

Fog had also rolled into the bay and was spreading across the city. Looking east LaDonna saw that the Sea Cliff district was obscured.

LaDonna could only think that she needed to get home to Ms. Wentworth. Something was wrong and here she was trapped on the beach. How could she have been so foolish to linger until it was too dusky to see her way home?

There was only one way to get home quickly. If only she could command her body to do it. Concentrating LaDonna closed her eyes and tried to make her body ascend. Several minutes passed. She was about to give up when she felt the familiar stirring in her brain and loins and she soared straight up. For only a moment she feared she might fall. Soon she was flying above the fog where stars twinkled ice-like in the black sky.

LaDonna flew for a minute or two until her body felt less unwieldy. It reminded her of swimming except her body felt more weightless. Flying was the most pleasurable thing she had ever done. The only experience to give her more elation was the feeling she had after the birth of her children. She wanted to fly ceaselessly, but she had to focus and get home.

Diving down, Ladonna knew she would have to follow the coastline to Ms. Wentworth's house. When she was about twenty from the ground the beach became visible through the roiling mist. She flew past a pelican; their paths so close she felt the tip of the bird's wing. It squawked loudly.

Shortly, LaDonna spied the roof of the house. Effortlessly, she landed on the terraced lawn beyond the pool. She ran up the stairs and down the path to the darkened house digging in her pocket for the backdoor key. Once inside she began calling out for Ms. Wentworth.

Delia heard LaDonna calling out to her and she headed with her cell phone to the back of the house.

Suddenly the cloaked figure moved from the shadows and blocked Delia's path. In the bluish light the phantom appeared to glow. She saw the face more distinctly. It was clearly a black man but not as young as she had presumed. He had a pained expression. His mouth opened but no words came out. His face became more contorted and then he vanished. As soon as he was gone the lights came on again.

"Are you all right, Ms. Wentworth?" LaDonna asked as they met in the kitchen.

"No, I mean yes. I got a little rattled when the lights went out."

"I'll have an electrician come out tomorrow to check the wiring."

They looked at each other urgently. Neither woman wanted to expose what had just happened to them.

"Why don't you sit with me here in the kitchen?" Delia didn't want to be alone. The spirit trying to reach her had her very unsettled.

"I'll make you a pitcher of martinis. I hate it when the lights go out too. Back in Springfield it happened all the time because of the storms."

"Yes, you're from Illinois, right?"

"No, Missoura, I mean Missouri. My brother Donald is trying to help me with my accent. I never knew I had one till I moved out here." LaDonna said as she expertly mixed the martinis and then poured one for Delia.

"It's only a slight accent. I'm convinced that television is eroding regional accents. Nearly everyone on television sounds the same."

Delia sipped her martini. "Why don't you pour yourself one too, LaDonna?"

"Oh, I don't know, Ms. Wentworth. I've never had anything stronger than some homemade elderberry wine my sister-in-law used to make and that didn't settle too well."

"There could be no comparison. I insist you try one."

LaDonna poured herself a glass and took a sip. She smiled. It tasted crisp and it burned her throat slightly. She liked it. She nibbled on the olive.

"I knew you'd like it. Now sit down here with me at the table. Tell me something important about yourself."

"I don't know, Ms. Wentworth." LaDonna thought of the flying and she reddened. "I have a son and a daughter but they aren't speaking to me right now."

"Why is that?"

LaDonna proceeded to explain what had happened with her former husband. She left out the activities of the mad hatters.

When she was done Delia asked her, "Why didn't you fight him?"

"I guess I was afraid of what would happen if I tried to go against him."

"What could have been worse than what happened to you? You lost your home and your children and your inheritance. I won't include your marriage because it sounds like you are well rid of this Jerry fellow."

"I guess you are right, Ms. Wentworth. Everything I feared would happen did happen. I suppose I seem pretty ridiculous to a successful woman like yourself." LaDonna swallowed her martini and poured another for herself and for Delia who had just finished hers too.

"I'm not successful. I'm an heiress. It was pointed out to me quite recently that I don't work for a living. I inherited my billion-dollar empire. I drink too much too. I guess some people would think I was an alcoholic, but I'm not. I don't crave it. I just get bored easily. I do have good managerial skills, though," Delia smirked.

"Well you must be good at business. A lot of people would have spent their fortunes."

"I know who to hire to manage my businesses and my money."

"I would consider that a great skill, Ms. Wentworth. I wouldn't know the first thing to do if I inherited a great sum of money. Just the thought of it frightens me."

"You mean you haven't ever fantasized about being wealthy?" Delia asked as she poured out the last of the martinis into LaDonna's glass and began mixing another pitcher.

"Maybe my book will be a bestseller and I'll have everything I want."

"I didn't know you wrote, LaDonna. What is your book about? I love to read." Delia didn't mention the ghosts or the fact that she had already read a passage of the book on LaDonna's computer earlier.

"Creative Writing was my major in college. Jerry said I had no time to raise a family and write books too. He said I didn't have the talent or discipline to be successful. But you know, now that I think of it, I don't think he ever read anything I ever wrote. Anyway, my new novel is about a woman seeking revenge on the man who killed her sister and was never punished for the crime."

"That sounds intriguing. You should never listen to abusive people. Surround yourself with people who are supportive of your goals. What would you buy if you made millions from your writing, LaDonna?"

"If I were rich I'd buy my children whatever they wanted."

"But what would you buy for yourself?"

"First I'd buy the hybrid Lexus I wanted when Jerry, Sr. insisted we get the Cadillac instead. It was my parent's money in the first place. I'd get my children cars too. Well, when Jenna is old enough. She won't be sixteen for a few months. Jerry, Jr. will be eighteen."

"My children are older."

"You have children, Ms. Wentworth?"

"Yes twins, a boy and girl. I'm a lousy mother. My family is the last thing I want to discuss. What *are* we going to do with your appearance, LaDonna?"

"I don't know. I know I'm a mess. It is so discouraging working for someone as beautiful as you. You're even beautiful in the morning when you don't have on any makeup."

"My sister is much prettier," Delia blurted out and then she stopped herself from speaking of it further. "I'm going to have to think of something to help you. You have very nice bone structure and very pleasing features. First though, I need to help you lose the extra weight." LaDonna and Delia spoke and drank martinis for over an hour. Many nights after for the next two months they spoke intimately. Delia was avoiding the ghost of the mystery man. Since that first night he visited her continually. He never said a thing he just lingered and looked forlorn. Delia hoped Grandmother Ingrid or even Anngelie might come to her but they didn't. Great-Grandmother Birgit and Aunt Agatha stopped visiting too. There was only the persistent man and the older couple. Delia had finally figured out from photos LaDonna had shown her they were LaDonna's dead parents. They never said anything either, but, unlike the unknown man, their spirits appeared tranquil.

Delia also still had grave doubts about ever finding Anngelie's child. Devlin Barlow's contract had been extended several times and he kept finding new evidence to support the claim there had never been a child. There was documentation of two pregnancies that ended with late stage miscarriages. Perhaps losing them had been too much for Anngelie and she had convinced herself one of her babies had lived. Delia had decided to give it two more weeks and then she was going to stop looking and go home to Beverly Hills.

It was another Friday evening and Delia had yet again had her usual frustrating meeting with Devlin. Delia was alone in the library. The pink light of dusk was settling over the house.

The light flickered on the desk and Delia looked up and saw the ghost of the man. His image was more defined than ever before. He zoomed across the ceiling and lingered just above her. As usual he opened his mouth as if he was trying to say something but no sound was uttered. Delia decided it was time to find out what he wanted.

"Is there something I can help you with? Do I know you?"

The man looked at her with beseeching eyes. She could sense his frustration. Finally he muttered, "Tigger." The lights flickered and he was gone.

Delia instantly recalled Anngelie's final words, "Look for Tigger." At the time Delia had considered Anngelie's vague reference to the character from *Winnie-the-Pooh* as delirium and she had quickly forgotten it. Now it all seemed so apparent. Tigger was someone Anngelie knew.

"Thank you, Tigger," Delia said as she called Devlin's phone number.

After speaking with Devlin and telling him to look for someone nicknamed Tigger, she rang for LaDonna and told her to bring a bottle of champagne and two glasses to the library.

Twenty minutes later Delia and LaDonna were sipping vintage Veuve Clicquot.

"This is delicious, Ms. Wentworth. I've seen people drink champagne in the movies and it looks so glamorous."

"I told you to call me Delia a long time ago."

"I'm sorry, Ms. Wentworth. I mean, Delia."

"You need to treat yourself more often, LaDonna."

"I have been. I bought myself that computer. I have the large savings account I always wanted. I've even been able to help Donald and his husband quite a bit. That feels like a real extravagance to me. You've given me so much besides the money too, all those clothes and shoes and handbags and cosmetics and jewelry. I've never had such nice things. I feel like a queen or a movie star."

"Those things are nothing, LaDonna. When you're rich and even slightly famous people want to give you things. It's all about marketing. I'm kind of losing my taste for all those luxuries anyway. I'm satisfied if my clothes are well made, comfortable and have a classic style. It seems like these days I gravitate to the same ten or so items I like the best. I can scarcely believe there was a time when I never wore the same thing twice."

"Well, I think it is awfully kind of you. Don't think I don't realize that thanks to you I have lost all this weight. Your trainer has been so helpful and encouraging."

LaDonna also wanted to tell Delia the job was a breeze. LaDonna had set up all household budgets on the computer, so bills were paid electronically. There was a staff to clean the house and two chefs and three sous chefs to handle the meals, which were most often only eaten by LaDonna and the resident employees. A lawn service maintained the grounds and a nanny tended to Delia's poodle, Isobella.

Delia didn't usually wake up until noon and her daily activities included working out with a trainer, drinking martinis, and reading. Twice in those two months she went to an exclusive spa in Napa for a facial and a body wrap. Every Friday she had her private meetings with Devlin Barlow. LaDonna had very little to do except for screening calls, setting up appointments, and making certain Delia was never bothered with the trivialities of running the house.

"You're looking so much better, LaDonna."

"Thanks to you, Ms. Wentworth. I mean, Delia."

LaDonna was self-conscious about her new physique but Delia seemed genuinely delighted. Several times she had treated LaDonna to a new haircut and a makeup consultation with her own stylist and makeup artist. For the first time in her life, LaDonna had confidence in her appearance. It was a new and exciting feeling, and it was all due to Delia's guidance.

"How is your novel going? I really enjoyed all you've let me read."

"I think I might be about half done."

The writing she had started as a whim at Ina Coolbrith Park, before being hired by Delia, was now turning into an actual novel. Each morning LaDonna would sit at one of the patio tables out on the back lawn where there were unobstructed views of the Marin Headlands, the Golden Gate Bridge, and the Pacific Ocean.

The Headlands always stirred LaDonna's creativity. The rugged hills with their hues of browns and blues and greens had definition and features. LaDonna imagined them as the shoulders and heads of Poseidon and Amphitrite and their children, emerging from the sea. The ocean was Amphitrite's sweeping ballgown and the whitecaps were the lace trim. The Technicolor orange, deco inspired Golden Gate Bridge straddled the sea to their mythical underwater home.

"That's great, LaDonna. Don't give up. You have a gift. I wish I had a talent or inclination for something worthwhile. You have to let me read some more tonight. I'm so hyper I'll never get to sleep."

"I'll print some out before I go to bed. I hope nothing is wrong?"

"Not at all. I've been trying to do something for my sister and it looks like things are going to work out."

"That's wonderful. I remember you mentioned a sister one time."

"She's my twin. I mean she was. She died several months ago and I miss her very much. I thought it might get easier with time but so far it hasn't. I think about her more than ever."

"I'm sorry for your loss. It is very difficult to lose someone you love."

"Yes, you miss your children very much, don't you, LaDonna? I can tell it bothers you a great deal to be separated from them."

"My heart aches, but I keep praying. I know one day they will realize how much I love them." LaDonna started to cry. "I lied to you, Delia. I have three children. Please don't think less of me. I got pregnant when I was fifteen by a boy from my church. Everyone said I did it so he would marry me, but marriage and having a baby were the furthest things from my mind. It was just me being afraid to say no to someone I love, as usual. My parents made me give the baby up for adoption. They were so hurt by what I had done. I often wonder if they ever truly forgave me. I wake up every day worrying that my son is safe. I learned later a distant cousin and his wife adopted my son. They live in Burbank. I'd love to just meet him and make certain he had a good life. I guess I shouldn't be so selfish."

"There is nothing selfish about that at all, LaDonna. He probably wonders about you too. You should try to locate him. I had a child when I was barely sixteen. I was sent off to Switzerland. It was the scandal of the family."

"Did you have to give your baby up too?" LaDonna asked tearfully.

"My Robert died when he was four weeks and a day old. He was born with a hole in his heart. The doctors said it was a miracle he lived as long as he did. It didn't seem like a miracle. My mother said it was a blessing he didn't live. Perhaps it was," Delia said wistfully.

"Let's change the subject. Where are your friends, LaDonna?"

"My brother and his husband Arthur are my only friends out here, besides you. People out here aren't overly friendly, or maybe they just don't take to me. I have a lot of friends back in Springfield. I was an honorary Red Hatter. You're supposed to be fifty or over to be a member but my group is more casual about the rules. We have some members in their twenties. We younger ones are Pink Hats."

"I read about the Red Hat Society online just the other night. I used to have a group of ladies I ran around with. We were quite close in our way. We got a little too wild most of the time. I guess you'd think we were pretty hedonistic, LaDonna."

"I think you are one of the best people I've ever known. I don't see anything wrong with wanting to have a good time."

Delia smiled. "My friends and I went beyond having fun. We did drugs like out of control teenagers. Sometimes I feel like I spent the past twenty years stoned on something. We slept around, often with each other's boyfriends or husbands. We travelled the globe and caused all kinds of havoc. It was all about parties, and shopping and men and being competitive with one another. We even got heavily involved with Guang Chi."

"I heard about that religion on the news."

"Don't believe what you learn from the media. I know firsthand the agenda behind what is reported. I'll simply say Guang Chi was a cult for people with too much money. I'd rather not go into it. It's quite embarrassing when I think about it. That life seems so far away. I was so vacuous back then. I probably still am."

"I would imagine it must be quite overwhelming to have billions of dollars. I'm surprised you are as down to earth as you are. I can't imagine the trouble I might get into with all that money."

"Please, LaDonna. You are too kind to be as wicked as I was. My friends and I were the clichéd decadent rich. I guess we were trying to buy meaning in our lives."

"That is very astute, Delia. Don't for a second think debauchery is confined solely to the wealthy."

"When I was young I wasn't such a self-indulgent bitch. It sounds odd now, but at one time I seriously considered joining the Peace Corps. I actually believed I could change the world."

"I had an aunt who was a doctor and after she retired from her practice in St. Louis she joined the Peace Corps and served in Cameroon."

"I don't know what happened to me. My mother said I was just being dramatic and wanting attention. I listened to her and got married and had kids just like everyone else, but that life felt stifling. I divorced and then I dabbled with the family business and then I just travelled and shopped. I can't think of a time when I didn't feel restless."

"I think you have just been trying to find yourself."

"Oh, God, don't say that. I don't even know if I'm worth finding. I'm just glad to be rid of my old cohorts. Though I've been so bored and lonely here in San Francisco that I almost miss them. But I better not speak of the devil."

17 ❧

LaDonna was just finishing chapter eleven of her novel when Mildred Drummond the maid in charge of the domestic staff came outside and interrupted her. "Hey, LaDonna, some gals are here demanding to see Delia. But of course she's still asleep and I know we're not supposed to disturb *her majesty* before noon," Mildred called loudly from the open French doors at the back of the house.

"Thanks, Mildred, I'll take care of it. Tell the ladies I'll be right in," LaDonna called out. Mildred shrugged her shoulders.

LaDonna hurried into the house. Delia had strict orders about unexpected visitors. When LaDonna reached the foyer, two women were standing just inside the still open front doors. They were chattering noisily at each other and inspecting the house.

One of the women was obese to the point of looking uncomfortable. She had glistening brown hair that looked a little oily, a pale almost chalky complexion, and a big round face with no definable chin or neck. In total contrast, the other woman was cadaverously thin with harshly bleached hair that had been moussed and spiked into irregular heaps on her tiny head. She had overly tanned, leathery skin, and a bony, angular face.

"I'm sorry, ladies, but Ms. Wentworth is unavailable presently." LaDonna walked toward the two boisterous women to herd them out the doors. "Now if you ladies will leave me your names, I'll tell Ms. Wentworth that you dropped by."

The emaciated woman pushed past LaDonna. She suddenly called out in a frantic, high-pitched voice, "Well, there is our little runaway. It's not nice to disappear without telling your best friend. Besides, Delia, we're cousins too, and you're supposed to tell me everything."

LaDonna looked up and saw Delia standing in the shadows at the top of the staircase that circled down to the foyer. She started to turn around, and then she sighed audibly and began to descend the stairs saying, "I told LaDonna last night I shouldn't speak of the devil. How did you find me, Constance? Who do I have to discharge?"

"Oh hush, Miss Grumpy. You know I have my ways of finding things out. Anyway, why did you leave Beverly Hills without telling anyone where you were going? Most people are speculating that you ran off with Gillian's husband Garvin. Garvin disappeared about the same time that you did. I thought it was just nonsense; you know I'd never gossip about you. Why, even when I was telling people that you had run off with Garvin, I didn't really believe it."

Delia felt trapped, but she realized now that Constance had found her it would be futile trying to avoid her relentless cousin. Further, if inane Constance had located Delia it was likely that everyone knew where she was.

LaDonna looked at Delia. She was still quite prepared to eject the uninvited guests. She started to clear her throat and make up some kind of excuse to get rid of the two women, when Delia told her, "Don't worry, LaDonna, I'll call you if I need you."

LaDonna started to walk away when Constance screeched, "LaDonna? What kind of name is that? And who is she anyway? Don't tell me she's your new PA?"

Delia nodded.

"Well, pickings must be pretty slim here in San Francisco. You never hire unattractive people. Of course, you know I won't tell a soul, but wait till everyone hears that Delia Wentworth has started employing the hopelessly plain."

LaDonna could feel her face flush as she turned to walk away with that despicable woman's words echoing in her head. Tears began to well up in her eyes as she realized the truth; she had obviously fooled herself into believing she had gone through a great physical transformation. Delia wasn't quite as candid as she had thought. Now, it was obvious to LaDonna that Delia had been attempting to transform her into a Personal Assistant she wouldn't be ashamed of. Obviously she had failed.

Delia watched LaDonna walking away and she wanted to call after her. But what could she say? LaDonna didn't seem to be the type to be affected by what other people thought of her appearance, and Constance's opinion of anyone or anything was beyond insignificant.

Unfortunately, it was true. Lillian would have said LaDonna lacked any inherent style. She ruined the costly and flattering hairstyles that Delia had paid for by restyling them with a curling iron and hairspray into the same matronly helmet shape she had probably been wearing since her late teens. LaDonna had lost quite a few pounds, but her body was still kind of fleshy and her posture was bad. The expensive designer clothes Delia had given to her usually looked preposterous or simply dowdy on her. Still, she was a superlative assistant and Delia could see the potential beauty that LaDonna seemed too frightened to claim.

Delia felt protective of LaDonna so she turned to Constance and said icily, "You are hardly the one to criticize another woman's appearance, Constance. It's quite apparent that Nino is just as tight with your allowance as ever. That coat you're wearing is obviously straight off the children's department clearance racks. And that home bleach job has fried your already butchered hair. It looks like matted clumps of excelsior. Moreover, there really is such a thing as being too thin."

Delia ushered the two women into the library and closed the doors. She barely glanced at the mastodon that had arrived with Constance, though the tired pageboy haircut, the round forlorn face, and the triple chins did look vaguely familiar.

Constance tittered as she pranced into the room. She tossed her jacket onto the floor and revealed the pink leotard and tutu she was wearing underneath. She clumsily attempted to do the splits on the floor by the fireplace but ended up in kind of an awkward heap on the rug. Laughing she said, "Oh, Delia, you're such a tease. I know I've never looked better in my life. My new psychic colonic therapist insists that these next few years are my time to shine. Something is retrograding, or aligning, or something. He says in a former life I was anorexic and I need to heal that person so I've stopped eating most of the time. Although my color advisor says I should consume a certain amount of a specific color of food on certain days. I'm down to eighty-seven pounds and two percent body fat. I can see every major bone in my body. I love losing weight. It's so transcendent. I've been having these moments of clarity where I have total recall of my former life as an anorexic. It's all so God-like. You know I've always existed on a more spiritual plane than the vast majority of people."

"Please, Constance, you're just hallucinating from malnutrition. I'm serious; you look wretched. Your skin is more wrinkled and your thighs are almost as narrow as my wrists," Delia said as she and the blob sat down in the leather armchairs by the window.

Constance danced across the room and then got on the floor between the two chairs and attempted to stretch her twig-like limbs. "I told you she would be eaten up with envy. My weight is finally lower than my IQ; I think that means I'm a genius, or something," she chortled. She tried to raise one of her bony legs over her head with one hand and with the other she poked at the squishy ankle of the woman she had arrived with.

"Why the leotard and tutu, Constance?"

"I'm taking neuroballet. My instructor is a revelation. She says that if you can conceive the movements in your brain you can persuade your body to achieve anything. I'll probably turn professional in a few months, but right now I'm concentrating on the little girl I used to be. You know how vengeful my mother was. Why, she stifled every natural inclination I ever had. I just hope I can summon the strength to heal all the inner children that exist or used to exist within me."

"Please, Constance, your mother and father gave you anything you asked for. Why, you were the only girl I've ever known who had custom designer outfits and real miniature jewels for your Barbie dolls. I even remember you whining about headaches in the fourth grade, and your parents sent for a specialist from Europe because your Beverly Hills pediatrician insisted it was psychosomatic. The specialist finally concluded that you were just over stressed so you got to be home tutored for two years, and he gave you a prescription for Valium and recommended a cruise to Europe. Remember that birthday party in Paris where Elton John performed?"

"Yes, but did either of my parents really care about the inner me? Anyway, I can't talk about it. It's too painful. I'm trying to deal with all of it in the novel I'm writing. That's why I came to San Francisco in the first place. You know the fabulous author Janelle Stone, Delia. She and I go way back. You remember, Delia, her parents were some titled nobility who were exposed as Nazi sympathizers. But hey, whose parents weren't? We were both married to the same prince of some tiny country in Europe that doesn't even exist anymore. She and I truly bonded during his trial in New York City for bigamy. We're both such romantics. I'm going to check with my past life regression guide and see if we were sisters in a former life. I've been staying with her for the past couple of months getting guidance for my new novel. Then suddenly she got called away to a remote place in Africa, I think. But a few weeks before she left, she hooked me up with this fabulous writers' group her gay daughter Althea found on MySpace," Constance said intently.

Unexpectedly the mastodon interjected loudly, "I've been losing weight, too. It kind of freaks me out because I haven't been trying to. I have a phobia of being too thin anyway."

Delia thought the woman was joking and she almost laughed but then she looked at her and realized she was serious.

"Let's not even get started on the subject of phobias. I'm the most phobic person you'll ever meet." Constance crowed, as she rolled herself into a ball and somersaulted across the floor.

At this, the gelatinous woman snorted out a few guffaws and her whole body quaked. It was a loud, self-conscious laugh and Delia recognized it instantly. It was her old chum from college, Ida Gurmen-Kensington. Ida had been famous for a time after publishing a few iterations of *The Pampered Princess* cookbooks. She had even had a short lived cooking show appropriately titled, The Pampered Princess that aired on the Foods and Travels cable channel that Delia's media conglomerate Royal Arts Communications owned. The last time Delia had seen Ida was in her cat infested Central Park West apartment. It was the same building in which Delia had owned the penthouse for many years.

"Ida, I almost didn't recognize you. What are you doing out here in San Francisco?"

Ida snorted again, nervously, and then her pasty round face grew as red as a lobster's shell. She sighed heavily. "Oh, it's all just too freakish. Believe it or not, I'm your neighbor. I live in the historic Fern McGowan Mediterranean across the street. The house has been in the family for years and I've been banished here indefinitely. Unfortunately, I'm sandwiched between the Chinese Embassy and some Middle Eastern prince's meth house. Between the squawking fowls being butchered daily by the cook at the embassy and the thunderous all night rave music at the meth house, I'm about to go mad. I guess you didn't hear about the ridiculous incident that sent me into exile?" Ida didn't even wait for Delia to respond. She was talking so rapidly she was wheezing through clenched teeth after every other word. "It was the number one topic of everyone on Long Island. I'd love to give you the gory details but that would take simply days. Anyway, I offered gratis, yet again, to cater a party my former BFF Rowena Roosevelt-Claxton was hosting for our new neighbor in East Hampton, Henri Bastin, the French media mogul. I'm sure you know the brute, Delia. Anyway, I made my famous vanilla coconut bars, zesty lemon chicken kabobs, and a mixed green salad with my homemade Roquefort dressing. Everyone raved about the food. But a few days later, several people who had attended the party fell ill, and Henri's seven-year-old daughter Willamina was transported by helicopter to a private hospital in Manhattan where she spent three weeks in intensive care. You won't believe it but my food was blamed for making Willamina and those other people sick. Some specialist supposedly ran tests and reported the food I had served was tainted with of all things, feces. Before I even had a chance to defend myself, word got out I had improperly handled the food and that I either got feces on my hands from one of my beloved Sphynxes, or that my personal hygiene was not adequate."

Ida was about to continue when Delia held up her hand and said impatiently, "Wait." Then she rang the kitchen and ordered a pitcher of martinis. "Would anyone else like something? Maybe you'd like half a leaf of lettuce, Constance, or a thimble of water?"

Constance snorted and replied, "Oh, Delia, you are such a kidder. Seriously, though, I haven't eaten a thing in seventy-six hours and I've never felt more centered. I guess I could have some bottled water, though."

"I'm so traumatized I can't even think of eating. But, I guess I'll have a diet soda and if you'll have your help bring me a plate and fork I'll just have a piece of this key lime pie I brought. It's one of the few things I can keep in my stomach," Ida said. She pulled a greasy box from the large purse she had been holding under her sweaty arm and continued her story, unconcerned whether Constance or Delia were even listening, "I'm convinced the real culprits of the tainted food were either my sweet Sphynxes or more likely the immigrant help who served the food. So I made a call to another former friend, Beth Steinman at the INS, and most of those miscreants were summarily deported. Of course I had all thirty-two of my precious babies euthanized, but that wasn't enough for the vigilantes in East Hampton. People were actually saying I was unhygienic, which is the height of absurdity. Why, I almost always wash my hands after I have a bowel movement," Ida scrunched her face and forced out three loud guffaws. Then she continued her harangue as Delia made a mental note of every surface that Ida had touched, "My family and my attorneys thought it advisable I uproot myself from the Hamptons and disappear, so to speak. I haven't seen a soul in the past six months except when I get my groceries delivered. Fortunately, I happened to be out in my yard when Constance recognized me, and she begged me to come with her to visit you. I had no idea you lived right across the street and I keep a pretty close eye on the neighborhood. Now it will be almost like when we were roomies that day at Stanford. We can see each other any time we want. Isn't it lucky I had just baked one of my famous key lime pies? I decided to bring it along as a housewarming gift. In East Hampton we only gave gifts that could be used or consumed in one sitting."

"I'll have to be sure I show Constance my gratitude," Delia said quite sarcastically, but she knew it would go over both of their heads, and it did.

Constance was still contorting herself on the floor. With one leg stuffed precariously behind her head she huffed, "I'm so excited. I've got the best news for you, Delia, and for you too I guess, Ida." She paused briefly and then stated with a grimace, as she removed her leg and let it fall, "Hello neighbors! I just closed on the house next door to you, Delia."

Delia was so startled that she barely suppressed a yelp. At that moment, LaDonna walked into the library carrying a tray from the kitchen having anticipated the situation that had developed.

"I told Hannah I'd bring you the things you asked for from the kitchen, Ms. Wentworth. You wanted me to remind you about the meeting this afternoon. Elliot will have the limousine ready in thirty minutes. Is there anything I can do to help you get ready?"

Delia gulped down her first martini and poured herself another before she responded, "You can have Sarah draw me a bath and set out my clothes. A simple brown pantsuit will be sufficient. I'll ring for you in a few minutes."

Constance studied LaDonna as she was handed a glass of water. LaDonna could feel her face flush as she quickly left the library and closed the doors. She hurried down the hall to her room when Delia's private phone started to ring.

Ida panted and stood up holding the grease-stained box. Nervously, she tried to hand the box that contained the pie to Delia. Delia ignored her; she finally sat back down and snorted out an uneasy chortle and said, "Well, since Constance isn't eating, I'll just take a few bites and leave the rest for you, Delia."

Delia was slightly surprised when Ida disregarded the plates and forks that had been brought from the kitchen and instead retrieved a crumb covered plastic fork from the breast pocket of her ever-dampening blouse. Within moments, she was digging into the open box and devouring the pie with loud lip-smacking bites. Every so often she would glance over her forkful of green colored pie at Delia and Constance and grunt out a laugh. Delia continued to monitor everything Ida touched. She would make certain it was all disinfected after the whale left.

Just as Delia was finishing the last martini and was about to tell Constance and Ida they were going to have to leave so she could get ready for her imaginary appointment, someone tapped lightly on the library door. Clearing her throat she called out, "Yes, come in."

LaDonna peeked into the room and said, "Excuse me, Ms. Wentworth, but could I speak to you privately? It's a rather urgent matter."

Constance eyed Delia suspiciously as she watched her leave the room. Standing, she went around the room inspecting the furnishings closely. Finally she hurried to the closed door to listen. Ida barely noticed as she continued to shovel large bites of pie into her mouth.

Out in the foyer LaDonna was speaking to Delia in a hushed toned, "I didn't mean to interrupt, but Mr. Barlow from the private investigation company called. I told him you were occupied but he insisted I give you a message when you were available. I offered to come get you, but he said he only had time to leave a message and that he would have more details later. You're supposed to call him after three o'clock this afternoon, because there has been a huge break in the investigation. He'll be unreachable till then."

Delia had been certain that the message about "Tigger" the night before would be the break the investigation needed. Maybe now she would find Anngelie's child if it existed. It was amazing to think about.

Then Constance came bursting through the doors of the library and demanded, "What is going on out here, Delia? You know I won't rest until I find out what you're hiding. Whose husband have you stolen this time?"

"Don't push it, Constance. You and your friend Ida are going to have to leave now," She gave Constance a pointed look and then stared behind her at Ida who was still welded to the chair by the fireplace.

"Ida is not my friend, Delia. I just met her early this morning when I caught her out in my bushes spying into my windows. Then, we got to talking, and she was really nice and I found out that the two of you used to be best friends. Later in the day, when she saw me coming over to your house, she barreled across the street and begged to come with me. I assumed she had already been here, she seemed to know all about the comings and goings, so I didn't see the harm in bringing her with me," Constance whined.

"Well, you brought her, so you tow her away. I've got business to attend to." Delia put her hand on Constance's bony shoulder and started shoving her toward the front doors. Then, she called out loudly, "Hey, Ida, you and Constance are going to have to leave now."

As Delia pushed her to the doors, Constance looked at her and panted, "I just know you've got a new boyfriend, Delia. Ida says some guy comes over here every Friday and that you hardly ever leave the house and when you do you're wearing a scarf and big dark glasses. She didn't even recognize you. Is it really Gillian's husband? If you don't tell me I'll just burst."

"Well, that's incentive enough to keep my mouth shut, Constance." Delia replied as she opened the doors and thrust Constance out onto the portico. She felt a tug on her arm, and fetid, hot breath wafted across her face as Ida walked up behind her and leaned in close to her ear and whispered, "Mustarnnaise."

Delia recoiled asking, "Pardon?"

Ida snorted out a laugh and then said, "I knew that would get your attention. I said 'mustarnnaise.' I thought I'd let you and Constance invest some capital to get my ingenious idea in production. I've decided to market my own line of good specialty foods and I'm going to start with Ida's Mustarnnaise. It's the perfect blend of good mustard and good mayonnaise for dressings, dips, and recipes. I just need some funds to get it launched and I'm giving my closest friends the first opportunity to invest."

Delia had easily forced Constance's skeletal frame out the doors but when Delia turned to shove "The Pampered Princess," she was immovable. She continued to lean into Ida and glanced over at LaDonna who rushed over to help.

Ida seemed oblivious as she continued to blather, "Oh, and I've got the perfect slogan, 'All good cooks use Ida's Mustarnnaise, it's a *must*.'"

"Ms. Wentworth doesn't handle any of her own investments, but I'll pass along the information to her financial advisors." LaDonna grunted politely as she and Delia finally managed to ram Ida out onto the front steps.

Delia quickly added, "But, I'm sure Constance would love to give you some of her husband Nino's money, Ida. She might have stopped eating but that doesn't mean she can't profit from other people's gluttony." Constance reeled and turned to glare at Delia.

"Oh that's wonderful, Constance. I'll come over later and give you the particulars. This is such fun living so close together. It's kind of like *Sex in the City* but without sex and without New York City. Well, I guess I better get back to my babies. I've adopted twenty new Sphynxes. I can't resist them. I guess it's the nurturer in me," Ida called out as she lumbered across the lawn. Then, as she was climbing the parched embankment of her own front yard she turned and hollered out, "Oh, by the way, Delia, I finished that key lime pie. I'll bake you another one tomorrow and drop it off."

LaDonna walked back into the house and Delia was about to follow her inside when Constance said, "All right, Delia, I'll go, but only if you promise to come with me later to my new writers' group. Otherwise, I'll be forced to call your mother and tell her I've located you. She's desperate to know where you've disappeared to."

"All right, Constance. I'll go with you, but remember I don't like to be threatened. I won't be available till late this afternoon. If my mother locates me, I'll make certain you regret it more than I."

"That's perfect, Delia. The meeting isn't until seven thirty tonight. Now, I don't want to hear any excuses later. I'll be by to get you at seven o'clock." Constance was still babbling when Delia slammed the doors closed. Delia was certain she or LaDonna could think of some plausible excuse for not going, before seven o'clock.

After closing the doors and locking them, Delia leaned back against them and looked over at LaDonna and rolled her eyes smiling. LaDonna had become a trusted friend. Delia had to help her somehow. She didn't know yet how she could help her but it felt good thinking about it. She'd have to consider it later though; right now she was consumed by the possibility of locating Anngelie's son.

"Would you please get someone to close the windows in the house and shut the drapes, LaDonna?" Delia could almost feel Constance spying on her from the house next door.

"I'll see to it myself."

"No, I need you to get me another pitcher of martinis and do whatever you have to do to locate Devlin Barlow. With the fortune I'm paying his agency, he'll not be unavailable to me. Have Mildred get someone to tend to the windows. And tell her to have all the surfaces in the library disinfected. I'll be in the second floor study. After you've brought me my martinis, don't disturb me for anyone but Mr. Barlow."

After she entered the study, she closed and bolted the tall heavy doors. She was about to light a fire when she observed the wide floor to ceiling windows that looked out over the front lawn. She hated being paranoid, but she knew Constance too well and she didn't want her scrutinizing her activities.

Of course there wasn't much for Constance to monitor. Still, Delia felt uneasy. Mostly because she was about to get some answers from Devlin Barlow about her beloved sister's child. It made her almost unbearably anxious.

Delia's heart was racing as she stepped over to the windows to close the curtains. Just as the curtains were nearly shut, Delia noticed Ida holding a wrinkled hairless cat, standing by a window on the second story of the house across the street. Delia could see Ida plainly. Only small front lawns and the narrow street separated their houses. Ida's pink stucco house was situated higher on the ridge from Delia's. Among the other palatial homes in Sea Cliff it looked so neglected. Shards of paint were peeling off all the window frames and a grayish-green mold was collecting along the edge of the dilapidated roof. The grass on the lawn was brown and worn. The few pitiful bushes looked spindly and decayed. It was difficult to imagine that Ida had once lived with her former husband in one of the most impeccable homes with one of the most lavish gardens on Long Island.

Ida too, was gazing out from behind curtains but her curtains were dingy and shredded. Delia nearly cried as she studied Ida. She recalled how beautiful Ida had been before she became fat and slovenly. Ida's once lovely dark eyes that had been so bright and happy were now puffy and full of a confused desperation.

Yet, as Ida stared out over the roof of Delia's house, in the direction of the restless Pacific Ocean, her expression became briefly resolute. Then her bloated, pink face wrinkled and Delia could see that Ida was sobbing. Delia walked away from the window and let the heavy fabric of the drapery close tightly, obscuring her view.

18 ❧

The crumbling, wooden walkway snaked out across the steep, jagged cliff ending in a circle like a coiled tail on a precipice above the gray churning waters of the Pacific Ocean. Alberta could sense that D.C. wanted to walk out to the end of the path but the wood railing was too dilapidated to be safe. Instead, she held tight to his tiny hand and stood a few feet back from the edge of the towering ridge and they stared out at the ocean pounding against the rocks about two hundred feet below.

Brisk, damp winds were blowing in off the water. The air was briny and pungent stinging Alberta's sinuses. Still it felt good as it filled her lungs. She could tell D.C. liked it too.

It had been an emotionally exhausting day but the ocean always renewed Alberta's spirit. She believed it might do the same for D.C.; he was worn down but too unnerved to rest. She had hoped the pure majesty and breathtaking beauty of this scenic location might give D.C. a bit of solace.

Alberta thought back to earlier that morning and a new wave of sorrow engulfed her. As usual she had woken up around five o'clock that morning. She recalled smiling to herself as she walked into the living room and saw Brownie had snuck up on the sofa and was sleeping curled up beneath D.C.'s tiny, almost weightless arm.

After Alberta had quietly finished her morning coffee, D.C. had walked up to her and made the noise for "cereal." Alberta made him a bowl of his favorite maple-cinnamon flavored instant oatmeal adding a heaping teaspoon of sugar and a pat of margarine. A cylinder of frozen grape juice was melting in the pitcher for him.

When his breakfast was ready, D.C. pointed at the back door and Alberta realized he wanted to eat outside. Parkmerced Apartments were laid out in blocks that formed squares, and the first floor apartments had back patios facing the inner courtyard. It was a rare sunny morning at Parkmerced so Alberta decided it would be a good idea for D.C. to have breakfast outdoors, and she could have a second cup of coffee out there with him. Once Alberta had set up a tray by the plastic chairs that were stained with tree sap from the spindly, old oak tree that shaded half of the patio, she placed D.C. in one of the chairs. She only had to call Brownie once and he came bounding outside. Alberta was surprised and tickled by the dog's energy. She and D.C. both smiled as Brownie looked up at them and wagged his tail as he sniffed the air. Alberta had set Brownie's bowl of dog food outside too, but he ignored it. He seemed content just to be near D.C. and Alberta as the heat from the sun warmed him.

As Alberta sipped her coffee she heard one of the backdoors next to hers rattle open and close again. Her neighbor Karla Kookla asked in her booming voice, "Alberta, did you hear that commotion last night?" Karla cleared her throat; something she did often.

Karla lived around the corner. Only an overgrown hedge and a slight incline separated their back patios. She had been living at Parkmerced for nearly as long as Alberta. They often spoke, with Karla monopolizing the conversation discussing her life's woes, but their relationship had never grown to anything beyond the trivial. Karla cleared her throat again and Alberta could tell she was closer to the hedge. She suffered from a chronic allergy to mold. After she cleared her throat a third time, Alberta looked over and saw Karla's beady eyes staring at her through an opening in the hedge. Alberta took a secret delight pretending she was ignoring her.

If Karla wasn't bemoaning being charged what was actually a pittance for another pass-through, or the few extra dollars of rent increase on her already rent-controlled apartment, she was griping about one of the other tenants making too much noise or breaking one of the stipulations in their lease. When she wasn't complaining, she was crowing about her "oh so successful" children, who, from what Alberta observed, shunned their aggressive mother.

"Well, did you hear the racket, or not?" Karla asked again more insistently.

"No, Karla, I didn't hear a thing but my own business."

"You know Marjorie across the way? She's always grilling something stinky. Well, her daughter Tessa moved in with redheaded Randy two doors down. The three of them were out there at about two o'clock in the morning lit up like Christmas trees. Marjorie and Tessa hollered at each other for a good twenty minutes about money and lawyers and all kinds of nonsense. Finally, Tessa balled up her fist and called Marjorie a crack whore and punched her in the stomach. Randy started yelling at both of them and the next thing you know Marjorie was outside with a steak knife stabbing Tessa in the arm. I called the police and as usual it took them about an hour to get here. I just can't believe you didn't hear any of it." Karla stated loudly in her nasally, grating voice, still mostly hidden by the hedge.

"I've got my own affairs to tend to. I just turn on my fan for a little white noise and I'm not disturbed by a thing," Alberta replied coolly.

Alberta took a sip of her warm coffee and observed Brownie with a smile. His face was pointed up at the sun with his eyes shut. He stood and rubbed up against Alberta's bare leg and licked it softly. He yawned and stretched before he walked over to a patch of sun-drenched patio where he circled twice before laying down again. He yelped excitedly twice as if he had recognized someone or something. After that he seemed to settle down and then he let out what seemed like a sigh. Just before Alberta noticed his chest had stopped moving, he looked up one final time at her and D.C. His dark cloudy eyes were full of a new kind of wisdom. Alberta was about to distract D.C., when he dropped his bowl of oatmeal and climbed down from his chair and limped over to Brownie. It was too late; D.C. was too connected to Brownie not to realize that Brownie had just expired.

D.C. plopped down next to Brownie and put his tiny hands on the now lifeless dog. He looked back at Alberta terrified. Alberta stepped over and knelt down beside him. When she put her hand on D.C.'s shoulder she could feel his body stiffen. His body trembled as he cradled the dog. Urgently he made the noise for "walk." Alberta realized he was trying to heal his friend. She held back her own emotions as she whispered in his ear, "No, D.C., Brownie can't be helped now. He has to go to heaven and be with the angels."

D.C. refused to let go. Instead, he shook the dog forcefully. It was the first time that Alberta had ever seen D.C. get angry. Finally, he fell on top of Brownie and let out the most anguished cry Alberta had ever heard.

"Good God, Alberta, What happened over there? Is D.C. hurt, or something?" Karla asked from the other side of the hedge with genuine concern in her voice.

Tears were streaming down Alberta's face and she couldn't stop her voice from quivering when she replied quietly, "Brownie just died," just saying the words made it true and Alberta bit her lip to keep from sobbing.

Now, hours later, as Alberta stared out at the murky, relentless ocean with the taste of salty sea air in her mouth, she allowed the tears to flow. She looked down at D.C. and he too was staring out at the water, but with a blank expression. Alberta could sense the enormity of his pain.

D.C.'s and Brownie's souls were bound in a way Alberta knew she could not begin to understand. Brownie had been such a devoted companion to D.C. He had adored the frail little boy without expectations or conditions. Somehow, Brownie intuited, more than the vast majority of humans, just how extraordinary D.C. was.

Overwhelming grief was making D.C. irrational. His mental disability made it impossible for him to express his sorrow, although, he had lashed out at Madison when she tried to separate him from Brownie earlier that morning.

After Brownie died, Alberta called Madison for help. It took her a while to get away from her downtown office, and it was nearly two hours later before she finally arrived. During that time, Alberta was finally able to convince D.C. they needed to bring Brownie's body inside.

While D.C. observed her intently, Alberta gently carried Brownie's body into the apartment and placed his lifeless body on the sofa. Alberta had to place a towel under Brownie because some dark urine and fecal matter had excreted from his bladder and intestines. D.C. thought this was a sign of life and he placed his head up against Brownie's and squealed with delight.

Alberta tried to distract D.C. but he could not turn his attention away from Brownie. Finally, when Madison arrived, D.C. managed to exorcise some of the rage and sorrow he was feeling. Madison had arranged to take Brownie to a local veterinarian and have the body disposed of.

D.C.'s pale little face reddened and he mustered a strength Alberta had never witnessed in him, when Madison attempted to wrap the dog's body in an old blanket and carry him away. D.C. shrieked and for the first time in his life there were tears in his eyes. He made the sound for "no" loudly and threw himself on top of Brownie and refused to let go. Though he had never been violent toward anyone or anything, he hit Madison and tried to bite her hand.

Alberta could only pray. She prayed for wisdom to comfort D.C. In her mind she imagined the white light of God's eternal love cradling D.C. Eventually, D.C. let go of Brownie and Madison took the dog away. D.C. retreated into himself and became unresponsive.

Madison agreed to return and take them out for a while. By the time Madison had come back, Alberta had decided D.C. needed to go to the coast to a place she considered one of the more scenic locations in the bay area just north of San Francisco. She hoped she and D.C. might be comforted by God's grandeur.

So here Alberta stood with D.C. braced against the strong northwest winds, staring out at the sea. The low gray clouds seemed as mournful as her heart. It was as if the harmony of the little family she had created with D.C. and Brownie had been shattered. It had been such a long day and D.C. was still impassive. But she held fast to his little hand and waited.

Although Alberta had suffered countless devastating losses in the past eighty years, it seemed the older she became the more difficult it was to let go. Each death seemed more profound and more painful than the last. Sometimes, it felt as if the weight of all the accumulated anguish was crushing her heart. It was only the firm belief she would one day be reunited with their spirits that kept her resilient.

It had been particularly painful to witness D.C.'s devastation and confusion after Brownie's death. Alberta couldn't get the image of the horrified look in D.C.'s eyes, when he had realized he had lost his best friend, out of her mind. How do you explain something so grave to a child, especially a child who is profoundly mentally impaired?

Brownie had shown no signs of being ill in recent days, but the dog was nearly sixteen years old. Alberta had recognized the loving little dog was getting tired and was nearing the end of his time on earth.

After a while, she scooped D.C. up in her arms and carried him to a weathered picnic table a few feet from where they had been standing. She set D.C. on the bench and pulled his knit cap down over his ears and wrapped his blue wool scarf more snugly around his neck. He stared at her blankly. A small busload of tourists hurried past them taking photos and grousing about the cold. When they left, Alberta, D.C., and a young couple who had wandered out to the top of the point beyond the guardrails were the only people left at the overlook.

Madison sat in her car in the parking lot reading a satirical novel about a madcap billionaire and her reckless coterie of friends. Occasionally, the book made her laugh out loud; it was a pleasant diversion. She felt compelled to periodically observe her mother and D.C. with their troubled faces and dismal old clothes. D.C. was so horribly handicapped and her mother ignored it. They looked like pitiable, frail phantoms as they sat at the table framed by the gray

ocean. It made her long for a wealth she would never have. If she had
limitless funds like the characters in the novel she was reading, she
could buy Alberta a nice home somewhere in Marin County where her
mother could finally have the garden she had long dreamed of. With
scads of money, Madison could buy her mother closets full of fine
clothes, and stock her pantry and refrigerator with fresh, healthy foods.
If Madison had a fortune she could locate D.C.'s real family and they
could take him away. She eventually set the book in her lap and started
to weep. She cried for failing her mother and for resenting D.C., and
she wept for Brownie, because she had loved him too.

Alberta had placed D.C. in her lap with her arms wrapped tightly
around him. The wind had grown fiercer, whipping her soft, fuzzy,
gray hair. The horizon seemed infinite as it stretched out before her
and blended with the grayish blue of the ocean. Her thoughts were of
nothing and of everything. In her youth she would have been seeking
answers, but age and experience had made her resolute to the pain. Still,
there was the anticipation of something undefined troubling her spirit.
She held tighter to D.C. and waited.

Later in the afternoon Madison left to go get sandwiches at a
grocery store in Mill Valley. Alberta stayed at the overlook with D.C.
Alberta was still trying to think of something she could say or do to
give D.C. a kind of acceptance. Not one thing came to mind, so she
continued to sit patiently with D.C. as the hours passed. She was
finding comfort in being near D.C. and being outdoors looking at the
scenery. Two fat crows kept swooping near, expectantly and cautiously.
Usually D.C. would have been delighted by their presence, but today he
paid no attention.

When Madison came back with the sandwiches and chips and
bottles of apple juice, D.C. refused to eat or drink. Alberta didn't feel
much like eating but she hoped that if she did it might encourage D.C.
to do the same. Alberta nearly pinched off a bite of food to give to
Brownie, forgetting briefly the dog was no longer right by their side.
Madison ate at the table with them and to please Alberta, she too tried
to coax D.C. to eat, without success. After she finished eating, she
rushed back to the warmth of her car.

Because D.C. loved popcorn, Alberta had asked Madison to buy
a bag at the market. Alberta opened the bag and shoved several kernels
into her mouth.

"Yum," she said loudly into D.C.'s ear. She tried to force two pieces into his mouth but he wouldn't part his lips and the puffy white kernels fell from her hand and were carried by the wind to a patch of grass a few feet from where they were sitting. One of the crows quickly flew to the ground and scooped the corn into his shiny black beak.

Alberta patted D.C.'s leg and said soothingly, "That's okay, D.C., you don't have to eat if you don't feel like it. We've got company and they're glad to share our food." She tossed a handful of popcorn onto the ground and the spying crows flew down and at first guardedly and then eagerly consumed the treat.

As D.C. sat expressionless in her lap, Alberta explained to him how intelligent crows were and she described the many legends about them in various cultures. She didn't know if D.C. was listening but she felt compelled to keep talking.

The chilly wind continued to blow in from the ocean. Various tourists and sightseers ambled past them while Alberta told D.C. about a crow she had kept as a sort of pet when she was a very young girl on her grandmother's farm in Niangua, Missouri. She and her family had lived there before they had moved to Springfield and years before they had relocated to Vallejo.

Alberta had named the crow Otis after her younger brother. The bird appeared the day her brother died of meningitis at the age of eleven months. Alberta and the other children had been sent outside while the adults tended to the mortally ill Otis. Even though Alberta had only been six years old at the time, she recalled the day vividly. She and her other brothers and sisters, and some of their cousins were playing on a bag swing her father had hung from a tall oak tree at the edge of the woods far from the two room, rough hewn house. Late in the day, just before sunset, her father came out to the woods carrying the nearly lifeless Otis. Alberta's father instructed each child to say goodbye to his infant boy and pray for his speedy entry into the gates of heaven. A few moments later, the baby stopped breathing and Alberta's father held him close and wept. It was the one and only time Alberta ever saw her father cry. At that moment the crow swooped down from the trees and landed at Alberta's feet.

After that, whenever Alberta would go outside the crow would follow her through the meadow and her grandmother's huge vegetable garden and into the woods. Alberta told the bird all her secret hopes and desires. The bird was her special friend and it just seemed natural and right to call him Otis. She fed it berries and cornbread, and in the frosty winter, pieces of hoecakes spread with blackberry jam.

Alberta's grandmother, Eugenia, was part Cherokee and she revered Otis as a herald from the realm of spirits. She spoke to him as if he were human and when she was troubled she would ask him for advice. Each caw or flap of his wings was a message only she could interpret. Grandma Eugenia even insisted it was Otis who came to warn her when Alberta's sister Dola fell into the well and nearly drowned. Grandma Eugenia would give the crow gifts of old brooches, beads, and bits of colored ribbon that the bird would carry off to his roost in the second story of the barn. Stories of Otis led to other tales from Alberta's past and she kept talking contentedly, as if D.C. was listening.

Finally, late in the day there was a break in the clouds causing patches of glistening light on the surface of the ocean. Off on the horizon the dark blue silhouettes of the Farallon Islands came into view. They looked mythical out by themselves in the middle of the ocean, which had now turned into a powdery blue, lilac color.

When more of the setting sun exposed itself, the whole overlook was bathed in a warm amber-tinged light. Prompted by dusk, two small brown gophers peeked out of knobby holes in the parched earth. D.C. looked down at them stoically; Alberta was glad he had noticed them. She stood D.C. on the ground and they began to walk along a pathway that snaked along the edge of the cliff to an isolated bluff just beyond a cluster of windswept cypress trees. The branches of the evergreens were draped with silvery green moss.

D.C tightened his grip on Alberta's hand as they approached the trees that were turning a shimmering yellow in the sunset. A regal flock of quails scurried out of the underbrush and across the field next to the path. Within moments, hundreds of chirping, tiny golden finches had perched themselves on the outstretched branches of the cypresses.

"Look, D.C., the birds have come to say good day to us," Alberta said.

She carefully led D.C. down steps toward the steep outlook. The scrubby and rocky hillside on the other side of the railing that bordered the walkway descended at a virtually ninety degree angle to the immense gray stones on the shoreline far below. In one of the larger boulders the persistent, pounding waters had carved a tiny dark cave. Alberta was pointing it out to D.C. when something glistening and ink blue, just yards from the shoreline, caught her eye. A plume of water shot straight into the air about thirty feet above the surface of the waves. Alberta was able to catch D.C.'s attention just as a large Blue Whale calf leaped out of the ocean. It dove back beneath the surface and then hurled its body out of the water a second time and sang out three notes. With a splash of its mighty tail it disappeared into the murky undercurrents. As if on cue, the hundreds of finches made a formation. Their tiny beating wings sounded like soft plucking on harp strings. They swooped just in front of D.C. One by one they alighted on his body and blanketed every inch of him like a feathery golden cloak. Moments later, they detached themselves from D.C. and glided out toward the ocean after the whale.

Putting her hand to her chest, Alberta caught her breath and looked down at D.C. She remembered vividly that day in The Headlands when the golden finches had mystically alighted on D.C. and Brownie. With tears filling her eyes, she told him excitedly, "Hurry up, D.C., say goodbye to Brownie. He's left us a message that everything is all right and he'll be waiting for us on the other side."

Finally, D.C. started to cry and he made the sound for "goodbye." His slender arm reached out after the whale and for the first time in his life he waved goodbye. Alberta picked him up and held him close and he wept against her neck. Finally, she felt reconnected to D.C. It comforted her because he was the only one who understood the pain she was feeling at having to let Brownie go.

Alberta and D.C. stood at the railing staring out at the water that had turned into a rainbow of pinks and blues and yellows. A lone white and gray seagull hovered soundlessly just above them. Their figures were golden on the bluff as they waved farewell to their beloved friend one last time.

19 ❧

When, at a little past seven o'clock that evening, Constance pounded on the front door, Delia was upstairs in her master suite. The stereo in her room turned on suddenly. The radio dial raced through the channels. It stopped on an oldies station playing "Mona Lisa" by Nat King Cole. Delia glanced into the mirror and saw the ghosts of LaDonna's parents materialize behind her. They were less transparent than usual and their figures glowed slightly. LaDonna's mother was reaching out her arms and whispering something so faintly Delia could not understand her. LaDonna tapped on the bedroom door and the spirits vanished.

After a bit of squabbling, Delia agreed to go with Constance to her writers' group meeting, but only after insisting on bringing an excerpt of LaDonna's novel to read. She had made copies of a short chapter without LaDonna's knowledge. Further, Delia demanded that LaDonna accompany them.

Constance announced she was driving even though Delia had called for Elliot to bring the car around. Out in the driveway the three women climbed into Constance's giant Hummer H1 Alpha. It was filthy. Every surface was coated in sticky grime. There were candy wrappers, empty bags of varied kinds of chips, and crushed diet soda cans strewn everywhere inside the sizable interior.

"Jesus Christ, Constance, don't you ever have this tank cleaned?" Delia asked disgustedly, as LaDonna was thinking it.

"Oh, Delia, you're such a clean freak. You need to evolve and learn to embrace dirt like I have. Anyway, I must have had it cleaned a week ago," Constance chimed back.

"A week and three years ago," Delia turned to look at LaDonna over her headrest and added, "It's just gross. Isn't it, LaDonna? Well, get going, Constance."

"Don't be so impatient, Delia. We have to wait for Ida. I think she's coming out now." The three women looked over at Ida's house. Before she could close the tall, blistered front door, two hairless cats slithered past her and scampered off into a hedge of rangy juniper bushes. Ida called after them loudly. Throwing her hands up in the air, Ida bounded down the embankment and rushed to the waiting car. A leather satchel, the size of a wardrobe trunk, was slung over her meaty shoulder. She was smiling widely.

Just as Ida was opening the back passenger door behind Constance, Delia whispered, "Please, why did you have to invite her, Constance?'

"She's your friend, Delia. When we left your house earlier she pleaded to come along so the two of you could catch up on old times. To hell with it, Delia, whenever I try to please you I fail. I couldn't care less about the fat cow. Maybe my life coach at the Yin Yang temple is right and our chemistry is preordained to be toxic."

LaDonna was listening to Delia and Constance but she was watching Ida who was having extreme difficulty climbing into the Hummer. Ida seemed oblivious to what Constance and Delia were saying, as she made nasally grunts and finally hoisted herself into the seat opposite LaDonna. LaDonna smiled at Ida and then she had to turn away. Ida had put on too much cologne.

"You two bicker like an old married couple," Ida said laughing loudly.

No one responded and it left an uncomfortable silence in the huge boxy cab. The engine rumbled and Constance pulled away from the curb and drove speedily and clumsily down the street. She looked at a passing vehicle and started to say something and the SUV went up over a curb and listed heavily. She giggled and then focused most of her attention on the heater and the stereo. The SUV nearly sideswiped two parked cars as it weaved down the residential street.

"San Francisco feels like the North Pole to me. It's always so cold here I can never get warm enough. All this fog is just too much. It's enough to make me want to slit my wrists," Constance moaned.

LaDonna tried to focus on the passing scenery but she couldn't keep from glancing over at Ida who was making tiny grunting noises. LaDonna noticed she would mouth words to herself grinning and snickering into her stubby hands. Occasionally, she pulled chunks of what looked and smelled like an egg salad sandwich out of her purse and shoved them quickly into her mouth.

Eventually, Constance smelled the food and demanded, "All right, who is eating back there?"

"Not me. I'm on a special court-ordered diet," Ida replied cryptically.

LaDonna wanted to ask her what a "court-ordered" diet was but she stopped herself from saying anything. She already felt uncomfortable about going.

LaDonna wished Delia had not insisted she come along to Constance's writers' group meeting. LaDonna didn't even really know what a writers' group was. She assumed you got together and critiqued each other's work. A few months ago the idea of exposing her writing to strangers would have terrified her but not so much anymore. She had just recently realized she was becoming less fearful since the encounter with the boy in the Headlands.

While Constance chattered on inanely to Delia, LaDonna kept very quiet and hoped to be forgotten. Silently, she stared out the window and smiled as she watched the cool fog swirl in gusts all about them obscuring the passing scenery. She loved the weather in San Francisco.

Eventually, amidst screeching tires and blaring horns, Constance swerved into a handicapped parking space. They were in front of a nondescript restaurant at the east end of a long strip of shops on California Street.

After slapping an expired handicapped placard on the dashboard, Constance chirped, "Okay, girls, here we are. Remember Delia, these women are serious writers, so don't embarrass me by exposing all of my dirty laundry." All LaDonna heard were Constance's words "serious writers" and her heart sank.

Delia muttered sarcastically, "Miz Brown's Feed Bag? It certainly sounds like a serious literary establishment."

Before she opened her door, Constance looked back at LaDonna and said, "LaDonna, you should forget about sharing your writing since this is the first meeting you've attended. You're not a legitimate writer anyway."

"Forget that, Constance. The only reason I agreed to come was so LaDonna would get the experience of hearing her work read in public. I personally intend to be the one reading the chapter from her book," Delia stated. LaDonna's dread was only slightly alleviated knowing she wouldn't be the one having to do the recitation.

"Well, don't say I didn't warn her, Delia. Remember writing isn't just a lark or a passing fad with these women. It is essential to their souls," Constance snapped.

"Please, Constance. I've known a good number of the most prolific and successful authors of recent history, intimately."

"That's the trouble, Delia. I know you think this is a joke. And

I'm sure your intention was to embarrass me when you insisted on bringing this LaDonna creature you've taken up with, but I refuse to be intimidated. If these ladies laugh your little protégé right out of here don't come blaming me," Constance exclaimed shrilly, as they entered the brightly lit diner.

LaDonna reluctantly followed the other three women as they snaked their way past crowded noisy tables to a room at the back of the diner. She wondered if Constance was correct about it being a joke to Delia. Though, the Delia she knew could never be so petty.

All thoughts of Delia swiftly left LaDonna's mind when she entered the back room. Four grim-faced women looked up at her and the others skeptically. With furrowed brows and firmly set mouths they hissed out a "Shh," or a "Hush," or a more declarative, "Silence!" Then they turned away and focused their attention on a petite woman with a stiff round head of coarse dark hair who was lying on the dingy linoleum floor reading from typewritten pages. Narrow framed glasses rested on the bridge of her broad nose. Occasionally, she would pause and let out a loud groan. Her voice was very quiet and LaDonna could barely understand what she was saying. She gathered the piece she was reading had something to do with incompetent male doctors, emergency rooms, and pain medications. Just before she finished, Constance handed one of the stapled mimeographed pages from a stack on the table to each of her companions.

LaDonna quickly scanned the pages and discovered she was right. The untitled story was about a trip to the hospital emergency room because of severe back pains. It was a self-conscious piece of writing with no nuance or substance. Surely, this wasn't the work of one of the "serious writers" in the group.

The other women surprised LaDonna when they all exclaimed to the woman they called Axel that she had surpassed even her own previous superlative work. Two of the women declared excitedly the story was "Thurberesque." Then they corrected themselves and pronounced it was better than Thurber.

Axel's only response was a smug, "Yeah, you gotta love that it lacked his myopic chauvinistic perspective."

For several long minutes they gushed over the supine woman's writing. She just kept grimacing, arching her back, and moaning dramatically. Then she laid the pages across her chest, stuck a pencil in her wiry, ball of hair and closed her expressionless, tar colored eyes.

The women in the room made no acknowledgement of Constance, Delia, Ida, or LaDonna, until the oldest one with bobbed white hair wrinkled her leathery nose and whinnied, "Oh my, Goddess, I might not be able to stay. I'm deathly allergic to lint!" She glared at LaDonna. Everyone at the table turned to stare too. LaDonna felt as if she had surreptitiously entered the room with her purse and her pockets stuffed with tufts of thread and clumps of fiber. The withered lady was wearing a low cut, knit blouse and she put her claw-like hand to her brown, bony chest. LaDonna couldn't help thinking it looked like a wooden stepladder.

Thankfully, Delia blurted out, "Well, I'm allergic to excessive body odor, but I think if I stand by the open door I'll survive." Ida, LaDonna, and even Constance chuckled, but the ladies of the writers' group frowned.

Axel, the tiny woman on the floor who seemed to hold sway over the group, called out with a moan, "Constance, aren't you going to introduce us to your friends?"

LaDonna learned the woman on the floor was Axel Peterson. The white-haired older one was Willie Chapman. Next to Willie was a pasty woman with catlike eyes named Jean Astin. At the far end of the table was a bloated looking brunette who insisted on pronouncing her own name, "Hi, I'm Dee Nah Swett," she declared placing severe emphasis on each syllable. When LaDonna replied, "I'm LaDonna. It's nice to meet you Dena." She corrected her and said, "No, that's not right at all. It's DEE NAH. Oh just never mind. You'll never get it right. Even my own family can't pronounce it correctly!"

About this time a waitress stepped into the room and asked Constance, Ida, Delia, and LaDonna cheerily, "Would you ladies like to order anything?"

Bony chest Willie offered a suggestion with a knowing wink but no hint of a smile, "We ordered the chicken fried steak dinner. You all should order it too. It's really tops here."

LaDonna and Ida both took the advice, but Constance ordered two servings of corn and a slice of lemon pie. She said something peculiar about it being her day to eat only yellow food. Delia rolled her eyes at Constance and told the waitress she didn't want to order anything unless by some miracle they served dry martinis. The waitress snorted and walked away stating, "I wish."

After complaining about men and subjects only familiar within the writers' group, Axel decided it was Dee Nah's turn to share her week's writing. Dee Nah looked flustered. She stood and rifled through her pages and then handed a single page copy to everyone in the room. LaDonna looked over, just as Delia let hers drop to the floor before leaving the room.

"I'll be reading from my updated résumé, again. It's week seven and I'm still looking for a new job. My boss at the Center is the typical aggressive male and he's driving me crazy," Dee Nah said. She stood holding a sheet of paper in her flushed, puffy hands and began to read very slowly and loudly. Frequently pausing for several moments as if she was having difficulty comprehending her own words. Although the résumé was only a single page, it took her nearly ten minutes to stutter her way to the end. When she was finished with her résumé she added bizarrely in a louder voice, "I've had terminal lupus for thirty five years! I hate my immediate family! I've told them for years how to fix their countless flaws and they never listen. I even thought if I destroyed their lives by saying our stepfather molested me it might break them down and make them take a good look at themselves, but that lie did nothing but make them a bigger burden on me. I really do *hate* them, but I still try to visualize them as happy."

Of course when she was finished the other ladies from her group praised her profusely. "You'll get whatever job you choose," they all clucked. LaDonna and Ida said nothing.

As Axel commanded it was Constance's turn to read, Delia walked back into the stuffy room. With a great flourish, Delia tossed a pile of copies of a chapter from LaDonna's book onto the long table. Axel and her faction ignored her.

Before going to stand in the doorway again, Delia leaned down next to LaDonna and whispered, "I canceled your chicken fried steak dinner order. When I was passing the kitchen to go to the restroom I heard our waitress telling the cook that customers were complaining the meat was rancid again."

"But shouldn't we tell the others?" LaDonna whispered back and Delia shook her head "no" emphatically.

Willie hissed at them, "Shush."

Delia rolled her eyes at LaDonna. Constance eyed them over her pages and continued reading more loudly. She lingered over each word, pausing between each paragraph to glance around the room. Delia snorted at a few lines. It was an elaborate and muddled tale of large ominous trees, unidentified abusive men, and a drive along a dangerous precipice surrounding a murky body of water. The hodgepodge culminated with Constance emulating someone's son wailing "Why?" repeatedly as the character perished suddenly without explanation. LaDonna tried to read along but the story was so convoluted that she set the pages in her lap and just listened.

It was obvious Constance was new to the pack because they fawned less over her work than they had over Dee Nah's résumé. Still they praised it and said she was showing definite improvement. Willie even stated it was nearly at the submission stage.

Suddenly, Axel cleared her throat and cried out noisily, "Ouch!" The room was silenced. The other members shouted out words of solicitude as they rushed over to Axel.

"Everybody sit down. Just stop making a big deal out of it. I'm learning to live with the pain. It won't destroy my bliss. It's not like I'm a man and I have to be coddled over every ache I have. Jean, it's your turn to read. Ouch! Damn that doctor! If I were a man he'd have taken my pain more seriously. Now everybody just stop talking about it. I hate being the center of attention," Axel bellowed, as she writhed around on the filthy floor crying out, "Goddess, damn this pain!"

Jean stood and handed out the copies of her single page of writing. LaDonna thought it must have been a mistake, or perhaps there were not enough copies for every person. There were only three typed lines on the page and Jean's name in bold print in the top right corner.

"Hidden below the carousel on the boardwalk, their agony hung in the air like putrid gas. Why am I in this wheelchair now, Popi? Popi, will anyone ever understand my empty womb the way my sisterhood does?" Jean recited earnestly. When she had finished the three sentences she continued, "Well, you can see I've totally reworked these sentences. I've spent the whole week on them. I rearranged the order and I made Lum's statements into questions."

Not surprisingly, the other women shouted over each other to lavish praise with words like "profound," "illuminating," "startling" and "superb." Delia smirked and gave her first evaluation of the night, "At least it was succinct." LaDonna smiled into her hand. She was beginning to feel much less intimidated.

Axel interrupted LaDonna's thoughts when she announced that of course Willie would not be reading. She conveyed why in terms only discernible to the five members. Then the waitress and busboy entered the room with plates of the steaming chicken fried steak smothered in flesh colored gravy. With much commotion and vocalizing, Axel at last decided she could just barely recline sideways. After many failed attempts, she was appeased when the clearly frustrated waitress finally placed the plate in the exact right location next to her.

"This looks really yummy," Ida exclaimed with a soft grunt.

"Be careful. It can become an addiction," Axel hollered, as she shoveled food into her mouth seemingly free of any back pain.

"Well, while you women enjoy those dinners, I'll read a short chapter from the fantastic novel LaDonna is writing," Delia announced. LaDonna was mortified and excited. Delia picked up the stack she had put on the table earlier and placed a stapled copy of the chapter in front of each lady in the room. She even tossed a copy down to Axel, who made a show of wincing and moaning when she retrieved it.

"Yeah, you know what, Deirdre, we don't normally allow nonmembers to expose themselves until after a few weeks of mandatory attendance, and only after a writing sample has been thoroughly evaluated," Axel said imperiously from the floor.

"I've already evaluated it, *Axel*. And LaDonna's novel is good. In fact it's better than good it's brilliant. So while you all eat your yummy little dinners, I'll read these pages. I think LaDonna needs to hear how good it sounds," Delia said determinedly.

Willie looked up from the plate of food she had been poking at and croaked, "And for goddess's sake, please don't go on too long." The other women nodded reinforcing Willie's demand.

Taking a drink of martini from the flask she always carried in her purse, Delia began reading loudly and animatedly. She announced the title, "*One Night Stan*, a novel by LaDonna Cofax."

LaDonna was petrified but soon she became captivated by the way Delia was reading the words. She gave emphasis in all the right places and commanded the perfect tone for the narrator, Evangeline Woodruff. Evangeline was a sweet, plump, naïve young woman who transforms herself into the amusingly lethal seductress Eva Wood to get retribution on the man who murdered her sister. In the passage Delia was reading, Eva is recalling the day she found out her pregnant teenage sister has disappeared after being turned out by their abusive parents. The words were enthralling.

It all sounded so new and fresh to LaDonna hearing it read aloud. She realized for the first time without a doubt her book was good; she was an accomplished writer. She glanced around the table and noted the women had stopped eating and were staring intently at Delia as she read. Finally she had done something in her life no one could diminish. She might have failed at being a good wife and mother and at trying to be beautiful, but no one could ever again make her doubt her ability to write.

LaDonna didn't necessarily expect any of the women in the group to like her novel. She did assume they would acknowledge the craftsmanship. Especially when it was compared to the other writing shared that evening.

When Delia finished reading she sat down next to LaDonna and patted her hand.

Jean said distractedly, "It was awfully descriptive."

"It was a little too cinematic for my taste," Dee Nah whined.

Jean responded, "Too cinematic, yes, that is the perfect description. I always prefer to read books I can't visualize. It gets in the way of the words."

"I couldn't help thinking as I was listening to your story go on and on that writers today have it easy. In the old days--I'm going back to cave dwellers here--storytellers were not so lucky. Cave dwellers used to sit around the fire and listen to the storyteller and when the storyteller was boring, she was killed and eaten and the tribe found a new storyteller. I guess you're lucky we all have these delicious meals instead," Axel said dryly. All the other members nodded their heads in agreement.

To LaDonna's surprise, Ida, who was sitting next to her, leaned over and whispered to her emphatically, "Well, I loved it." Delia heard her too and she smiled at Ida for her encouraging words.

Delia was furious though at the women in the group. She wasn't going to allow them to dishearten LaDonna. She stated defiantly, "I know it is a great book. When it is completed I'm going to contact Basil Prousse, the editor at Hampton House Books, and tell him I've got my hands on his next bestseller."

"Oh, Delaney, it's hardly as simple as that. Your little friend here first needs some remedial writing courses. She has to learn how to map a novel. After she has honed her craft and finally completes a book that is really readable she'll have the onerous task of having to find agent representation. Before she begins a book she needs to decide on the genre and ask herself who her audience is going to be. Everyone is so naïve about the publishing world. Why my own book was rejected many times before my agent and I decided on self-publishing," Willie said pompously, as she picked at nonexistent lint on her blouse.

"That's right. Why it took Willie eight years to get *Love's Enduring Journey* published and nearly that long to get an agent, which only happened through a business connection of her sister's. It's one of the best historical romances I've ever read," Axel boomed from the floor.

"How do you women dare disparage LaDonna's hard work? Where are you're bestsellers or acclaimed books? There is nothing constructive in your criticisms. Do you honestly think Van Gogh or Beethoven or even Hemingway asked themselves who their audiences were going to be? A novelist who is an artist does not combine A+B to get C. Novel writing is not a science and definitely not marketing. It makes me so mad that Madison Avenue and Wall Street are marketing the art out of art. In any case, Basil won't mind if I contact him. I was the one who appointed him to his position as Executive Editor of Adult Fiction."

"Oh, Delia, don't you think if the book was any good that Willie, who is a professional, would be the first to recognize it? Honestly, sometimes you go too far with your little pranks. I know you too well, Delia. You never interfere with the running of your companies; you're much too busy shopping," Constance said with a knowing smirk.

"I think it's time to end this week's meeting. LaDonna, you're welcome to come back and apply to be a member when you've developed your writing skills to a higher level," Willie wheezed.

"Yeah, I have to get home to my cats. My back is killing me and now my stomach is cramping," Axel called out as she slowly got to her feet with much theatricality.

Simultaneously, Jean and Dee Nah replied, "Yes, my stomach is hurting, too."

"Crap, I hope we all don't have that bug I've been hearing about," Willie growled.

"Yes, I've heard about that stomach virus," Delia said and then she looked at LaDonna with the hint of a smile.

"Delia never gets ill. I think all the alcohol she consumes keeps her sterilized," Constance chuckled.

"If the male gender would only learn to clean properly we might rid the world of all disease," Willie said as she swiped at a drop of gravy that had fallen on the table and then licked it off her finger.

"Please, we need to get out of here now, Constance," Delia

ordered.

As the ladies left the back room of the restaurant, Constance explained to Delia that she had promised to give Willie a ride home. Axel, Jean and Dee Nah needed a ride too. They had parked their cars at Willie's and the four women had taken the Golden Gate Transit into the city. They all lived in Marin.

"I'm going to phone for my car, Constance," Delia said.

"Delia, you know my sense of direction is terrible. I'll never make it back to San Francisco without getting lost."

"Ida will be with you."

"You're not foisting her off on me."

Delia glared at Constance, emptied her flask, and pushed past the other women abruptly and hurried outside.

Once she was outside, Delia folded her arms across her chest and searched the sky for stars, but fog obscured the night. She comforted herself with the thought she would make certain LaDonna's book would be published. It was nice knowing she could help LaDonna achieve her dream. Perhaps the same would be true for her sister. Delia hoped for Anngelie's sake that Devlin was going to inform her he had found the child. As she stood by the Hummer waiting for the others, a seagull squawked loudly in the sky and she felt she was being mocked.

20 ꧑

Three meteors streaked from the sky and disintegrated just above the windshield of Constance's Hummer.

"Did you see that, LaDonna?"

"My goodness. What was it?"

On the way home from the writer's meeting Constance had stopped at the Whole Foods Market in San Rafael. The Whole Foods in Mill Valley was nearer to where they were going but Willie was certain they didn't carry the brand of sour cream she preferred. Earlier that day, apparently assured someone would drive her to San Rafael, she had called the store bakery to reserve a dairy-free lemon torte for her partner Francis's birthday. The other women, except for Delia and LaDonna, claiming they needed various things too, had accompanied Willie into the store.

"I'm sorry you were subjected to that nonsense this evening, LaDonna. I had no idea what kind of people would be at that writer's group."

"I didn't mind at all."

"Why they all suddenly had a desperate need to go to the market is beyond me. I'm sorry about Constance too. She is definitely the worst of the bunch I used to associate with. It's so odd how I was talking about my former friends and then she turns up. My old life seems so unreal to me now. Maybe it was a good thing Constance showed up again. I know I don't want to live like that anymore."

"I'm glad I'm not living my old life, too. Not that I don't miss my kids like nobody's business. I was so scared back in Springfield. I was afraid all the time I was going to disappoint everybody or something awful was going to happen. I'm learning to trust and that it's okay if you don't please everyone." LaDonna wanted to tell Delia about her experience with D.C. in the Headlands. She wished she knew his name. "Here I go again. I'm afraid to tell you something because I think you'll think I'm a nut. I had a kind of supernatural experience in the Marin Headlands where I saw this magical little boy. I know it sounds crazy. I can't put it into words yet. Hopefully some day I'll be able to write about it. I know it sounds weird but since I saw that boy I feel less and less fearful."

"I think that is a very good thing, LaDonna, you shouldn't be afraid. I believe very strongly in the paranormal." Delia turned to look at LaDonna. On either side of LaDonna were her mother and father. LaDonna's father was speaking this time. His voice was too low to discern. Their expressions were sad and urgent.

"Is anything wrong, Delia? You look concerned."

Delia didn't answer. There was just silence. LaDonna didn't mind being quiet. She looked out the starry sky, smelling the cool night air. Vaguely, she sensed that summer was ending. Except for an occasional Indian summer, autumn's arrival back in Springfield was obvious and distinct. It was surprising how much she missed the vivid colors of the leaves and their smell as they collected in damp cold piles on the sidewalks and streets. Though, ultimately, she was sure she was going to prefer the subtler and less violent seasonal changes of San Francisco.

Delia listened intently to LaDonna's father's gravelly indistinct voice. She tried to determine what words his mouth was forming but it was unclear. Their images began to fade away.

As they were disappearing Great-Grandmother Birgit materialized in the row of seats behind LaDonna. She looked troubled too.

"Gå til din sønn, mitt barn," Great-Grandmother Birgit said urgently.

Delia was completely bewildered. The other side was obviously trying to send her a message but she had no idea what it was.

As LaDonna was gazing out the window she glanced at the car parked next to theirs. As soon as she looked at the car the dogs inside began barking frantically.

"It's okay, little doggies."

Great-Grandmother Birgit disappeared and Delia too looked over at the dogs, saying, "Everything is fine, babies, we won't bother you."

"Maybe if we ignore them they'll calm down," LaDonna replied.

Just then Madison parked in the empty space on the other side of the car containing the dogs. She and Alberta and D.C. were coming back from the overlook.

Alberta stepped out of the passenger side. LaDonna realized she was the lady from the Headlands.

Alberta stood next to the car. LaDonna noted her head blocked out the tail of the Scorpion constellation in the night sky.

Madison stepped from the driver's seat. The dogs LaDonna and Delia had been observing frantically snapped and clawed at the closed windows. LaDonna was watching intently as Madison was lifting D.C.

out of his car seat and standing him on the ground. LaDonna wanted to tell Delia that he was the boy from the Headlands. Some impulse, not fear, told her not to mention it.

Delia was looking at D.C. now also. Before Madison picked him up Delia thought she saw her father, F.S., sitting next to D.C. She quickly convinced herself it was not possible because her father was not dead and D.C was a stranger to her.

Delia's cell phone vibrated in her blouse pocket. Looking at it she saw there were three messages from Greta. She decided to check them later at home.

As she watched D.C., from her seat in the back of the Hummer, LaDonna realized she hadn't noticed before that his tiny body was bent and misshapen and that the expression in his eyes was disconnected. She was shocked no one was holding on to him; she was even more surprised when he limped to the other car and fearlessly put his hand up on the car window. He wasn't tall enough to see into the vehicle so Alberta raised him up. D.C.'s round, icy eyes fixed on the two raging dogs.

Alberta said softly, "Tell them feisty creatures they don't have a thing in the world to fret them, D.C."

The fascinating boy's name was D.C, both LaDonna and Delia heard.

After hearing her words, D.C.'s expression became majestic and he made some unintelligible sounds. Immediately, both dogs whimpered once and then were silent. Wagging their tails contentedly, they stood at the windows staring at D.C.

Once the dogs were soothed, Alberta and Madison took D.C.'s hands and walked slowly toward the entrance of the market. Remaining silent, the dogs curled up on the seats. Just as D.C. was about to walk around the front of the market he turned and looked back at LaDonna and then for a longer moment at Delia. There was knowingness in his eyes. LaDonna felt as if he had looked inside of her and divined the true nature of her soul. LaDonna didn't know why, but she began to weep. It wasn't long before she got that unusual feeling in her body like she was going to levitate. The seatbelt she was still wearing kept her body from rising.

Delia was so overcome seeing D.C. for the first time that she was oblivious to LaDonna. It was strange to Delia that a boy she didn't possibly know enthralled her. She couldn't get him out of her mind.

A few minutes later, as LaDonna continued to cry quietly, staring up at the crescent moon, she heard Constance and Willie and the gang returning to the SUV.

Axel bellowed, "Hey, did you see that spooky kid with the two black gals? He really freaked me out."

Willie replied, "He looked pretty brain damaged to me. People should keep kids like him at home."

Jean and Dee Nah said in unison, "He had the creepiest eyes."

"The way he was staring at me made me furious. It's a good thing I'm so evolved. He's lucky I didn't slap him," Constance said as they all stepped back into the SUV.

Just as Axel was about to climb in next to LaDonna she noticed the dogs and said loudly, "This dog looks just like the Lhasa I used to have." She paused for a minute and then LaDonna watched her pound on the driver's side window. "Hey, doggie, get up so I can get a better look at you," Axel continued to bang on the car window with the side of her clenched fist. "Hey, get up, sleepyhead. You stupid dog, I said get up!"

"Tell her to get in this car now, Constance. I'm ready to go home," Delia said firmly. Then she called out to Axel, "Stop provoking them."

It was too late, both dogs lunged at the window barking and scratching more viciously than before. Axel pounded at the window harder and screamed, "Cool it dogs! Holy goddess, what is wrong with you two?" Axel continued to bang on the car window shouting at the dogs to shut up. They grew more frenzied.

Eventually Axel stepped back and bawled, "Those dogs are bonkers. They're so damn aggressive. I bet they belong to a man." She turned to LaDonna and demanded gruffly, "Scoot over, Loni. I've got to get away from those belligerent dogs. Hey, does anyone have a piece of paper and a pen? Make it quick. I'm going to leave the owner a message."

Axel fretted over the note for a long time. At last she was satisfied, and she recited her letter so loudly it was impossible to ignore her.

"I think this is perfect, guys. Now listen to this: *Your dogs are a noisy, aggressive nuisance! Have you never heard of obedience classes? How dare you destroy my bliss?*" Axel finished reading and stepped out to pin the note under the wiper blade of the car.

One last time she pounded on the car window and screamed at the dogs, "Shut up!" Then she shoved into the backseat again and ordered,

"Okay, Constance, get me to my car. I work so hard to maintain my bliss. I try to be such a pleasant and thoughtful person, but some asshole always comes along and sabotages me. First it was that freakish kid and then the dogs. Sometimes I wonder if it is worth the effort to be so nice. Damn it, Loni, or Lodi, or whatever your name is, could you move over? Your elbow is digging into my side and the stench of your perfume is about to make me vomit."

"Her name is *LaDonna*, Axel. I thought the boy in the store was truly special. When he looked at me I felt like he saw value in me," Ida replied unexpectedly, as Constance backed out of the space. LaDonna glanced at Ida and saw she had tears in her eyes. They smiled at each other. No one noticed D.C., Alberta and Madison getting into their car.

Delia was silently staring at her nails. D.C. haunted her thoughts. He seemed so pitiful. There was something hauntingly familiar about his large, silvery eyes. For some reason, he reminded her of Anngelie.

Madison drove out of the parking lot behind Constance's SUV. Madison had paid close attention to the five women that were in the Hummer; she found Delia particularly compelling because there was something familiar about the woman's flawless features. Madison was certain she didn't know the striking lady. It was a fleeting thought. Soon she was observing how recklessly Constance was driving. Madison slowed to keep her distance. A few blocks after leaving the market Madison purposely stopped following Constance, unaware they were headed for the same rarely used cut-through.

Alberta turned to pat D.C.'s hand. She was still only focused on D.C. It had been a long day. It still didn't seem possible Brownie had died that morning. Alberta was pleased that D.C. had finally eaten a little while they were stalled in the heavy traffic. Alberta had asked Madison to stop at the market for croissants and black cherry yogurt. They were two of D.C. favorites. Without any persuading, D.C. ate half a croissant and almost an entire container of yogurt. Alberta could sense he was still in mourning for Brownie, but something about D.C.'s spirit had changed at the overlook earlier that day after the golden finches had covered him. At that moment, sitting in the back seat of the car, D.C. looked at Alberta with an intensity and intimacy he had never conveyed before. The passing streetlights gave his skin an uncanny glow. Alberta was startled by D.C.'s powerful expression, but instead of recoiling she lifted her hand and touched his soft cheek. It became obvious to Alberta, as she searched his eyes, his thoughts were no longer disjointed and fractured. Very soon, she was convinced; D.C. would be able to communicate more effectively. Alberta even dared hope he might one day soon say his first words. Alberta thought of mentioning this to Madison but she stopped herself, because she was certain Madison would only say she was projecting her own desire onto D.C. Alberta was reminded D.C. was still a small child when he made the sound for "hungry." Alberta reached into the sack of food and pulled out a glossy red apple. She wiped off the piece of fruit with a napkin from her purse and then bit off a large chunk. Juice dribbled down her chin and she chuckled before she handed it to D.C.

For the next half hour Constance drove down every meandering lane in San Rafael. Madison went another direction and got caught in traffic headed for the highway. Willie, Axel, Jean and Dee Nah commiserated over Axel's lost bliss. They talked endlessly in hushed but adamant tones about the autumnal equinox coinciding with a celebration for their "*womb*anliness." Ida cried and tittered quietly to herself as she snuck bites of some odorous food hidden in her huge purse.

Finally, Delia snapped, "Can't you drive this ludicrous behemoth any faster, Constance? Please, at this rate we won't be home till dawn," just as Constance had pulled into the turn lane.

Madison had driven up behind Constance at the light. She said, "I thought we got away from that Hummer. I noticed they were ahead of us a couple of blocks back. The lady who is driving must be drunk or something. She's nearly skidded off the road twice."

Alberta looked at Constance's Hummer in front of them just as it ran the stop sign and swerved wildly to turn south onto Coyote Grade Road. "My goodness, Madison, shouldn't we take another way home?" Alberta exclaimed.

After running the light, Constance recklessly sped up the sharp incline of Coyote Grade Road. She swerved wildly around blind curves. LaDonna heard someone gasp but she wasn't frightened. Something about the experience seemed preordained. About a half a mile from where they had turned onto the grade, a large shadowy object came into view and Constance rammed into it. After which, she let go of the steering wheel and the Hummer veered off the road nearly hitting a tree.

"Turn off the engine, Constance, and give me the keys this instant! Don't you realize that you just hit someone or something! I'm fairly certain I saw a pair of eyes flash in the headlights."

"No, Delia! I just lost control for a second. I don't think I ran into anything but an old tree stump. We're all perfectly fine. That's why I love this machine so much. For Christ's sake, I hit things all the time. Me and my passengers have never been injured."

"I said turn off the engine and get out and see what you struck, Constance, stop being so infantile! I'm calling 911," Delia said, reaching to turn off the engine and take the keys out of the ignition.

"All right, Delia, but I'm not getting out. I won't get out! I won't! I won't! I won't! I'm not acting childish. You're just being a big bully as usual. Anyway, look, someone is pulling up behind us now. They'll check on whatever it was I supposedly hit."

Madison had parked about ten yards behind Constance. Delia was astounded when she recognized the car. The car doors opened and the interior light shone. Delia thought she glimpsed F.S. again. Then he vanished. She was puzzled at seeing her father but she was more confused by how much the boy, D.C., fascinated her.

LaDonna had been watching and waiting for D.C. It was like a dream. Unexpectedly, she had precognition of what was going to take place. The miracle of it frightened her and filled her with true awe. An intense affection for D.C. overtook her.

While Delia and LaDonna watched D.C., Alberta and Madison, Constance suddenly shrieked, "I've killed again!" Then she snatched the car keys from Delia's hand. Within seconds she had started the engine and was backing out into the road. The other women tensed and said nothing.

Alberta stood next to Madison's car and watched Constance's SUV speed away. Shaking her head with disgust, she searched the embankment and the roadside illuminated by the car headlights. Almost immediately, she glimpsed a large buck bleeding and mangled on the edge of the road several yards away. His large eyes were filled with fright and shock. Alberta caught her breath and pulled D.C. back when she noticed a slim coyote creeping down the side of the hill toward the injured deer.

D.C. tried to loosen Alberta's grip on his hand and she told him, "No, D.C., it isn't safe. Let nature take its course."

D.C. showed his newfound strength again that day and pulled free from Alberta's grasp. Alberta screamed, "D.C., come back!" She started to run after him but Madison put both her arms around her mother

Doctor Cotton

and took a tight hold.

"Mother, stop. I'll take that stick over there and get D.C. I don't think we should startle the coyote. He just wants the deer."

Madison let go of Alberta and jogged to pick up a hefty branch a few feet in front of them. Alberta ignored her daughter and went running after D.C. but she tripped on a stone and fell hard.

D.C. had plopped down beside the huge, antlered animal instinctively placing his hands on the areas of the deer's body that had been injured. The coyote warily stepped closer. Brandishing the tree branch Madison ran toward the coyote but he inched closer and bared his fangs. Madison hit the ground with the stick and shouted, "Go!" The coyote loped away. After a moment the deer scrambled upright. He nuzzled D.C. with his furry, bloodstained snout and then darted up into the woods and the darkness.

Madison went to pick up Alberta who was about twenty feet away. Alberta shrieked, "Madison, get D.C.!" noticing the coyote skulking back, headed for D.C.

Madison turned to get D.C. as the coyote snarled and lunged on top of the still seated and oblivious boy. Alberta screamed, "Oh, Lord, no!" and then passed out. A chill ran through Madison's body. There were many known and unknown reasons why she hated D.C., but she didn't want him to be harmed.

The coyote let out an unnerving howl as his body covered D.C. He buried his head in the boy's chest. D.C. uncannily put his arms about the animal's neck. D.C. said something unintelligible and the canine stretched out belly up passively on the ground beside D.C. When he spied Madison racing toward him with the limb raised high, the coyote too bounded into the dark wood.

Alberta roused and seeing that D.C. was unharmed she felt much better. He came to her and she hugged him close. Madison helped her to her feet, but she was a bit unsteady.

"Mother, I should call for help. You fainted and your legs are cut."

"Nonsense, sweetheart. I've just twisted my ankle and cut my knees a little. I'll dress the wounds when I get home. I'll be plenty fine after a good nights rest."

Madison helped them both to the car. Just before she stepped into the driver's seat, Madison looked into the black firmament at the countless, twinkling stars. "Thank you, God," she whispered, as she watched a satellite race across the sky. She heard the sound of beating wings, but she could not see the plump gray gull circling overhead.

21 ❧

After sleeping fitfully for an hour or two, Delia awoke early that morning expecting Devlin's call. She was certain now D.C. was her nephew. She couldn't explain how she knew.

Devlin phoned around 10 a.m. He seemed disappointed when Delia didn't act surprised upon learning he had located her nephew. Devlin also informed her the boy, known as D.C., was living with an older African American woman named Alberta Sommers.

It didn't seem unusual her nephew was referred to as D.C. They were the initials of Daniel Christopher, the name Anngelie had given to him. Delia thought perhaps this Alberta woman had known Anngelie or maybe it was just synchronicity. Delia had grown to believe life was full of meaningful coincidences.

Delia was also remembering F.S. When she arrived home from the ridiculous writers' group meeting the night before, she had learned her father had died. Somehow he had wheeled himself to the ocean. On a steep beach he had let his wheelchair roll into the water. His body was found near a pier in Pacific Palisades.

Upon being told of her father's suicide, Delia quickly realized it was the reason she had seen F.S.'s ghost with D.C.

Delia didn't know how she felt about her father's death. She had never been close to F.S. but he was her father and there were some pleasing memories she couldn't keep at bay.

Delia felt so many things that day. She was sad, ecstatic and slightly panicked. Her father had passed away but she had actually found her twin sister's child, though he was obviously at least somewhat mentally impaired. She had discerned it in his expression.

Delia stood in the hot shower for nearly an hour trying to imagine how she was going to raise D.C. Firstly he would now be called Daniel Christopher. She would also have to contact the finest specialists for him. Most importantly, she must get him home to Beverly Hills.

It was now past noon as Delia stepped out of the shower still thinking of Daniel Christopher. The bathroom was full of steam. As she was stepping up to the mirror above the sinks she saw the gauzy figures of LaDonna's parents. The father floated to within inches of Delia. Delia could almost feel his form pressing into her back. He was trying to utter something.

"I'm sorry. I don't understand, Mr. Beck," Delia told him. He groaned more unintelligible sounds. Delia shook her head. Finally he reached his arm out and wrote, *Baby Sorry LaDonna Is Good Girl - Tell Her* in the steamed up mirror. The stereo speakers in the bathroom crackled and Nat King Cole's "Mona Lisa" started playing just like it had that night, weeks ago.

"I'll tell her," Delia said.

Delia heard Isobella bark. LaDonna's parents disappeared and the music stopped. Isobella barked again as someone pounded on the bathroom door.

"Just a minute," Delia called out. She slipped into her robe. She unlocked the door and Constance flung it open.

"God, Delia, this place is like a mausoleum, and that woman who answered the door downstairs, Mildred, is straight out of some horror movie. I expected to be greeted by your obsequious charge, the weepy LaDonna. Tell me you've finally come to your senses and discharged her."

Delia groaned as Constance skipped ahead of her through the dressing room into the adjoining bedroom. She was wearing a grease stained, child sized artist's smock, control top pantyhose under the too short smock, and scuffed Manolo Blahnik heels three seasons old.

"Please, Constance, I most certainly did not dismiss LaDonna. I'll never forgive you for getting me involved with that coven of hags last night. They were the most pompous, mean-spirited lesbians I've ever met."

Constance snickered and said, "Delia, you are so silly. None of the women in my writers' group are gay. They're all either married or living with their boyfriend. Why, Axel and Jean each have two lovely children."

"Please, ninety percent of the gay celebrities in Los Angeles are closeted. As far as calling themselves writers, even if you combined all four women you wouldn't have one competent writer."

"No, Delia, I won't listen to you denigrate those women. They are four of the most talented ladies I've ever known. Willie has self-published two historical romances and she's saving up to publish a third. The other women are also writing historical romance novels. Willie is going to refer them to the same press she uses so they might get a group discount. Those women are generous enough to help me find my voice as a writer."

"Well, if that muck you read last night is any indication of your voice, I'd advise you to get literary laryngitis quickly," Delia replied dryly. Recalling the accident, Delia added, "By the way, I haven't forgotten the collision you had last night. If I read that some pedestrian or bicyclist was injured or killed, I won't hesitate to contact the authorities."

"I don't know what you're talking about, Delia."

They sat down by the fireplace. Constance fingered her dull yellow, crunchy, hair; pieces of it fell off in her hand.

"So, what are our plans for the day, Delia? I'm expecting writer's block so I thought I'd let you spend the day with me. There are so many things we can do here. I love living in San Francisco, it inspires the artist in me. Maybe it would be fun to play tourists and hang out at Fisherman's Wharf. We could take the ferry to Sausalito. Later we could ride the cable cars and go shopping at Saks."

"Please, you know I hate department stores. I have no intention of spending the day with you. I already have plans. Later, I suppose I'll be making arrangements to move back home to Beverly Hills." It was evident now to Delia that Constance's companionship was only tolerable when several martinis or some kind of recreational drug leavened it.

"That is wonderful news! I hate San Francisco. It's old and it's cold and there's absolutely nothing going on. It's as bad as being in Europe. You know while I was staying at Janelle Stone's we lived like hermits. I'm certain she was delighted to have my company, although I didn't see a great deal of her because she spent most of her time locked away in the attic with two apprentices. They must have been writing away like mad up there. Anyway, she has that huge, crumbling house in Pacific Heights with a three thousand square foot ballroom; you know it used to be the Decker mansion. The whole time I was there she only had one party and it was some fundraiser for juvenile obesity or diabetes or some kind of kid's disorder. It was such a bore. There were no celebrities, only a bunch of senators and governors. I miss L.A. There is constantly a party or premiere or awards celebration going on. Everyone here is so political and wrapped up in current issues. In Los Angeles you can go for months without having to hear about anything depressing and important."

"My plans don't include you, Constance. If you want to move back to Beverly Hills, that is fine; and if you decide to stay in San Francisco that's fine too. I couldn't care less where you go," Delia said as she stood and took hold of Constance's arm. Lifting Constance out of her chair, Delia started shoving her to the door.

As Delia escorted her down the stairs towards the front doors Constance exclaimed, "When we get back to Beverly Hills things could be like they used to be. Do you know it has been two years since you and Adrianna and Melody and me got together as a group? Adrianna said you refused to join us in Paris. I miss the days when we all did things together. That LaDonna has turned you against me. She doesn't like me and I don't know why. I have a really evolved orange aura. I'm so angry I'm tempted not to tell you about my new plans. When we get home I'm giving up writing for painting. I'm going to hire a watercolorist to actualize the pictures in my mind. God, being an artist is so exhausting; you have to organize so many things."

"I owe you an apology, Constance. It isn't you. I've changed. You probably won't understand but the life we used to lead seems so empty to me now."

"Okay, well I'll call you later and see what our plans are," Constance said as she was leaving. Delia smiled and shook her head.

Delia rushed back upstairs to dress. She had asked Devlin to come get her at four o'clock for their meeting. He was going to tell her the details of Anngelie and D.C. and help with the arrangements to secure custody. That morning he had informed Delia, after she asked, that Anngelie had given birth to D.C. while Cornell was incarcerated. Before Devlin picked her up she needed to meet with LaDonna.

LaDonna had spent the day in her room. After seeing D.C. the night before, she had been even more compelled to figure out the significance of the five objects he had given to her in the Headlands. After arriving home from the writers' meeting, LaDonna had studied these seemingly mundane items well into the night. Finally, the meaning dawned on LaDonna and it was profoundly clear: the harmonica stood for music and art; the feather was an example of all the animals; the acorn, marked by tiny wormholes, exemplified the symbiosis between plants and insects; the smooth gray pebble was the earth; and the photo of the little boy together with the older woman and the dog was a symbol of the souls we cherish most. Art, in all its forms as the language of human experience, the earth and the life that exists on it, and the people we love and are loved by; all of these were God. It was so simple yet so profound; we were born to cherish and honor them as our gifts from God because they were God.

LaDonna also believed the five objects held another essential truth. She would have to keep pondering them. One day she was certain she would know the answer.

So much of what she felt could not be put into words, but LaDonna now knew she could never look at life in the same way ever again. She felt conscious of the entire planet and every living thing inhabiting it. Things that had never troubled her before, like the precarious state of the environment and the way creatures were often mistreated, suddenly seemed of great consequence. The things she used to avoid thinking about like worldwide poverty and armed conflicts were now monumentally important to her.

Being so aware was painful, but it made her feel stronger as a person. She knew she could effect positive changes, even in small ways, by making more informed choices and by trying to be the best person she could be.

LaDonna had always made an effort to be a good person and do the right things, but it was by other people's prescribed standards. Recently she had been trying to be good and competent in Delia's estimation. Now LaDonna's attitude had shifted and she was going to rely on her own instincts.

LaDonna had been so inspired, she had spent the rest of the night and the early morning hours sequestered in her room writing and rewriting, compelled to finish her novel. The theme of the book had shifted from a tale of vengeance to a tragic and sometimes comic but ultimately inspiring story about the redemptive power of love. There was a chance Delia had been joking about getting the book published, but LaDonna was resolved to see it in print. She didn't know how it would be accomplished but she wasn't going to give up.

LaDonna also trusted she would soon have the dearest desire of her heart and be reunited with her children.

The final page of LaDonna's novel was printing when the house line rang and Delia asked LaDonna to meet with her in the library. A few minutes later they were sitting alone together.

"LaDonna, I have something quite strange I need to discuss with you. Do you believe in ghosts?"

"I suppose so. I've never seen one."

"I have a special ability. I've had it since I was young. I see apparitions. Sometimes they try to communicate with me."

Delia could see from LaDonna's expression that she was confused. "I've seen your parents. I didn't know who they were until you showed me your photographs of them. They've been visiting me for many months, even before I moved to San Francisco and met you. Today, after I took my shower your parents came to me. Your father's message was, 'Baby sorry LaDonna is good girl' I don't know what it means but I told your father I would give you the message."

LaDonna looked even more confused.

"Oh, and they played Nat King Cole's 'Mona Lisa' on my stereo."

When Delia said this LaDonna started to cry instantly.

"My daddy used to play that for me. He called me his beautiful Mona Lisa when he was especially proud of me. He must be trying to tell me that they are sorry about my baby. They were really disappointed in me when I got pregnant, especially my daddy. They insisted I give him up for adoption. I felt like they never really forgave me."

"Then I did the right thing in telling you? I've never delivered messages from the dead. I thought you might think I had come unhinged."

"My goodness, it's the best thing you could have ever told me. Now I know I didn't fail my parents. They said, 'sorry', too. I'm very, very happy you told me, Delia," LaDonna wept.

Across town, Alberta was readying D.C. for an outing. He was still mostly unresponsive because of Brownie's death the day before. Alberta too was grieving mightily. She had to force herself many times not to cry. She didn't want to trouble D.C. further. But they both needed to get out of the apartment.

Fortunately, Alberta had made plans weeks before to go see the upcoming eclipse of the harvest moon. A few days prior she had purchased the groceries to make a picnic. First, Alberta intended to take D.C. to Lafayette Park where they would eat their meal on a park bench with views of the North Bay. Later in the afternoon they would get the bus connections that took them within a few blocks of the crest of Lombard Street at the intersection of Hyde Street. Before sunset she and D.C. would find a place to sit with a good vantage point near the top of Lombard and observe the rise of the moon. The full lunar eclipse was to occur about an hour after sunset. She had checked out a book from the library that explained eclipses and their different forms and she had read it to D.C. early that morning. He was fascinated by celestial occurrences.

"Look here, D.C., yum." Alberta smiled down at D.C. She named each item as she put it in the large grocery bag. Alberta didn't see that D.C. was nearly smiling.

After packing up the sack Alberta put it in the cooler and set it by the front door. Then she put two old sweaters and a knit cap on D.C. His heavy, faded brown, denim pants were a size or so too large, but he would be warm and that was what was important. Alberta slipped on the old car coat she had bought probably thirty years ago. She and D.C. would be out for the rest of the afternoon and part of the night and she wanted more protection than her usual scarf. The only hat she had was an old fedora Armand used to wear when he couldn't tame his hair to his liking. Alberta chuckled and retrieved it from the closet by the front door and pulled it down tight over her ears.

Before Alberta left the apartment with D.C. she thought she better try to call Madison, who was at work, one last time. She wanted to apologize to her daughter because she had gotten annoyed with her. It seemed to Alberta that she and Madison had been arguing more often lately and usually the quarrel concerned D.C.

That morning had been no different. It was after breakfast and Alberta was sitting with D.C. on the sofa. She was reading to him when the phone rang. It took a while for Alberta to answer the call because she couldn't find her bookmark. Alberta was certain her voice was agreeable when she finally spoke into the receiver, "Hello."

"Mother, are you okay? Why did it take you so long to answer the phone?"

"Oh, it's you. Good morning, baby doll. Yes, D.C. and I are right as rain. You don't usually call until your lunch break."

"Why did it take you so long to answer the phone?"

"I'm sorry, honey. I was reading to D.C. and I couldn't find my bookmark."

"Oh, don't tell me. I bet I can guess. You were reading him the *Sutta Pitaka*."

"Don't get sarcastic with me, Madison. I think it is important to expose D.C. to the teachings of the major religions of the world. I've told you many times D.C. can't go a day without hearing one of the 'Pooh' tales. This morning I even recited a little bit of Molière to him," Alberta told Madison, and then wished immediately she hadn't.

"You don't mean Molière the seventeenth century dramatist? That is simply weird. Even I find Molière a bit obtuse. D.C. barely has a functioning brain and he can't even speak."

"Well, he sure can hear fine. He sits and listens and barely moves until I'm finished. Like with the world religions, I feel compelled to expose him to every important writer from every era. Nancy Adamo, a clerk at the Lakeside Branch Library, recommended it to me. She knows all about the classics. Besides, I don't really see how it is any of your business," Alberta was beginning to get annoyed.

"Mother, D.C. sits and listens because he doesn't know any better. D.C. needs professional care. I'm beginning to think you might need to go see a doctor as well. You don't seem to realize how you are harming that poor mentally handicapped little boy. He's not even related to us. I think you are suffering from depression."

"Now I'm getting very angry, Madison Kay. I read holy books, classic literature, history and science books to D.C. And I read children's books to him too. I know he understands, and I am as certain as I am sitting here he has a miraculous mind. I give him more credit than any fool doctor ever would. If that makes me crazy then I don't care," Alberta stated emphatically.

"Mother, I didn't say you were crazy. I don't know why you never listen to me. I said you might be clinically depressed or maybe you're exhibiting early stages of dementia. I think all you might need is a good multi-vitamin and a mild antidepressant."

"Oh, Lord, You've been talking to your cousin Sondra again. Sondra is twice your age. I've told you, Madison, that your Aunt Jewel spoiled her rotten and all she ever cared about was her own self. How she could have been sweet Jewel's daughter I'll never know. Madison, I'm about wore out with you carping at me about D.C. If you can't accept my relationship with him, well I don't know."

"I feel like you are choosing a stranger's child over me. Why am I an afterthought with you? First daddy got all your attention and then Phillip, and now that brainless child. I've done more for you than anyone but I never come first with you. No wonder I love accounting so much. Numbers are clean and fair. You get a provable solution and things make sense if you follow the rules."

"People are not numbers, young lady, and life is mostly unfair. My marriage to your daddy was my business. You were barely two when he died. At this time in my life, yes, D.C. is my main concern. You may not like it or understand it but D.C. is the love of my life. I did not give Phillip any more attention than you. The attention I gave you was different and definitely more positive. Wasn't I the one who paid for your college education? And didn't you and your children live here with me rent-free after Rick died? I won't go into all I've done for you. Yes, you have been a very thoughtful daughter and I am very grateful."

Madison was barely listening to Alberta. She had noticed a man in the outer office step up to her secretary, Tyler's desk. She was nearly certain it was the detective Devlin Barlow. He had called her earlier that morning, and they had spoken at length about her brother Phillip and D.C.

"Mother, I've got to go now. Maureen is here and she needs to ask me about this trust account we've been working on," Madison lied.

"Alright, Madison. I wanted to remind you that D.C. and I are going to the top of Lombard Street to watch the eclipse and we'll being going to Lafayette Park before that for a picnic. I'm sorry we fussed about D.C."

Madison saw Tyler look into her office through the window as her line began to ring. Hurriedly she told Alberta, "That's fine, Mother. Maybe it will all be resolved soon. Anyway I've got to run."

Alberta didn't have a chance to say goodbye before Madison hung up. As soon as she placed the receiver back in the cradle Madison's words started to disturb her. What had she meant by "maybe it will all be resolved soon?"

Since awakening, Alberta had felt like something bad was going to happen. She had felt dread for the two days before Brownie's death and now, the day after, a sense of doom was still with her. She had sensed tragedy the days leading up to both Armand's and Phillip's deaths. Once they had passed the feeling was gone. It was unthinkable, though Alberta was nearly certain another loss was coming.

Now, it was hours after Alberta had talked to Madison. She tried to call Madison one last time to apologize, before she and D.C. left the apartment. Alberta was trying not to dwell on the foreboding or her conversation with Madison. She wanted to be lighthearted for D.C.

"This is going to be exciting, D.C. You've never seen an eclipse. And we've got all this good food for our picnic," Alberta said to D.C. as they were walking out of the apartment. Alberta was even able to smile when she spied the Molière book sitting on the coffee table as she was closing the door.

Alberta was glad she was filling D.C.'s mind with the greatest thoughts, ideas and discoveries that had been put to paper. He understood so much more than anyone could believe. Why didn't Madison realize that by educating D.C., Alberta was also acquiring knowledge?

Alberta had often expressed to Madison her envy of people who had been privileged or driven enough to get a college education. Armand had expounded upon the importance of obtaining a degree. He was extremely knowledgeable, but mostly self-taught, as he had been forced to quit school after the second grade. It was true Alberta would probably never earn a diploma from a university but she was still proud, and she knew Armand would be too, that she was finally taking the initiative to learn.

Alberta was still smiling when the bus pulled up to the corner. Carefully she assisted D.C. up the steps. Even though she was now certain she was again going to lose someone treasured, she had the wisdom to cherish the moment.

As the bus lurched, Alberta told D.C. who was sitting in her lap, "We're going to have a glorious day."

Downtown, Delia was fuming because Devlin had called to say he would be unable to come get her. Because Elliot had taken the limousine for servicing, Delia had been forced to take a cab to her meeting at Devlin's offices in a building in the Financial District.

Sequestered in a private office, Delia spent a good portion of the afternoon being ignored. She distracted herself by glancing through countless, seemingly identical magazines. Eventually she was staring thoughtlessly out of the window down into the alleyway next to the building where a gray, dusty homeless woman was loudly railing at the universe and every hurried, disinterested passerby.

"I am Cass, asshole! Where is my fucking baby?" Delia heard the woman screech several times, before she plodded away. She couldn't help but think of Anngelie. Perhaps, she too had stood in that dank alley, delusional and strung out on drugs, crying out for Daniel Christopher.

Occasionally, Devlin's pear-shaped assistant flitted into the room and offered up coffee, tea, soda, a slice of birthday cake from a coworker's celebration, and scads of excuses and apologies. This charade went on for nearly two interminable hours.

When Delia had had her fill of waiting and was about to leave, Devlin emerged from the adjoining, shadowy office and expressed his profuse regret for keeping Delia waiting for such a long time. He complained that he had been occupied by another client's pending litigation, but the glint in his eyes made Delia believe he wasn't being honest.

Devlin rolled a heavy leather chair in front of his desk and held it while Delia seated herself. He lingered a moment and the strong scent of his cologne started to irritate Delia's sinuses. He tentatively put his tanned hand on Delia's shoulder and she abruptly shoved it away.

Devlin seated himself and tried not to stare at Delia but he couldn't stop himself; her silky hair the color of a white-hot sun and her golden glowing skin were stunning. She was as perfect and unattainable as a crowned jewel. Her eyes were astonishingly blue amethyst hues. When he was in her presence, it took all of his will to keep his composure and remain professional. She was so lovely and inaccessible that it made him angry. Devlin tried to not sound terse but he knew he did when he finally cleared his throat, leaned across the huge polished desk, clasped his hands and said, "Ms. Wentworth, as I told you on the phone we've found your sister's son. I also informed you I've learned all of the facts of how she got pregnant and the people she was associating with during that period."

Delia inhaled deeply. Delia could not look at Devlin. She was only able to gaze at his hands. His fingers were long and the nails were neatly manicured and buffed like polished coins. Delia's head started to ache. Devlin didn't know how truly beautiful and sweet Anngelie had been. Devlin didn't know Anngelie had been too gentle for this world. He only knew the facts of Anngelie's sordid life as an addict and a prostitute.

Delia needed to see Daniel Christopher. She only wanted to see him again and soon.

Several blocks northwest of Devlin Barlow's offices, Alberta was with D.C.; they had transferred Muni buses downtown from the 1 California and were now on the 41 Union to Hyde Street. During the afternoon they had snacked on the picnic food as they strolled around Lafayette Park. The last hour they sat at a bench where they had views of the North Bay. A majority of the fog had receded and the sky was a powdery blue; it reflected in the water darker like a shadow.

On the bus, D.C. sat on Alberta's lap in the front seats. Alberta stroked D.C.'s arm and studied the other passengers. An older Asian man, with three pink plastic bags at his feet, sat next to them directly across from two raucous teenage girls from St. Peter's Academy.

The spastic girls shouted about boys and enemies and creepy teachers. The Asian man was even louder than the girls. He was round with slumped shoulders, an immobile face, and clabber-colored skin. Faded brown trousers, inches too short, showed his pale hairless legs and a shrunken T-shirt exposed his protruding belly. Alberta couldn't help thinking he looked as pitiful as she and D.C. did and she smiled.

Alberta patted D.C.'s arm and closed her eyes as the bus staggered up Union Street. Alberta listened as the Asian man continued to bawl in Mandarin into his cell phone that was held together by duct tape. There was an appealing sort of rhythm in the enunciation.

Three blocks later, before the intersection of Union and Hyde Streets, Alberta reached up to pull the cord to ring for her stop. As the bus slowed, Alberta placed D.C. on the floor, picked up the cooler, and stood with a firm grasp on D.C.'s hand. The Asian man, still shouting into his cell phone, stood too and got up behind them at the front of the bus and pushed past them; D.C. tumbled down the steps. Alberta was barely able to catch him before he hit the pavement.

Furious, Alberta turned to the older man, and tugging at his coat sleeve to stop him from skittering away asked him heatedly, "What is wrong with you? Can't you see this child is disabled?"

The man jerked his arm from Alberta's grasp and replied languidly, pointing to a battered aluminum cane stuffed under his other arm, "Same thing!" He walked purposefully up Union Street brandishing his cane like a divining rod.

Alberta felt compelled to chase after the man. D.C. made a noise and she looked down at him. There was so much love in his expression. Alberta squeezed D.C.'s hand tenderly and said, "You're right, D.C. I should respond with kindness and not anger." D.C. mumbled something Alberta couldn't understand, but she thought she recognized a smile.

Alberta suddenly felt energized. She lifted D.C. effortlessly. Carrying the cooler and D.C., Alberta rounded the corner and began climbing the steep incline to the top of Hyde Street. The colorful, gingerbread Victorians butted up against fat, deco apartment buildings, reminding Alberta of the miniature townscapes displayed in stores at Christmas time; she loved this street. At the crest of the hill, as a backdrop to these decorative structures, was a view of the Flemish blue water of the bay and fog-enshrouded Alcatraz Island.

Alberta gazed at the views and kissed D.C.'s soft white neck and whispered excitedly, "You and me, we're going to have a great time, D.C." She had just about said, "You and me and Brownie," but luckily she stopped herself.

As they were reaching the crest of the hill D.C. wriggled in Alberta's arms and she knew at once he wanted to walk. As she was standing him on the sidewalk, a cable car filled with watchful tourists clanged as it passed by. The smell of the singeing wooden brakes reminded Alberta of a cozy fire. She wished she had the extra money to spend on the cable car ride but it would have depleted that month's grocery budget, and Alberta had already spent extra money on the food for the picnic. As she was thinking about this she perceived that D.C. was reading her thoughts, and she told him out loud as a response, "It is fine by us, though. Isn't it, D.C.? We like to walk because it keeps us strong. Plus the air feels good in our lungs. Someday soon we'll take a ride on a cable car."

D.C. looked up at Alberta with a knowing fondness and he did smile even though his heart was aching for Brownie. Alberta didn't see him because she was paying attention to the traffic and the crowd converging at the top of Hyde Street where it intersected with Lombard Street. She worried that the large number of people would make D.C. uneasy.

Alberta needn't have been concerned about D.C.'s reaction to the swarm of people. Strangers no longer distressed D.C. He had gained confidence and strength of will he couldn't yet convey.

"Come on, D.C., let's you and I sit over here on the steps. We'll have a clear view of the horizon," Alberta said casually as she walked D.C. through the throng of thoughtless sightseers with their flashing cameras to the steps on the north side of the street.

After helping D.C., Alberta seated herself on the step below him to guard him from falling down the steps. She placed the cooler between her feet. They were backed up against the concrete retaining wall, a few steps from the top, making sure to leave room for people using the stairs.

"I'm about starving again, D.C. We still got us some luscious treats in here." He had surprised her earlier at the park by eating more than he ever had. She assumed that D.C. was probably still full and she didn't have much of an appetite either but she couldn't let food go to waste. Alberta searched inside the cooler and pulled out the container of cold, spiced shrimp. After opening the box of crackers she put a shrimp, an olive, a hunk of smoked cheese, and a dab of pepper jelly on one of the salty wafers and handed it to D.C. assuming he would probably refuse it.

Alberta was surprised when D.C. took it and ate it without being urged. He consumed it hungrily. He didn't make any noise but Alberta noticed there was something different in his eyes. They had lost their remoteness. Now she noticed how really blue they were; not like ice but like the sky or shallow ocean waters near the shore.

As Alberta was pouring red cherry cola into a cup for D.C., she heard someone screeching nearby. Looking around she spied a woman heading toward them. Moving swiftly, the howling lady descended upon Alberta and D.C.

The late afternoon sun was disappearing behind the top of the hill and its waning light was casting long, black silhouettes. The woman was now within steps of D.C. and Alberta. A dusty blanket was slung over her shoulder like a soiled cloak and a large bottle of golden beer dangled from her hand.

"What the hell are you goddamn assholes staring at? You're goddamn right I'm mad! If you all didn't have shit for brains you'd have enough sense to be pissed off too! Instead you wander around with your thumbs up your butts wondering what worthless crap you're going to buy next to make yourselves feel alive! I've got news, your souls are dead. Let your leaders go to war for profit while you watch television! Oh fuck it! Remember I warned you that the goddamn world is burning up!" The woman screamed, as she climbed within a step of where D.C. and Alberta were sitting. Alberta turned back and put her arm around D.C. She smiled at D.C. calmly and tried to blend into the wall. D.C. was looking up and Alberta knew he was staring at the woman. Alberta remained silent and still and kept her eyes only on D.C.

"Yes, I'm filthy and I'm drunk you gawking motherfuckers! But at least I'm not as goddamn ignorant as you people! You're like lambs being led to slaughter, but you're too stupid to even bleat!" The woman yelled at the crowd who were mostly ignoring her.

Suddenly, the lady stopped braying and unexpectedly stepped past Alberta and sat down next to D.C. Alberta kept her arm about D.C. and then leaned back to shield him with her body.

"Oh don't be so concerned. Most of my hollering is for the tourists. They expect it," The woman said softly in Alberta's ear as she leaned close to her. Alberta still didn't want to look at the woman. Silently, Alberta lifted D.C. and placed him in her lap with little commotion.

Alberta stiffened when the lady continued, "Seriously, you can relax. I'm only homeless and it isn't contagious. I used to live around the corner on Greenwich in a great flat but my boyfriend kicked me out for partying too much. I'm waiting for a check so I can lease a new apartment. Until last semester I taught sculpture at the Art Institute one street over. My name is Cass, you know like Mama Cass the singer. She and I were great pals years ago. I sang backup on her first solo album. We bummed all around Europe together. But she got all pissy with me when we fell in love with the same guy; an Israeli soldier who was vacationing in Brussels at the same time we were there. He preferred me, so Ellen, that was Mama Cass's real name, got all shitty acting and we stopped being friends. I should have let her have Isaiah as it turned out. He was a freaky deaky in the sex department. And when we broke up he stole my transistor radio, my suede fringed vest, and my first edition of *Winnie-the-Pooh*." Cass sounded more lucid than Alberta would have supposed but she wouldn't let her guard down.

Cass grew silent and Alberta thought she was finished but she started speaking again, and it became quite apparent how unstable she was. "Of course that all happened years before my involvement with the C.I.A. and my tempestuous affair with Colonel Sanders. All those years are a blur now. Sometimes it seems as if nothing really ever happened at all. But I do remember Mercy. I remember his tiny feet most of all. His toes were so little and the skin was so soft. I didn't think anything could be that small. This little guy knows what I'm talking about." Cass's voice had grown plaintive and hushed. Before Alberta could stop her, Cass reached out and rubbed D.C.'s cheek with her brown, soiled hand. Alberta expected D.C. to recoil but he didn't. He returned Cass's gaze with understanding in his eyes.

"Don't you see how he stares at me? How does this little guy know?"

Alberta reached into the cooler and retrieved a napkin that she blotted with water and then quickly wiped D.C.'s face where Cass had touched him. Alberta barely glanced at Cass when she replied quietly, "He doesn't mean to stare. He doesn't feel good today."

"I never feel good. Who could feel good in a world like this?"

Alberta ignored Cass. She was about to pick up the cooler and move with D.C. to another vantage point when Cass grabbed her arm and sobbed, "How can I be happy when I've lost my Mercy? You haven't seen my little boy have you?"

Alberta turned to Cass and said commandingly, "Your child is not around here. Now if you're hungry I'll feed you but I don't have anything else I can offer."

Alberta hadn't gotten a good look at Cass until that moment and she was surprised to find Cass's features were strikingly delicate and childlike. Her mouth was small and rosy pink and perfectly shaped. Her face gave no indication of her circumstances, although her matted, brown hair, and her filthy hands and grubby bare feet made her homelessness apparent. Glancing at the stained and rumpled slacks and T-shirt and the tattered, blanket hanging over her shoulders made Alberta realize it had been a long while since Cass had had proper care and shelter.

Alberta's heart went out to the unfortunate Cass but Alberta's primary concern was D.C.'s welfare. So, Alberta started to pray silently. She prayed that God's love would surround Cass and heal her torment. She claimed "the peace that passes all understanding" for Cass, in the name of Jesus Christ.

Within moments Cass muttered, "Mercy, mercy me." She stood and climbed the remaining steps to the top. Alberta watched as she disappeared noiselessly into the crowd. Alberta continued watching to make certain that Cass was gone. D.C. fidgeted and Alberta realized she was holding him too tightly and he was sweating. Kissing his forehead she placed him back on the step behind her. Alberta leaned over slightly so that D.C. had a clear view of the sky. She barely noticed when a polished, black limousine pulled up and stopped at the intersection. Limousine drivers often rented their services to wealthy vacationers.

As the final light of the sun was making the sky a dark Persian blue, Alberta turned back around and saw a distinctive pink glow framing the Oakland Hills on the other side of the bay. The straining, burning sun had relinquished the sky to the passive but quickly rising, iridescent moon.

"Look at that Harvest moon, D.C. It is as red and glowing as a fired piece of coal," Alberta leaned back and spoke softly into D.C.'s ear, pointing at the moon. D.C. observed the radiant orb with fascination. The lunar light reflected in his wide, open eyes.

"I'm so grateful that you and I are sharing this together, D.C.,"

Alberta said. She wanted to mention that she felt Brownie's presence, but she didn't want to upset D.C. She reached back and petted D.C.'s tiny leg.

The limousine that had pulled up earlier was still stopped at the top of Lombard Street. It sat beneath a streetlight gleaming like a blade. Alberta didn't look at it twice. She was too enraptured by the moon. But D.C. kept glancing back at it intently.

An hour later the moon had risen halfway to Midheaven and the creeping shadow from the earth was nearing a full eclipse of its solitary satellite. D.C. was still sitting on the step behind Alberta and he was munching on a chocolate chip cookie twice the size of his hand. The night air was crisp and fragrant but there was very little breeze. Alberta kept turning to D.C. and pointing at the darkening moon. She spoke of the moon and its effect on the earth and she explained how the moon was gradually and imperceptibly wrenching itself from the pull of the earth's gravity. She described the moons of other planets like Jupiter's; the immense Ganymede; the largest moon in the solar system, and the mountainous, volcanic Io, and Saturn's Titan with its lakes of hydrocarbon. D.C. listened, fascinated. To Alberta, viewing the eclipse of the harvest moon with D.C. was utterly thrilling. And even though he could not speak, Alberta was certain D.C. enjoyed it as much as she.

Several minutes later, Alberta had stopped talking. The moon was completely shadowed and the dark grayness that had inched across its surface had acquired an orange cast. Without the unshielded light reflecting from the sun, the moon gained dimension. It glowed in the shade like a phosphorescent rubber ball suspended in the sky. Its appearance seemed mystical and ominous. Alberta was awed. Beholding this celestial event would hearten D.C., Alberta thought. Simply witnessing the grandeur of what God fashioned would give him solace from his grief, because he would be made aware that there is a great design to the universe that could only be divine.

"Thank you, God. And thank you, D.C., for being here with me. Isn't it a wonder, D. C.?" Alberta said quietly. Suddenly she became aware of the night that had surrounded them, and Alberta knew without looking that D.C. was gone. Panicked, Alberta bolted up the stairs crying out for D.C.

The shadow of the earth was still engulfing the moon. The air was as still as granite and strange warmth now cloaked the darkness. Suddenly, the earth quaked. Alberta paid it no notice as she frantically searched through the bewildered crowd for any trace of D.C. A scavenging gray and black seagull with a battered yellow beak, pink ringed eyes and a missing webbed foot swooped down from its perch on the streetlamp by the limousine. The earth grumbled again and the gull wailed loudly as it indiscriminately devoured the picnic food Alberta had left out on the paper plates.

22 ❧

"Whoa, did you feel that? That's the biggest quake I've felt in years," Devlin, said breaking the long silence that had echoed in the limousine since he and Delia had been chauffeured from his office building.

Delia didn't respond. She was leaning against the back passenger door opposite Devlin, staring out the window and trying not to want a cigarette. The earthquake didn't disturb her. She had spent her entire life in California and she had grown accustomed to tremors. Very few of them caused any real damage, and instinct usually alerted you when to be concerned. Anyway, Delia found earthquakes bracing. It was good to be reminded how powerful the earth was.

Devlin was still uneasy about the quake but he was more distracted by Delia. He tried to sound officious when he stated, "I still believe we could have better served ourselves by waiting for the supervised visit we've arranged for tomorrow. Even though the subject's daughter informed me her mother would be here with the child tonight, I don't think we're likely to spot your sister's child amid this crowd in the dark. We don't even know what the child looks like." Devlin was glad it was dark because he couldn't take his eyes off of Delia. Even in the dimness, her hair and skin were radiant and her purple eyes sparkled as if she were lit from inside.

"I'm paying you and your firm a small fortune, Devlin. I think you can grant me this one evening's indulgence," Delia replied firmly. She didn't want to divulge to Devlin that she already knew what her nephew looked like and that she had spotted Daniel Christopher and the woman he lived with, Mrs. Sommers, the moment the limousine had pulled up to the intersection. It was the same woman and little boy she had seen the night before at Whole Foods and then later at the accident. Delia knew her intuition or precognition or whatever you called it had been right.

Delia was thankful she had insisted on going because now she knew the kind of life her nephew was being subjected to. Before the first quake Delia had looked on with horror as a screaming, homeless woman had accosted her nephew and Mrs. Sommers. Luckily, the unhinged, dispossessed woman eventually walked away. As she kept watch, even from yards away, Delia had noticed the intensity of Daniel

Christopher's eyes. They were haunting and disturbed. Probably due to his mental disability that Devlin had confirmed.

Ignoring Devlin, and the earth when it rumbled again less severely, Delia continued to stare out of her window. She was distracted for a minute or two by a passing cable car and when she turned to look for her nephew again he was gone. Mrs. Sommers was scrambling through the thinning group of people when Delia briefly caught sight of her frightened face and knew instantly that Anngelie's son was lost. Catching her breath, she put her hand up to her mouth.

"Is something wrong, Ms. Wentworth?"

"I'm perfectly fine," Delia answered dismissively.

Then Delia glimpsed the homeless woman she had seen earlier. The grubby woman was holding her Daniel Christopher's hand and walking him toward Mrs. Sommers. Her nephew and the homeless woman were blotted with something dark and shiny.

It was all just too wretched to comprehend. Daniel Christopher and Mrs. Sommers looked almost as destitute as the homeless woman; she in her tattered clothes and shabby man's fedora, and he in his faded, oversized trousers and threadbare sweater. Why were they roaming the streets at night? She owed him a much more advantageous life. It was his birthright.

"Take me home, Devlin."

As Devlin's limousine drove away Delia didn't even look back at Daniel Christopher.

Alberta barely glanced at the limousine that Delia was sitting in when it pulled away from the curb. She was too relieved to notice anything but D.C., when she finally spotted him walking to her holding Cass's hand.

Alberta couldn't stop herself from dropping to her knees on the sidewalk and proclaiming tearfully, "Oh, thank you, God, thank you. Praise you, Heavenly Father."

Alberta didn't even care that some of the tourists stared at her disdainfully. But her elation abruptly turned to panic when she saw stains on D.C.'s face and hands that looked like blood.

Alberta took hold of D.C. and he let go of Cass's hand. She looked him squarely in the face and asked, "Are you okay, D.C.?" He looked into her eyes plainly and made the sound for "yes."

Alberta pulled him close anyway and started to inspect his body for injuries. There were no wounds on D.C. and he appeared unharmed. Still there were wet, sticky patches of blood on his face and arms and hands. It was a dark red and it had a strange perfumed odor like an exotic tropical flower. Alberta took a dampened rag and wiped D.C. clean.

Alberta gazed at Cass and realized she was soaked in blood. Cass sat down opposite Alberta with D.C. between them. Alberta searched Cass's eyes until Cass said, "Your little boy is perfectly fine. But I promise I didn't hurt him and I didn't take him. He came looking for me."

"Where did the blood come from?"

"I don't know for sure. Don't worry; all the blood came from me. I don't remember it all. I know I collapsed on the sidewalk around the corner on Chestnut Street. My mind was so muddled. I remember I had this excruciating pain in my head and my hands and my feet and even on the side of my abdomen. I called out to God and the blood came oozing out of me where the pains were. Then I looked up and your little boy was standing beside me. He touched my forehead and I swear I felt a heat go through my soul and my thoughts became coherent. The pain and the bleeding stopped instantly. Your son helped me to my feet and then we walked back to you. Right now I'm overwhelmed. I'm elated and ecstatic and humbled. Your boy knew I needed help and he came to find me. I think it was meant to be. He is beyond remarkable. I hope you realize what a gift he is to the world."

Alberta studied Cass in the illumination from the streetlamp and was certain she was coherent and her spirit was calmed. She looked at D.C. again and his expression told her that what Cass had said was true and he had gone after her. D.C. had duties to perform beyond her comprehension. He was maturing and she was going to have to strengthen her trust in God's will for his life.

The earth rumbled again and the aftershock felt more like a gentle pulsation. As the brilliant white edge of the moon began to steal from the shadow of the eclipse, Cass stood. She was crying but she managed to smile warmly when she looked down at D.C. and Alberta.

"Thank you. Thank you, both." Cass turned back one last time and said triumphantly, "I think it is time to go home. Yes, after all this time I'm finally going home."

Both Alberta and D.C. watched Cass walk away then together they walked back down the steps to where the cooler was still sitting. Alberta laughed and pointed out to D.C. that some creature had eaten all the food they had left out. Alberta placed D.C. in her lap and they shared the last chocolate chip cookie from the bag in the cooler. Together they stared at the moon until it emerged whole again.

Alberta didn't awaken the following morning until nearly nine o'clock, and only then because the phone was ringing. Groggily she picked up the receiver of the phone that was on the table next to her bed and said hoarsely, "Hello."

"Hello, Mother, I was beginning to wonder if you were home. Are you ok?"

"Oh, I'm just fine, honey. I'm just a little lazy this morning. D.C. and I had a late night. Remember we went to Russian Hill and watched… "

Madison interrupted Alberta, "Mother, I need to see you this morning. I'm coming with some people around noon. I've got to finish this tax return for Bob before I can get out of here. I'll try to be there early. I have to go now, goodbye, Mother."

Alberta didn't have a chance to say anything before Madison hung up. She didn't get a chance to ask her why she was coming over, or who were these people she was bringing with her. Before she could think more about this, she needed to have coffee and to feed D.C. his breakfast.

After breakfast, Alberta finished reading D.C. the final chapter of *The House at Pooh Corner*, again, and then she read him a literal translation of "The Book of Exodus" from the Old Testament. None of the words had penetrated her worried thoughts but D.C. was enthralled as usual. When Alberta closed the book and set it on the coffee table he gave her a pointedly sorrowful look. Alberta smiled and assured him that they would go back to reading after Madison and the company left. D.C.'s expression grew graver and Alberta, intuiting his fears, wondered if he was right, and they would not be reading together again anytime soon.

At twelve o'clock there was a knock on the door. When Alberta opened the door she was relieved Madison had arrived alone. Rushing into the apartment, Madison's cell phone began to ring before she could even greet her mother and D.C.

Anxiously, she told the caller, "Yes, I'm here now. Sorry, I was running late."

Madison slipped her phone into her purse. Sighing heavily, she looked at her mother. Alberta noticed Madison didn't even glance at D.C. Madison asked Alberta to sit down. D.C. stood by Alberta clinging to her pant leg. Madison started to say something and someone knocked loudly on the door.

Madison answered the door and two nearly identical looking men in tailored suits and a plump, white-haired woman strolled into the tiny living room. But it was the second woman who walked in after these three who really caught Alberta's attention. It was Delia. Alberta noted she was tall and almost too slim, with golden skin and very light blonde hair. The symmetry of her face was perfect. So perfect it reminded Alberta of an expensive handcrafted doll. Alberta had to convince herself the Delia's striking dark eyes could surely not be purple as they appeared. She was probably the most beautiful woman Alberta had ever seen. Still there was something unsettling about her face. At first Alberta wondered if it was too perfect. In some ways looking at her reminded Alberta of gazing at a lifeless, department store mannequin.

Delia was extremely uncomfortable and she wished she had never asked to accompany her attorney and the two men from Social Services. She glanced around the bleak small apartment. It was clean enough but pitifully furnished and Anngelie's son deserved so much better.

Interminably, Alberta heard the plump woman talking at her. Sometimes the men interjected. They all spoke in puzzling terms that seemed to purposely confuse. All Alberta gleaned was that they appeared to be leading up to words that would take D.C. away.

D.C. eventually crawled into Alberta's lap and leaned back into her. Alberta wrapped her arms around him. None of the strangers ever looked once at D.C. Alberta observed, for what seemed like the first time, how gray everything in the room looked when it was foggy outside. Then her hands began to ache and D.C. sensed it and took hold of them. But there was no connection. He began to panic and sat motionless in her lap and tried to disappear.

Alberta finally was informed that the slender, purple-eyed woman was D.C.'s aunt. No one ever told Alberta Delia's name. They only told Alberta that they were going to take D.C. away. It all seemed too unreal. Alberta sobbed and pleaded and threatened and D.C. screamed but they still took him. D.C.'s anguished shrieks frightened Alberta terribly because they were the most human sounds he had ever made. Alberta thought she might go mad. Madison had to physically restrain Alberta to stop her from running after D.C. Then D.C. was just gone. Alberta knew she was defeated. She had no money to hire fancy lawyers and she was not related to D.C. What court in the world would grant her custody? Alberta's heart was crushed but she feared more for D.C. They could never understand him or care for him the way he needed. She knew he would end up locked away in an institution.

Alberta grew very weary. She went back into her apartment and sat down in the old chair by the back patio door that Armand used to sit in and closed her eyes. Her entire body ached fiercely, but she didn't care.

Madison stayed and talked to Alberta. She effused about the privileged life D.C. would have. At length, she spoke about him being reconnected with his real family, and how he would finally obtain the proper care he required.

Alberta listened silently until finally she stood unsteadily and stated, "You got what you wanted, Madison. Now please leave me alone for now. I have no more words for you."

"All right, Mother. I'll go back to work for a few hours and then I'll bring you some dinner later. I'll get you that Thai cashew chicken you like so much and some rice noodles," Madison replied. She stepped to the door; relieved in ways she couldn't understand.

Alberta opened her eyes and waved after her daughter's gray silhouette and mumbled, "Goodbye, Madison." She didn't feel compelled to tell Madison that her eyesight was failing fast and that she could feel sickness invading her being.

Then Alberta sat alone as the objects in the room vanished. She felt like she should pray but she was so anguished and confused.

Alberta whispered a passage from *Romeo and Juliet* her Great-Grandfather Desmond Charles had read to her thousands of days before, "Eyes look your last. Arms take your last embrace."

When Madison arrived back at Alberta's apartment with dinner later that evening, she knocked and her mother never answered. She tried the door and was surprised to find it unlocked. A chill went through her as she stepped into the noiseless, darkened apartment. Hurriedly she set the containers of food on the floor and switched on the overhead light. She gasped when she saw Alberta lying on the floor. She rushed over to her mother and felt for a pulse. At first she couldn't discern one and she started to cry. She pressed her hand on Alberta's neck and felt the blood pulsing weakly. Panicked, she dialed 911 on her cell phone. Slumping to the floor, Madison cradled her mother's head in her lap.

"Oh, God, what have I done? Please don't die, Mother," Madison cried out.

After getting custody of Daniel Christopher, Delia's attorneys arranged for a specialist in childhood developmental disabilities and two private nurses to accompany Daniel on his trip to Delia's home in Beverly Hills. They would all be driven in a hired ambulance and the specialist, Dr. Ruben Bunch, would evaluate Daniel and give his recommendations for his long-term care. Delia would arrive before them on her private jet.

Once Daniel Christopher was on his way to Beverly Hills, and as Delia was being chauffeured back to her house in Sea Cliff, he plagued her thoughts. He had seemed so placid and almost normal at Mrs. Sommers's pitiful little apartment. When he was taken away, he instantly became distressed and inaccessible. Later Delia was informed that from the moment they left Mrs. Sommers's dwelling till they arrived at the parking lot of the Pacific Medical Center, Daniel Christopher had never stopped screaming. She had witnessed his uncanny and anguished yowling and the beseeching and terrified expression on Daniel Christopher's face as he was carried to the ambulance.

When her limousine pulled into the driveway of her house Delia stepped out of the vehicle and rushed inside where she was shocked by how impossibly empty the spacious house felt. A strong fog laden wind was blowing in off the ocean and it whistled eerily through the eaves and the vents in the attic. She wanted to feel a sense of relief at having finally fulfilled Anngelie's dying request, but she mostly felt sad and mean. Running up the stairs, Delia locked herself in her bedroom suite where she immediately lit a fire and fixed herself a pitcher of martinis.

After drinking two martinis quickly, Delia rang for LaDonna. Delia would be closing the house in San Francisco and heading back to Beverly Hills with her poodle Isobella in a couple of hours. She had already spoken to Greta and apprised her of her plans. Greta had informed Delia that Lillian and Gigi and the rest of the family had vacated the estate four weeks prior. Delia was more than relieved but too anxious about Daniel Christopher to be elated.

A few minutes later, LaDonna tapped on Delia's bedroom door. She entered the room looking somehow different.

"I'm leaving tonight, LaDonna. Please make arrangements to close up the house and prepare the notices for the staff. You can write letters of recommendation for the personnel you think earned them and I'll sign them when you've faxed them to me in Beverly Hills. Inform the resident employees in writing that they have two weeks to vacate the premises. And contact a service to maintain the property. I haven't decided yet whether I'll be putting the home on the market."

Briefly, a dejected look flashed in LaDonna's eyes. Delia seemed aloof and she didn't understand why.

"I'll take care of it straight away, Ms. Wentworth." She started to leave the room but she paused in the doorway and added quietly without looking back at Delia, "Thank you for giving me a chance and hiring me. Working for you has changed my life. It may sound inappropriate, but since I won't be working for you any longer; I want you to know that I've grown to care a great deal for you. I think I admire you more than just about anyone I've ever met."

"Wait, LaDonna. I think you've misunderstood me. I won't be dismissing you until you've completed your novel and it has been published. And only then if you decide you no longer wish to work for me. I'm depending on you to remain in San Francisco until I've made a decision about the house. I presume that will give you enough time to finish your manuscript. After it is finished, I can give it to Basil Prousse for publication. He's been told about your book and he is anxious for your final draft. After that I can make room for you as part of my personal staff in Beverly Hills. You are writing a bestseller LaDonna and I don't think you'll need a job before long. I'm going to arrange to have my studio put a bid on the movie rights as soon as you've submitted it."

LaDonna's eyes widened and she said a bit breathlessly, still unable to glance at Delia, "Your cousin Constance said you were joking."

"LaDonna, I thought you had more sense than to listen to anything my ditzy cousin says. You should know me well enough by now to realize I'm quite candid. I want you to finish your book soon. I have a controlling interest in Hampton House Books and your novel is going to make you and me scads of money. So continue to reside in this house and take the next few months and write the remainder of *One Night Stan*. It may be the final thing I order you to do."

"Oh, I finished my book earlier today. Anyway, I think, I think I'm done."

"Well, I'm very pleased to hear that, LaDonna. Print a copy for me and I'll read it on my flight home. I didn't realize you were so close to completing it," Delia said and she almost smiled. Earlier Delia had felt like such a beast when she had removed Daniel from the only home he had ever known. He and Mrs. Sommers were so distraught that Delia couldn't help but wonder if she was doing the right thing. But now she was changing someone's life and there was no question it was for the better.

LaDonna glanced around the room observing its opulence. The glistening marble floors warmed by plush rugs with subtle tones of color, the fireplace flanked by a wall of windows that looked out across the bay waters reflecting the light inside. On the opposite wall was the bed of hand carved woods the size of a small sailing vessel. LaDonna had always wanted to live like this. It was luxuriant and beautiful but it suddenly struck her how insignificant it was.

"I was convinced you had been discouraged by those bitches at the writers' group the night before last," Delia said.

"I guess we both underestimated each other. And excuse my language but I said S.H.I.T. on those women. I knew my writing deserved more credit than they gave it. No, they did not discourage me at all. I don't know if you remember after we left the meeting and went to the grocery store and we saw a little boy in the parking lot and then later at the accident?" LaDonna paused and Delia nearly shuddered. LaDonna continued, "I know it sounds bizarre, but something about that little boy has really moved me. That day I saw him in the Headlands he was with that older lady then too. Maybe she is his grandmother. They exude so much love for each other it is indescribable. It is the greatest love between two people I think I've ever witnessed. It brings me to tears just thinking of it. But there is something so familiar about him. It's like I've always known him. Oh, I just can't explain it. Anyway, I feel like a new person. When Constance dropped us off the other night I came home inspired to complete my book."

Delia didn't react to LaDonna mentioning Daniel Christopher. She stared into the fire as LaDonna excused herself and left the room.

She immediately poured another martini. Alone in the room, waiting for one of the maids to come and start packing her suitcases, Delia stepped to the window. She unlatched it; cool wind gusted into the room and Delia braced herself. Gray fog was obscuring the hills to the north in Marin. Out on the lawn beyond the pool Delia saw a tar black crow swooping down to harass a lame, bone white gull that was pecking at some kind of food on the ground.

23 ❧

Three weeks passed. Even in temperate Beverly Hills you could discern the change of the season to autumn. The deciduous trees that flanked the broad streets and clustered in the canyons had begun to shed their leaves immodestly. Daylight shadows had shifted and elongated. The glaring white blaze of the summer sun had turned to amber in the October afternoons.

Like an arctic fox or a rainforest plant, Anngelie's troubled son never acclimated to living at Delia's Beverly Hills estate in the arid desert of the L.A. basin. During the first week, Daniel Christopher screamed day and night even after he was sedated. Refusing to eat, and sleeping only in snatches, he eventually weakened. On the seventh day, just like God, Delia joked, he finally was coaxed to bed and he slept for nearly three days straight. During this time he was fed intravenously. When he finally awoke he ceased making any noise at all and he retreated into a silent, unreachable world. He began to consume solid food but in a mechanical manner and only enough to sustain himself.

Delia put him in the suite next to hers in the south wing of the mansion. The only people allowed access to his room were four registered nurses and various doctors. None of the household employees or even Greta were told of Daniel's presence. Most importantly, Delia kept the knowledge of Daniel's existence from the rest of her family or any of her friends.

Delia led the staff to believe that she had a sick and highly contagious friend occupying the suite. Delia did all the cleaning in that part of the house and she prepared all of Daniel's food—duties she had never performed before. Lovingly, she even bathed her nephew daily. Never, not even with her own children, had Delia felt so protective of another person; Delia utterly adored Daniel Christopher. There was something so special and fragile about him and being with him had changed her irrevocably.

Delia hovered over Daniel Christopher and doted on him. She stayed in his room nearly every minute of the day. She even slept in his room on a chaise lounge. Petting and cooing she tried everything in her means to soothe him and draw him out of his stupor. By the third week Delia was frantic.

All the specialists Delia had brought in to look at Daniel

Christopher recommended that he be institutionalized. They all concurred he was hopelessly brain damaged, most likely due to trauma imposed on the brain by Anngelie's drug abuse during pregnancy. Each one of them was certain his cognitive functioning and adaptive behavior would never progress beyond the infantile stage and rated Daniel as profoundly mentally disabled. The treatment recommended by all was to have him raised by professionals who could evaluate his progress daily and administer to his specific needs in a controlled environment. Even the renowned Swede, Dr. Hager Angstrom, an authority on developmental disabilities, suggested long term lifelong residential care. But Delia would not give up hope. She saw something in Daniel Christopher's eyes.

Finally, twenty days after taking custody of Daniel Christopher, Delia made a decision. It was late afternoon and Delia was sitting in Daniel Christopher's bedroom beside his bed. The nurse on duty, a slight, pallid woman was out on her dinner break. The windows were open and a slight breeze was wafting into the room.

Outside, someone's laughter echoed. It startled Delia briefly because there were no neighbors nearby and usually all you heard was the wind rustling in the trees.

Minutes later Delia's son Winston exploded into the room. His eyes were wild and ranging and the whites as red as a brake light. His pale yellow hair was matted and disheveled. Delia knew instantly he was high, probably on methamphetamine.

"They tried to stop me from coming in downstairs but I snuck in the back entrance by the pool house. I told them they can't keep a guy from seeing his own fucking mother," Winston panted. He was gaunt and his skin was pitted and pale. Keeping his gaze mostly on the door, he scratched hard on his sweaty scalp and fidgeted about the room as if his legs were charged with electricity.

Delia got up quickly and sat on the bed blocking Daniel Christopher. Remaining placid so she wouldn't agitate Winston further, Delia replied softly, "Of course you can come see me anytime, Winston."

"What did you say? Oh yeah, you're fucking right I can."

"Did you need something, Winston?" Delia inquired calmly.

"Why? Do I need an invitation or a reason? Can't a guy just want to talk to his mother?" Winston stopped and glared at Delia his eyes wide and as steely blue as a thunderhead.

"I'm right here and I'm not going anywhere," Delia said, as she matched Winston's movements with her own to shield his view of Daniel Christopher. She hoped he wasn't getting frightened.

"Yeah, but you disappeared for several months without telling me anything. You didn't even call to check on me."

"I called Greta and she kept me updated on how you were doing."

"That's just great. Greta doesn't even really know me. How would she know if I'm okay or not?"

It was at that moment when Delia spied a revolver with a cylinder as fat as a gray fist stuffed in the pocket of Winston's baggy jeans. The barrel glistened like a mirror.

Winston paced around the room anxiously for several long minutes. Delia watched him guardedly and said nothing. Huffing and muttering to himself Winston would occasionally glare at Delia for an instant. The expression on his puckered face gave the impression that he was trying to form an idea or find a solution to a puzzle.

Finally Delia grew so panicked she couldn't keep silent. Defensively she asked, "Why are you here, Winston? What do you want?"

Winston suddenly rushed to Delia and shoved his face down next to hers. Delia leaned back over Daniel Christopher. Winston's hot breath smelled metallic as he hissed in a low menacing tone, "I told you, I just came here to see you, Mother. What the fuck do you think? Are you afraid I came here to put a bullet in your brain? Maybe I blame you because I can't stop taking this damn meth. Aren't mothers supposed to take care of their children? Do you value anything, Mother?" Winston whipped the gun from his pocket and pressed the nose against Delia's temple. Delia could feel the tremble in his hand as he cocked the hammer.

Then Delia heard Winston breathe deep and he mumbled something low and unintelligible. Briefly the pressure of the gun eased. Delia knew that Winston had finally seen Daniel Christopher.

Before Delia could stop him Daniel Christopher had climbed from behind her and was reaching up to try to take a hold of Winston's hand. Winston heaved mightily, and beginning to cry he started backing away from Delia and Daniel Christopher. Now his gun was pointed at Daniel Christopher.

"Daniel Christopher, stop! Winston, please don't hurt him," Delia stood and started to reach after Daniel Christopher.

"Sit down, Mother, and shut up," Winston snarled through his tears as he continued to back away. His hand holding the gun was visibly shaking but it was still pointed straight at Daniel Christopher who was unfazed and kept limping unsteadily toward Winston. His gait was weakened by the weeks in bed.

"Who is this kid, Mother? Why does he keep staring at me like he knows my insides? Tell him to stay away from me."

"His name is Daniel Christopher and he doesn't know any better, Winston. I'm sorry if I failed you but don't harm him because you're upset with me," Delia tried to sound calm.

"Why does he look like us? I feel like I've seen this kid before. Oh, Christ, I just can't take it anymore. This shit is driving me crazy but I can't stop using. My own mother acts as if I had nothing more than a cold. No, worse, you act like you don't care. Hell, what am I doing? See this shit has me so fucked up. I'm not here to hurt anybody but myself, Mother," Suddenly Winston stopped a few feet from the doorway and put the gun in his mouth. Daniel Christopher had finally caught up with Winston. Winston patted Daniel Christopher's head and told Delia in a muffled voice with the revolver pressed against his tongue, "Mother, come get this little guy and take him out of here." He smiled eerily at Delia and added, "Don't worry about the mess, you can pay someone to clean it up."

Delia rushed over to Daniel Christopher and tried to pick him up but he squealed and resisted her with an amazing amount of strength. Still trying to hold Daniel Christopher back, Delia looked up at Winston just as he was pulling the trigger of the gun. She had never before realized how incredibly blue her son's eyes were and how anguished. Fearing the worst, Delia attempted to cover Daniel Christopher's eyes and pull him close but he determinedly resisted her and instead he took a tight hold of Winston's free hand. Winston's eyes grew more panicked and he trembled. D.C. closed his eyes and continued gripping Winston's hand. Winston eventually sighed and his eyelids fluttered. Delia could see her son's body become less tense. Tears ran down Winston's cheeks. For a moment it appeared as if they both levitated a few inches into the air. Minutes passed.

"Thank you, Daniel," Winston uttered when Daniel Christopher finally let go of his hand. Daniel Christopher made a noise that neither Delia nor Winston could decipher, and then he hobbled back to bed and became as noiseless and still as an ancient sarcophagus. Delia rushed to his bedside and spoke soothingly to him but he never even glanced at her.

Winston came up behind Delia and put his hand on her shoulder. It was the first time he had touched her in years. It felt right to both of them.

"I don't know what happened, Mother, but when that little boy took hold of my hand I felt this heat travel through my entire body and through my head. I was so tormented and now I feel restored. I haven't felt this much peace since I was really young and you and dad were still together," Winston said, his voice was no longer strained.

"Trust it, Winston. I can't explain it. Perhaps we'll never understand it, but you can trust," Delia replied. She took hold of Winston's hand and kissed it and added, "Forgive me for being so foolish all these years."

"Who is Daniel Christopher?" Winston asked.

"He's just a little boy I thought I was supposed to take care of. But I already have two children who need my attention. His real name is D.C., and it's time for him to go home." D.C. looked at her for the first time and Delia was certain he wanted to smile.

At that moment Delia noticed the unmistakable odor of Chanel No. 5 and she instantly thought of Grandmother Ingrid. "Yes, you take that boy back home now, Delia Aurora Wentworth," Delia heard her dead grandmother command. Delia glanced around the room but she didn't see her grandmother.

Four hundred miles north of Beverly Hills, and another world away, at St. Luke's Hospital in San Francisco, Alberta's life was slipping away quietly like the midday fog. The only sounds in her room came from the machine monitoring her weakening heart and Madison's muffled crying. The fluorescent light leeched the color from everything in the room.

The doctor had reported so many things wrong with Alberta that Madison had forgotten most of them. All she knew was that her mother's lungs were filling with blood and she was too weak to be operated on again. The word from the doctor was that Alberta would probably not last through the night and Madison had given the consent to not resuscitate.

It seemed impossible, only weeks before Alberta had been vigorous and joyful. Since the day D.C. had left she had been completely unresponsive. Twice they had operated on her heart and she went into cardiac arrest both times but was revived. Madison kept praying that Alberta would rouse even for a few minutes so she could tell her how terribly sorry she was for helping the people who took D.C.

Madison had even waited a few days to tell the rest of the family about Alberta's condition hoping she would get a moment alone with her mother. A week before though, she had realized it wasn't fair to wait any longer and she had called her Auntie Roberta who of course was devastated, and she too had been spending many long hours by her beloved sister's bedside.

Once Roberta had been told of Alberta's impending death, it wasn't long before the entire family found out. Madison had been with her mother day and night and she had seen a seemingly endless parade of people coming to visit and express their concern and regret. Many of them were friends and distant relatives Madison pretended to remember. She was informed of dozens of prayer groups who had been asked to add Alberta to their list. Knowing that so many people cared about Alberta was heartening to Madison. Still she wasn't prepared to lose her mother and Madison had been begging God to spare her.

Madison stared at the clock which seemed to tick away the seconds faster each time she looked at it. It was nearly six o'clock and this was the first time she had been alone with her mother since early morning. Roberta had gone home about an hour before to bathe and change clothes, but her son Jay had promised to bring her back that evening.

Madison continued to watch her mother and weep. Then she wrapped the blanket one of the nurses had brought to her about her body and she leaned back in the vinyl recliner that had been her bed for the past three weeks. Closing her eyes she began to pray aloud, "Please, God, heal my mother. But if it is her time to go don't let her suffer, and let her know how much I love her and that I know now how wrong I was. I ask that you can forgive me, too."

When Madison finished she kept her eyes closed and continued to pray the same prayer again silently. She was exhausted. She hadn't had a good night's sleep since Alberta had been admitted to the hospital. A few minutes ticked away and Madison fell asleep.

Hours later Madison awakened. The room was mostly dark except for a dim light above Alberta's bed. It took her a moment to realize someone else was in the room. Before her eyes adjusted to the darkness, Madison's Auntie Roberta patted her arm and said softly, "Our sweet Alberta is about to leave us, Madison."

Madison stood and started to cry again as she stepped to her mother's bed. In the harsh light Alberta's complexion was as ashen-black as a burned log. The only sign of life was her open mouth gulping weakly and indifferently at the air.

Roberta took hold of Alberta's hand and in a trembling voice said softly, "You just go on now, sister. There is no need for you to stay here and suffer. There are many people on the other side waiting for you."

Aunt and niece stood together; each remembering different things about Alberta. A terrible loneliness for her had already overcome them. The heart monitor had slowed and barely pulsed. Alberta took one deep breath that sounded like a sigh and Roberta and Madison both assumed it was her last.

An instant later, the door opened and a shaft of light flooded the room. Madison and Roberta turned to look and they both cried out, "My God," when they saw a nurse holding D.C. walking toward them. He squirmed from the nurse's arms and thrust himself to the floor. He hurried a bit clumsily but steadfastly to Alberta.

No one said a word, but Madison helped him as he attempted to climb on the bed. A silence more intense than the peeling of church bells enveloped the shadowy room as D.C. took hold of Alberta's inert, cold hand. The monitor had flat lined and Alberta's chest had stopped moving. Undeterred D.C. lay across her body and stared into her face.

A fraction of a moment later that seemed to last an eternity, Alberta's chest began to move again. Madison, Roberta, and even the nurse gasped when Alberta's eyes fluttered open. She glanced around confused briefly and then she noticed D.C. and she pulled him close, smiling and crying.

D.C. pulled back, and still staring at Alberta he said the first words he had ever uttered distinctly and without hesitation, "Alberta, Love."

24 ❧

A few months later, Delia and her poodle Isobella were being driven north along the coast of California from Beverly Hills. It was December 23rd, two days before Christmas. It was the first Christmas she had been excited about since she and Anngelie were young girls. The bond she had formed with her children after D.C. had come into her life had not been fleeting, as she thought it might be. In ways she had never dreamed possible, she found her love for her son and daughter expanding.

Delia dialed LaDonna's cell phone.

"Hello, Delia. I was going to text you but I still haven't figured out how to do that. I think I have a mental block."

"Don't worry. I hate texting and twittering and all that nonsense. I think I was born too late or too early for all this mass communication stuff. I still think of computers as being like HAL in *2001*. Never mind that, though, how do you like L.A.? And how are your children?"

"You're so funny, Delia. I'm going to write a book about you someday."

"Please don't. It's already been done."

"Jeena and Jerry, Jr. are having a blast. They've never gone swimming in December before. We're going to spend Christmas Day at Disneyland. I have to tell you I don't think Los Angeles is fit for human habitation, but everyone seems to love it here. I can't wait to get back to San Francisco."

Delia laughed. "Yes, it is definitely an acquired taste; unless you were born there, as I was. I should warn you that all of the locals go to Disneyland on Christmas. It can be really crowded."

"The kids will love it, anyway. I'm looking forward to it too. I haven't been since I was seven years old. I only wish Disneyland wasn't down here."

"I shouldn't think the rewrites for the film should take more than a couple of weeks. Then you can go home to your beloved San Francisco."

"That sounds so good, Delia. Thanks to you I have a better life than I ever dreamed possible."

"Let's not go into that. You earned everything you have. I merely opened a few doors."

"Are you still going through with the plans you told me about the other day? It sounds so exciting."

"Yes, definitely. I'll call you in a few days and give you an update. Listen, I better hang up now. I've got a lot still to do. I just wanted to check on you."

"Thanks for calling, Delia. I love hearing from you. If I don't speak to you before then, Merry Christmas."

"Merry Christmas to you and your children too, LaDonna, goodbye." Delia hung up the cell phone and put it back in her purse.

"What are these mysterious plans of yours, young lady?"

"Grandmother Ingrid!" Delia shouted.

"Not so loud, Delia. What will Crawford think?"

"I don't care anymore, Grandmother. I'm so delighted to see you. Where have you been?"

"You don't think I would allow your sister to pass over here without welcoming her do you? I couldn't allow your Grandmother Stanhope to get all the accolades. She's a lovely woman, but she can be a bit demonstrative."

"How is Anngelie?"

"Lovelier and happier than ever before. I love showing her off to everyone."

"Tell her I miss her and I love her."

"You may tell her yourself, any time you please."

"Does she know I found Daniel Christopher?"

"Indeed she knows all about D.C."

"Why did you leave me before I found him? I really could have used your advice."

"Of course you could have. But you had to make those decisions on your own. This was your journey, Delia. It was one of those life altering experiences that sometimes have to be done alone."

"I really have changed, Grandmother. I took cooking lessons so I could make an early Christmas dinner for Gigi and Winston and Josh."

"I smelled your attempts."

People who knew Delia well would not fathom that she had burned two turkeys and half a dozen roasts teaching herself to cook so she could prepare an early holiday feast. She had wanted to do it all alone as a surprise for her children. Still, Delia found this new domesticity a bit embarrassing so she hadn't wanted to ask anyone for assistance and she had relied on a dearth of cookbooks, which had been as confusing to her as studying the Cyrillic alphabet or advanced trigonometry.

Finally, she had capitulated and had hired the head chef from her favorite restaurant in Los Angeles to come give her private lessons. After several frustrating weeks of trying to get the knack of basic cooking, dumpsters of inedible food, and a kitchen that smelled like the inside of a chimney, Delia had decided to let the chef cook the meal and she had been in charge of setting the table.

"How could you have smelled it, Grandmother? You are dead."

"Don't be tiresome. We've been through all that. You must stop making assumptions about the afterlife. It's nothing like the movies portray it to be. You still have yet to apprise me of your plans, Delia."

"I know, Grandmother. I don't want you to think I'm crazy. Lillian is livid. She insists I only want attention. She says her astrologer informs her I'll never go through with it."

"Perhaps you do want attention, but I hardly see anything wrong in that."

It was nearing two o'clock in the afternoon, the limousine pulled off of the highway and parked in a sandy lot overlooking windswept dunes dotted with tall grasses, scrub, and a generous shoreline to the sparkling ocean that had as many variations of blue tones as the gossamer wings of the Mission blue butterfly.

Delia got out of the car.

"Young lady, what are you doing?"

Delia tapped on the driver's window. Crawford rolled it down and asked, "Yes, Miss Wentworth?"

"Crawford, the car is yours. Think of it as a Christmas present. You may go on now. David, if you don't mind that I be so familiar as to call you by your first name, you have been an extraordinary employee. I've also learned over the many years of your loyal service that you are also a great guy. I will no longer be requiring your services. Where I'm going I won't need a driver." Delia handed him an envelope. He opened it and found a letter of recommendation and a check for one million dollars inside.

Crawford stared at the check at length and then stuttered, "I don't understand, Miss Wentworth."

"It's okay, David. I'm letting you go."

"Is there anything wrong?"

"Everything is finally wonderful, David. Now take your money and your car and have a good life."

"I don't feel right leaving you here, Miss Wentworth."

"I'm a big girl, David. I've already made other arrangements. Now wish me well and be off. I'm serious, Crawford. As my last command I'm ordering you to leave."

Crawford started to drive away slowly. There were tears in his eyes. "God bless you, Miss Wentworth. You're one of the nicest women I've ever known. Don't tell my girlfriend, but you are also by far the prettiest."

Delia watched him driving slowly away. He called out, "Oh and, Merry Christmas, Miss Wentworth!"

"Merry Christmas to you too, Crawford," Delia replied but he was too far away to hear.

"What is this all about, Delia?"

"I've given it all away, Grandmother. I'm not an heiress anymore. I set up trusts for Winston and Gigi and D.C. and I gave the rest of my money to charity. Gigi has adopted Isobella. I also couldn't resist giving my share of Royal Arts to Katherine's sister Wendy. She'll know what to do with it, better than I. Besides I couldn't resist getting one final dig into Katherine. I'll never be completely reformed."

"All your inheritance? My, my."

"Well, I did keep one gold card and a little sum in my Swiss account."

Delia started walking through the parking lot and then up a dune that looked out over the beach. Midway up the incline she asked, "Grandmother, I need to ask you something I've been wanting to ask you since you first came to me, but I've been afraid."

"Go right ahead, my dear. Though, I can't imagine you being afraid of much of anything anymore."

"Is my Robert there? I've always wondered."

At that moment Aunt Agatha appeared and glided to Delia. She was holding something in her arms.

"Of course he is here, my dear. We take very good care of him. Your Aunt Agatha has been bringing him to you since his spirit crossed over. Would you like to hold him?"

"Oh, my God, yes, Grandmother! More than anything in the world."

Aunt Agatha placed Robert in Delia's arms. Delia could see his sweet face plainly. He smiled up at her.

"I can feel him, Grandmother. I can actually feel him." Delia started sobbing for the first time in over twenty-five years.

"He's always been with you, my dear. You simply had to open your heart again. Now, where are we off to?"

"I've joined the Peace Corps and I'm flying out of San Francisco late tonight. I'll be in Mongolia the day after Christmas. Are you coming too?"

"Certainly, I'm coming. I love travelling and new adventures. I'm an Aries. We're going to meet a lot of fascinating people. One of them is a nomadic Tuvan throat singer. I'm going to buckle up for the ride of my afterlife."

"I hope some of these people are alive?"

"I'm sure some of them will be."

Grandmother floated ahead of Delia. "Bring Robert up here, Delia."

Delia walked to the top of the sandy bluff where the ocean came into view again. A strong winter storm had just battered the West coast and the beach was teeming with the large gray trunks of pines and bunches of coral-colored kelp. About twenty yards away, up against one of the dunes was a familiar looking, makeshift timber structure made from felled trees and decorated with ropes of seaweed.

Just beyond, where the tides smoothed the sand, D.C. was running. A fluffy brown poodle pup was bounding devotedly after him. Alberta watched after them standing strong.

"Look, Delia, Alberta is clapping her hands. You can hear her laughter echoing. Delia, we're all witnessing our D.C. run for the first time in his life. He has a staggering destiny."

Delia observed them. The sun beamed down unwavering through the cloudless sky. Delia regarded D.C. and Alberta and their newly adopted puppy for several minutes and then quietly started walking to the highway. She had seen what she had come to see. Turning back, Delia took one last look at D.C. and Alberta. She was still holding Robert and still sobbing. She whispered, "Your son is a miracle, Anngelie." Before she lost sight of D.C.'s and Alberta's golden silhouettes she spotted a seagull gliding over D.C. Its outstretched wings were as pure white as a thousand stars.

Stephen Barrett was born in Springfield, Missouri, the 'Queen City of the Ozarks' in the last century. He never pronounced it Missoura. He escaped to San Francisco in 1999. He lives with his partner and dogs high on a hill with views of the bay.